Doc probed deeper

"The question remains unanswered. Is there any of the poisonous old tech still on the premises, the rancid remnants of a bygone and perhaps best forgotten age? Some relic of that pernicious evil known as the Totality Concept?"

Doc hadn't idly brought up the name of the Totality Concept. He had spoken the name in the hopes of eliciting some kind of reaction.

The baron hadn't recognized the name at all, and had seemed genuine in his bemusement at the use of the term. But then, Doc hadn't been watching the baron. His eyes had been kept firmly on Jenna, and he had seen her sharp features harden as the words were spoken. The raven eyes had fixed on him, met his full on and tried to fathom his intent.

There was old tech here. Old tech related to secret government projects of the past. And maybe there was something that would link this ville to the main body of the Illuminated Ones, and the place in the North they were searching for.

Other titles in the Deathlands saga:

JAMES AXLER

DEATH LANDS®

Sunchild

A GOLD EAGLE BOOK FROM
WORLDWIDE®

TORONTO • NEW YORK • LONDON
AMSTERDAM • PARIS • SYDNEY • HAMBURG
STOCKHOLM • ATHENS • TOKYO • MILAN
MADRID • WARSAW • BUDAPEST • AUCKLAND

First edition December 2001

ISBN 0-373-62566-9

SUNCHILD

Printed in U.S.A.

...there have always been secrets, and there has always been power. It's just that some of it has been out in the open, and some of it has been in the shadows. That's the worst—you can never be sure what's going on in the shadows. That twilight world where there are only half-truths and half-lies, and no such thing as trust.

—From a report to a Congress
Committee on hidden cabals
and covert operations,
August 23, 1954

THE DEATHLANDS SAGA

This world is their legacy, a world born in the violent nuclear spasm of 2001 that was the bitter outcome of a struggle for global dominance.

There is no real escape from this shockscape where life always hangs in the balance, vulnerable to newly demonic nature, barbarism, lawlessness.

But they are the warrior survivalists, and they endure—in the way of the lion, the hawk and the tiger, true to nature's heart despite its ruination.

Ryan Cawdor: The privileged son of an East Coast baron. Acquainted with betrayal from a tender age, he is a master of the hard realities.

Krysty Wroth: Harmony ville's own Titian-haired beauty, a woman with the strength of tempered steel. Her premonitions and Gaia powers have been fostered by her Mother Sonja.

J. B. Dix, the Armorer: Weapons master and Ryan's close ally, he, too, honed his skills traversing the Deathlands with the legendary Trader.

Doctor Theophilus Tanner: Torn from his family and a gentler life in 1896, Doc has been thrown into a future he couldn't have imagined.

Dr. Mildred Wyeth: Her father was killed by the Ku Klux Klan, but her fate is not much lighter. Restored from predark cryogenic suspension, she brings twentieth-century healing skills to a nightmare.

Jak Lauren: A true child of the wastelands, reared on adversity, loss and danger, the albino teenager is a fierce fighter and loyal friend.

Dean Cawdor: Ryan's young son by Sharona accepts the only world he knows, and yet he is the seedling bearing the promise of tomorrow.

In a world where all was lost, they are humanity's last hope....

Chapter One

Ryan Cawdor opened his eye.

A sharp, stabbing pain shot through his head, piercing to the back of his brain like a red-hot needle pushed through the center of that diamond-hard blue orb.

No matter how many times he made the jump using the mat-trans, no matter how often he steeled himself for the inevitable agonies of recovery and regaining consciousness, it still amazed him that it could hurt so much. He'd lost count of the number of times his scarred and pitted torso had been injured in combat, racked with pain in torture; still, any of that seemed preferable, right now, to the agonies of regaining full consciousness after a jump.

Ryan's muscled body, honed by years of travel and combat, trained to cope with a harsh existence, complained in no uncertain manner as he rose from his prone position onto one elbow. His curly black hair, matted with sweat, hung down over his active eye and the empty socket, protected by a patch and scored by a long, livid and puckered scar.

The lead in his muscles moved as the lactic acid dispersed, and the oxygen from the stale air he breathed so heavily started to traverse his bloodstream. He looked across to the seemingly slight but deceptively wiry frame of J. B. Dix, the man known as the Armorer, a position he had fulfilled for Trader, and where Ryan had first met the man he could call friend in a land where such things were rare.

John Barrymore Dix was slumped across the frosted floor of the mat-trans chamber, across the now still disks that glowed when the chamber was about to activate. A faint tang of ozone remained in the brackish air, a sign that Ryan hadn't taken long to regain consciousness after the final stages of the jump. J.B., on the other hand, was still out cold, his chest moving visibly as he tried to gulp in air. His precious and battered fedora lay beside him, along with his Smith & Wesson M-4000 scattergun, his Uzi and the Tekna knife that had been invaluable when the aging tech of the blasters had given trouble.

Not that it often happened. The Armorer was an artist, if such a thing could be said to exist in the Deathlands. His eyes would sparkle behind his wire-rimmed spectacles—now safely stored in his pocket against the trauma of the jump—when he talked of weaponry, and his knowledge of blasters, grens and any other weapon was second to none. He made sure that the group with whom he traveled kept its weaponry in excellent condition at all times, taking pride in his work. A pride that was far from idle, as a misfiring blaster in the middle of a firefight would mean buying the farm when survival was much the preferred option.

Beside the prone J.B., her hand reaching out to him protectively, was Dr. Mildred Wyeth. Sometimes cynical in the face of adversity, her phlegmatic attitude in some ways echoed that of the Armorer, and had led to their relationship and understanding deepening

over their travels. Despite the horror of the postapo-
calypse world into which she had been thrown, Mildred's predark idealism still powered her onward.
Trapped in cryogenic suspension following compli-
cations during a minor operation, Mildred had awakened into something that for her was a nightmare.
Initially, she had clashed with Ryan Cawdor, questioning his right to assume leadership of the group.
But Ryan's fighting skills and survival instincts had
won her respect, as had his strong sense of justice,
albeit tempered by necessary pragmatism. Besides
which, she noticed that although assuming leadership
and thus having the final say, Ryan believed strongly
in teamwork, and played to the strengths of his companions.

Mildred's beaded plaits hung over her dark face,
almost a pallid gray as the waves of nausea from the
jump dragged her toward consciousness.

A low moan, tortured and like a wailing lost soul
seeking rest, drew the one-eyed warrior's attention,
causing him to turn slowly. As it came from the inside
of the chamber, and was in a tone he knew well, he
allowed himself the luxury of taking his time, allowing his still complaining equilibrium to adjust to the
movement of his head. If he hadn't recognized the
sound, or if it had originated outside the chamber, he
would have steeled himself, ignored the sudden diz-
ziness and nausea and reached for his panga and his
9 mm SIG-Sauer P-226 blaster.

This time there was no need: the moan emanated,
as he knew it had to, from the bony and angular figure
dressed in a frock coat who lay propped against the
far wall of the chamber. Dr. Theophilus Tanner was,

in real time, somewhere in his mid- to late-thirties. Yet his real age was incalculable, as he had been plucked from his own time into another, and then tossed back into the stream of time. Doc's muddled and bemused memories told of a time before the turn of the twentieth century, when life was sedate and ordered. The unwilling and unwitting subject of an experiment by the whitecoat scientists of a time immediately prior to skydark, Doc had proved too quarrelsome, too much trouble, and had been used as a test subject in an experiment to project forward in time.

It was an irony that the experiment had probably saved his life, landing him as it did nearly a century after the devastation of the nuclear war known as skydark. However, the damage to his physical and mental states was a subject of speculation. Mildred often referred to him as a crazy old fool, but was the first to own that this was merely irritation with his more unstable moments. The truth was that the Oxford- and Harvard-educated Tanner had weathered experiences that would have broken a lesser man. He looked weatherbeaten and aged—strangers would take him for twice his probable age—and from time to time was inclined to ramble in a seemingly senile and illogical manner, though these bouts were not as common as they used to be.

Yet he was also capable of a tenacious and wiry strength, and possessed a razor-sharp mind that could cut through the stress and strain of his most unusual life. For a man whose first experience of the Deathlands had been near death under torture at the hands of Baron Jordan Teague and his psychopathic sec chief Cort Strasser in the ville of Mocsin, Doc was surprisingly able to hold his fragile sanity together.

"I know—how much more of this can he take? Right, lover?"

Ryan turned back at the sound of Krysty Wroth's voice, which sounded like a sonorous bell in the enclosed space, clear and ringing, yet quiet and controlled. The flame-haired woman was sitting with her knees drawn up to her chin, wrapped in the bearskin coat that hid the toned and shaped curves of her body. She flashed Ryan a smile that sparked through her green eyes. Yet she still showed signs of the strain caused by the jump.

Ryan allowed himself a smile in return, and cursed as he felt the muscles of his face ache as they moved. "Always read my thoughts," he replied. Then he indicated Doc. "It's true enough. Hurts bad for us, let alone what Doc's been through."

"Crazy old coot'll outlive us all, you'll see..." Mildred tentatively raised herself onto one foot, remaining half-kneeling until she was sure of her balance. J.B., still on his back but now conscious, allowed himself merely a grunt of assent.

"Okay, people, how are we doing?" Ryan asked. It was a rhetorical question. They were doing well, so far.

By now, Ryan and Krysty were on their feet, both massaging life back into their aching and dulled limbs. It was a luxury they knew they could allow themselves. J.B. was checking his blasters, which was no more than second nature to him. Mildred was checking Doc, pulling back his eyelid to see his rolling eyeball as his muttering grew less incoherent.

"My dear woman, I would appreciate a less heavy hand on my optic nerve," he murmured from his incoherence, the eyeball beginning to still and focus.

"No thanks, not a bit of it," Mildred replied with an indulgent smile, breathing silent thanks that Doc had made it once more.

There were still two members of the group who had failed to completely surface from the jump. Jak Lauren, the whip-thin and immensely strong albino, still lay on the floor of the chamber. His patched camou jacket, littered with the leaf-bladed throwing knives that were his specialty, seemed almost to smother him. As always seemed to happen during a jump, he had vomited, wretched strings of bile that dripped from his nose and mouth, forming small acrid puddles around his face. His breathing was regular and shallow, and he showed little sign of regaining consciousness. The boy beside him, however, was beginning to stir.

The casual observer would think that it was Ryan Cawdor who was prone on the chamber floor, then would notice that under the black mop of curly hair, the chiseled face was bereft of scarring and still held two eyes. The limbs were rangy, the musculature strong but still taking shape. But there was no mistaking that the boy was of Cawdor blood.

Dean Cawdor, recently turned twelve years old, was his father in miniature, and for Ryan it was an uncanny experience to look on his son and see himself some twenty-odd years previous. He even recognized the bridling brashness and overconfidence in his abilities that Ryan himself had been prone to at that age—except that Ryan had gone through this

stage in the comparative safety and security of Front
Royal, under the patronage of his father, the ville's
baron. Dean had to go through this learning experience in an environment where one wrong move could
mean instant death, or worse…a lingering, tortuous
death. So perhaps sometimes the older Cawdor was
harsh in slapping down his son's brazen self-
confidence, but only because he was aware of what
was happening inside the boy and felt an urgent need
to quell the impetuousness that could be Dean's un-
doing.

Even as this passed through the one-eyed warrior's
mind, Dean groaned softly and raised his head slowly,
opening his eyes and then raising himself in the same
manner as his father.

With Doc also now on his feet, Mildred devoted
her medical attentions to taking care of Jak. The albino's tolerance to the bodily stresses of the jumps
was lower than the others.

Slowly, Jak came round, wiping the sticky mucus
and bile from his face with his sleeve, and hawking
a glob of phlegm from his throat.

"Okay to go?" Ryan questioned him.

Jak nodded. "As ever be."

"Let's do it."

THE DOOR to the chamber had unlocked automatically
when the jump had been completed. It was a safety
facet of the mat-trans system that the doors on both
the sending and receiving chambers had to be shut
before the transfer could take place, and that the comp
systems would automatically lock and unlock the
doors when the transfer got underway and ended. Or

at least, the aging and mostly uncared-for tech had worked that way thus far. Any deviation was beyond their control, and so not really worth consideration or worry.

They exited the chamber singly, checking the immediate area as they went, prepared to provide cover and defense for those who would follow. As always, Ryan took the lead, with J.B. at the rear.

The anteroom and control room outside the mat-trans unit were empty. The comp consoles winked and chattered softly in the semidarkness, with much of the lighting having fallen prey to the passing years and lack of maintenance. The lack of dust was due to the antistatic air conditioner, which still worked.

There were no signs of life.

It took little time for them to ascertain that the redoubt was, on these lower levels at least, completely deserted. It was in a reasonable condition. There were signs of stress in some of the walls, suggesting that earth movements resulting from the tremors and quakes following skydark had made some impact on the redoubt, but most of the lighting was still working, and there was some circulation of air through a purification plant. The air was clean, but a little thin, suggesting that the plant was damaged.

"Can't stay here too long," Mildred remarked as they explored the empty rooms. "The air's fine now, but it won't last that way forever."

"Why not?" Dean countered. "It's been okay up to now, right?"

"Think about it, my boy," Doc interjected with a sardonic note. "The air is, shall we say, a little thin down here. Suggesting, I should imagine, some malfunction of the ancient technology keeping this place alive, albeit perhaps in a wheezing and somewhat dubious manner... A little like myself, in fact.''

''So?'' Dean prompted, still in the dark.

''So, it's thin and strained when the redoubt is empty. But now it has seven people breathing in at a ridiculous rate. A rate made, with some irony, even faster by its very paucity.''

''Big words for say we use faster than made,'' Jak commented with an amused look at the old man. Doc merely shrugged.

''So how long you reckon we got?'' J.B. asked Mildred.

She shook her head, the ends of her plaits moving rhythmically as though caught by a much needed draft of air. ''Couldn't say for sure, John. It's like being at a high altitude. I don't think we'd suffocate for a few days, but the more rarefied it gets, the more it might affect us. Hallucinations, maybe.''

''Great. Like jolt only not so good,'' Jak muttered in a dour tone.

''Think we can risk a night?'' Ryan asked Mildred. ''I'd like us to get some rest before tackling whatever may be out there or risk another jump.''

''I'd say we could do that,'' Mildred replied after some thought.

''Good. Now let's try and find the shower stalls, mebbe some clean clothes. That'd make me feel better for a start,'' Krysty added.

''Right. Stink like mutie polecat on heat,'' Jak grunted.

It didn't take long to find the shower stalls and washing facilities. Like most redoubts, this one was laid out to a specification that had been generally used. There had been exceptions, but for the most part it could be assumed that if a person had explored one redoubt, he or she had a fair chance of navigating every other one he or she came across.

The showers were still working. As with several of the redoubts they had encountered so far, the lighting in this one was erratic. But the water was still on, and the heaters still worked. The first streams of water were lukewarm, flecked with some decay and foreign matter from the pipes, but after a minute or so by Ryan's wrist chron the water was clear, flowing freely and of an even temperature.

They took turns to shower, keeping a guard at all times. It seemed that the redoubt was deserted apart from their presence, but they could never be too sure. The friends had been taken unawares on a previous occasion.

It was a simple matter to find clean clothing. The store rooms for all redoubts were situated in the same place, and in this redoubt they were lucky enough to find underclothes and thermally insulated outerwear that had lain unused for over a century. They took the opportunity to change clothes and would later launder what they usually wore.

One strange thing, though—the clothes weren't the usual regulation khaki and olive-green, or white. Some of the clothes were in colors that seemed, under the dim lighting, to be black or a dark blue. Some of it, under the better lighting of the corridor, even revealed itself to be purple, a color rarely if ever seen in predark sec conditions. And the lighter colors were yellows and sky-blues. It was a small but significant difference.

"These make a change," Dean remarked as he dressed, "but it doesn't seem right to me."

"You're right," Krysty agreed. "The armies from before skydark would never have used this." She held up a purple T-shirt that seemed, in the light, to have streaks of a faded pattern running across it. "This is no ordinary military redoubt."

"Built on the same lines, though," Ryan said thoughtfully. "Odd. Most of the nonmilitary redoubts we've jumped to have been different. But this…"

"I know," Mildred said. "It's uncanny, and maybe just a bit creepy. It's a military base, but with so many nonmilitary touches. If only it wasn't so damned dark…I'd swear that these rooms are just a bit smaller than the usual size. It's like someone got the military blueprints but had to downscale just a bit." Mildred shivered. "It just gives the place a screwy atmosphere, like looking into a distorting mirror."

Jak looked at her, puzzled. "Not feel danger here," he said simply. "Old sec weird. Seen plenty weirder."

Doc, who had so far been silent, leaned thoughtfully on his swordstick, hands clasped over the silver lion's head. "I wonder…" he mused, then lapsed into silence.

"Wonder what, Doc?" Ryan asked gently, knowing that when the old man was straining to recall, it was best to keep patience and coax it from him.

"Whitecoat paranoia," Doc continued. "You know, those fools always believed there were secret cabals out to overthrow them—private armies, hidden money and knowledge. All power, I suppose. But perhaps…''

''If this was such a place—another sec force—then mebbe it's got a good armory.'' J.B. almost smiled as he jammed his fedora onto his closely cropped scalp. The twinkle in his eyes betrayed his excitement.

''We could do with a few new blasters, mebbe some grens,'' Ryan said. ''Should be easy to find the armory if this follows standard layout, right?''

They all nodded agreement.

''Well, I vote we get some sleep first,'' Krysty said with a sigh. ''We know we can't stay here too long, and I can't feel any danger at all, lover.''

''Okay. We'll search for the armory after we've slept, mebbe see if we can access some information. This place seems to be in good order, so mebbe the comps won't be too fucked up.''

The weariness with which his companions agreed and the fact that the Armorer was content to leave the weapons search until after sleeping were sure signs that the friends badly needed some rest.

As they had all suspected, the dormitories were easy to find. Echoing Mildred's impression that the redoubt was on a smaller scale than most old sec installations, the dorms housed only a few beds per room. In fact, it looked as though the total personnel of this redoubt couldn't have been more than thirty at most.

Dean, Jak and Doc took one room. Mildred and J.B. another, leaving Ryan and Krysty to take their pick of the remaining dorms.

Shutting themselves away from the others, and

gaining a rare privacy since the beginning of their travels, they settled into one of the beds. The controlled environment of the redoubt had kept the linen fresh, and little dust or dirt had accumulated over the preceding century.

Krysty moved closer to Ryan, molding herself to his body and running a fingernail over the ridges of the one-eyed warrior's ribs.

"Still tense, lover?" she asked, feeling the knotting of his muscles.

"Mebbe it's got to where I've forgotten how to relax," Ryan replied. "It's too quiet, too calm. I don't like it…. It's not right. Too easy."

Krysty drew circles with her nail on his rippling muscles. "Mebbe so… I can't feel anything, and I'm cherishing the calm. Gaia knows we don't get too much of that. It's not a calm and peaceful world, so finding an oasis of peace for just a little while… Do you think you'd be able to settle if we ever did find the promised lands?"

Ryan smiled at her choice of words, knowing that she had deliberately picked them to amuse him, relax him. "Mebbe. And mebbe I just can't think of that now when there's a fight around every corner. Guess I've spent, hell, we've all spent too long having to be on our guard. Peace like this just feels like the calm eye of some rad-blasted storm."

"Well, we're in the eye of that storm right now, so we may as well make the best of it," she replied softly, moving on top of him, using every muscle in her body to coax the tired warrior away from his concern and into focusing on her. And their togetherness.

Krysty was so skilled, and moved so intuitively,

that Ryan found his restlessness draining away, and
his attention drawn entirely to his lover's body as she
roused him to a passion that they had too little time
to consummate.

And afterward, he slept his first entirely dreamless
and restful sleep since he couldn't remember when.

Chapter Two

Both Ryan and Krysty awoke the next day refreshed. Ryan felt easier, and on examining his wrist chron found that they had slept for almost twenty-four hours.

After he and Krysty had risen and dressed, they ventured out of the dorm. The unearthly quiet that always accompanied a deserted redoubt was broken by the distant and muffled sounds of talk and the clatter of dishes. Exchanging puzzled and amused glances, they followed the sounds until they became more audible.

"...don't give shit. Not eating slop when self-heats there."

"C'mon, Jak. Doc's done his best, and it would make more sense to keep the self-heats and take them with us." Mildred's exasperation was showing through in her edgy tone.

"Yeah, but this crap'll kill us before we get out of the main door, so then we won't need self-heats anyway, will we?" There was a wry edge to Dean's tone that suggested he was enjoying helping Jak to exasperate the more sensible Dr. Wyeth.

Who was looking for backup. "John, don't just sit there and say nothing. Help me out on this one."

"Leave me out of this, Millie," came J.B.'s laconic

tones. "This crap isn't really edible, but then I don't like self-heats much, either."

Ryan and Krysty entered what was obviously the redoubt's kitchen to find their companions arguing at a table, with the exception of Doc, who was standing over a pan that bubbled busily on a hot plate. He greeted them with a sheepish grin.

"I fear I may be the cause of some discontent," he began. "Upon finding a supply of self-heats, but also some foodstuffs that had been dried and preserved, I reasoned that it would be sensible to try to make a meal from the latter, thus preserving the self-heats for our travels. However, I must confess that my attempts at the culinary arts have not been altogether—shall we say—successful."

Krysty wrinkled her nose at the stale stench emanating from the pan, then glanced at Ryan. He, too, had noticed the smell. Doc noted their silent exchange.

"Precisely," he replied to their unspoken question. "The desiccated foodstuffs and—well, what they were I can only assume—seem to be as stale as the spices with which I have endeavored to enliven them. Also, the consistency leaves a lot to be desired."

"It's not going to kill us," Mildred argued. "It'll still be nutritious, and that's the main thing. We can't waste self-heats."

Ryan looked from Mildred to Doc. The old man shrugged once more, and smiled, revealing his eerily perfect teeth.

"I suspect I know exactly what you're thinking," he stated. "If I had merely dismissed the dried foodstuffs as so much dross, and merely pointed out the discovery of the self-heats, then all this argument could have been avoided.''

Ryan laughed. It was the first time for ages that he had felt able. "Don't worry about it, Doc. Guess you're right, but it's nice to just be somewhere for a while where we have the time to argue about nothing.''

Doc grinned, his gleaming white teeth in his tightly drawn and lined face giving him the appearance of a skeletal jester. He said no more, but tossed the one-eyed warrior a self-heat, which Ryan opened.

"Let's just enjoy it for now," Ryan added, opening the container and setting off the process by which the contents were heated.

Doc distributed some more of the containers, and even Mildred conceded that, as poor as some self-heats could be in terms of taste, they were still superior to the bizarre hotchpotch, still bubbling gently if a little malevolently, Doc had thrown together on the hot plate.

They ate in silence, none of them realizing until that moment how hungry they were, and how tired they had to have been to sleep without even thinking about food prior to this.

When they had finished, Jak placed his container on the cluttered table and belched. "Air getting bad," he muttered.

"And you're not helping," Dean pointed out.

"Seriously, though, Jak has a point," Mildred added. "We're going to have to think about leaving. The air-conditioning plant won't be able to cope with us for much longer, and the air's just going to get worse.''

"Okay, we'll find the armory, check it out, then head on out," Ryan said decisively. "Let's check ourselves first, though—don't want to be too relaxed."

The group ran through their weapons and supplies. As well as his leaf-bladed throwing knives, Jak also carried a .357 Magnum Colt Python with a six-inch barrel. It was, as always, in immaculate condition. Dean checked his Browning Hi-Power, Mildred her Czech ZKR 551 .38-caliber target revolver, which she favored because it fitted in with her predark shooting skills that had seen her win an Olympic silver medal.

Doc's favored blaster was a LeMat double-barrel percussion pistol, usually firing two different kinds of shot. It was effective as a scattergun at longer ranges, and deadly in close quarters. A .38-caliber Smith & Wesson Model 640 was Krysty's preferred blaster, and this was also checked. Ryan shouldered his Steyr SSG-70 rifle, and inspected his SIG-Sauer handblaster.

Mildred and Krysty made sure that they had gathered the remains of the self-heats and tucked them into their backpacks.

They were ready, if still relaxed. Now to check out the armory.

As with everything else in the redoubt, it was ridiculously easy to find. And there was no sec lock on the door, which was easily opened.

"Dark night," J.B. growled. "I knew it was too damned good to be true."

The Armorer and Ryan walked into the room that

had once housed the armory. It was empty, apart from one open crate, which contained several rifles.

"Something's better than nothing," Ryan commented, removing one of the rifles from the crate and handing it to J.B.

"Guess I was mebbe expecting too much," J.B. replied, pushing his fedora back from his forehead and taking the rifle with his other hand. "But what's this?"

"I was kind of hoping you could tell me that, partner," the one-eyed warrior replied as he, too, examined one of the rifles.

They were of a fairly conventional shape, although the lines of the barrel and stock seemed to almost blur as they molded into one. The blaster was of some alloy with which they were both unfamiliar, and had a large, round red sight on the top, which was nondetachable. There was a crystal in a cage at the end of the barrel, instead of an opening, and there was no way of inserting ammo.

"You thinking what I'm thinking?" Ryan questioned.

J.B. put the rifle down and carefully wiped his spectacles. "Yep, guess so. Mebbe some kind of laser tech. Who knows how that kind of shit works? Never come across enough of it to figure that out. So if these were left here because they're defective…"

"Then we leave them because they're just dead-weight to us."

The Armorer nodded. "One way to find out."

Ryan nodded agreement. Making sure that the armory was clear apart from themselves, they tried each rifle, toying with the settings. None would fire; most wouldn't even fire up the digital displays that came up in the red sight. Those that did had low power readings and error messages that made little sense without a trained tech or a manual.

J.B. threw the last one to the floor in disgust—a disgust measured by his treatment of something he would usually cherish.

"Knew it was too good," he repeated.

"Guess we better just watch that it's as bad as it gets," Ryan said quietly.

He and J.B. returned to the others. There was no need to explain, as they had gathered the results.

"So we head out?" Mildred asked.

Ryan assented. "Recce on the way to see if we can pick up anything of interest."

They began to walk the corridors that led toward the elevators, emergency stairwells and upward ramps that would take them to the surface. The corridors were dingy, with just enough light to see in front, but not enough to stop the corner of vision from being obscured by shadow. They passed through several sec doors that were permanently open.

"Hey, has anyone noticed something weird?" Dean asked suddenly as they passed through yet another open door.

"How would you define *weird?*" Doc queried.

"Well, because all these doors are open I wouldn't swear to it being the same all the way through, but I've looked at the last couple of sec panels, and they haven't got numbers scratched on them."

Ryan frowned. It was something and nothing. Predark sec men sometimes scratched the sec-code numbers onto the scratch plates on the reverse side of the sec door, in case they forgot the number sequence.

"So you think what?" he asked his son.

Dean shrugged. "Don't know. Guess mebbe this wasn't a regular military place. Whoever was stationed here, was here all the time, and wasn't likely to forget."

"And why all open?" Jak added. "Not usual."

Ryan shook his head. "No, this isn't an ordinary redoubt. What—"

He looked round sharply, guided by an instinct that told him Krysty had stopped behind him. She was staring at a closed door, and the hair around her nape had formed tendrils that hugged her neck.

"Mebbe we'll find an answer in there," she said. "It feels bad, but not like danger...just residual bad feeling."

"If it can't hurt us," J.B. remarked, throwing a glance at Ryan. The one-eyed warrior gestured, and the Armorer stepped forward to the door. It had a computerized lock with a blank digital display, and when he tried the handle underneath, the door failed to yield.

With a shrug, he took a small piece of plas-ex from one of his pockets, added a detonator fuse and set it. Waiting until the others took cover, he activated the fuse and hurriedly stepped back himself.

The lock and display on the door was of glass and a soft metal, and the small blob of plas-ex was enough explosive to make the metal buckle and yield. Waiting for the friction-heated metal to cool for a few seconds, the Armorer tried the door once more, and it swung open. The smell of the explosion lingered in the poor air, catching at their throats.

Personal artifacts were strewed across the desk and the carpet, as though someone had wrecked the room in a rage. A swivel chair lay overturned on the door side of the desk, and the remains of a body were visible in the hollow beneath the desk.

Mildred moved around to get a better view. The body was dressed in a black T-shirt and combat pants, with scuffed boots. It looked paramilitary rather than military to her, reminding the woman of the punks and metalheads from her own predark days who had become obsessed with apocalyptic and militaristic imagery. Strands of hair still clung to the skull. The skeleton still clutched a gray service-issue Colt .45 with a customized mother-of-pearl pistol grip. The cause of death was obvious: part of the skull was lying across the room, splintered by the bullet that had passed through the right temple and out somewhere above the left ear.

Ryan noticed a poster on the wall. It was faded and crumbling, and over a dreamlike image were written, in gothic lettering, the words "Grateful Dead."

"Guess he was," Ryan said grimly, indicating the poster.

The comp terminal on the long-dead man's desk would give them no clues. It had been thoroughly trashed and was beyond repair, with the keyboard dismembered and the screen smashed. There were only a few pieces of paper scattered about. They were fragile with age and crumbled when Dean or Ryan bent to pick them up. The fragments that remained were so faded with scrawled ink that they were unreadable.

"It seems to me that we are in the hands of some apocalyptic cult or other," Doc commented mildly, squinting to read several posters that were still hanging—just—from the walls. They were faded, and the light was poor, but there was enough for him to see that they all had biblical imagery or photographs of dead, dying and starving people. The slogans beneath spoke of humankind—what was left—rising like a phoenix from the ashes of mass destruction.

"Creeps knew what coming," Jak commented.

"I don't think this was anything to do with the military," Mildred said, looking around her. "Can you imagine predark soldiers having these weird posters?" She gestured at the walls, and then looked at her companions. "No, I don't suppose you'd know, really," she added lamely, suddenly feeling the weight of her years.

Doc broke the silence. "From my somewhat limited knowledge, I would have to agree. I suspect this truly is some kind of nonmilitary base. In which case, it may be worth our searching for clues, as we may find information—if not weapons—that can be used to our advantage."

J.B. acknowledged Doc's point. "Okay, but where do we look?"

"There's as good a place as any," Krysty said, pointing to a poster.

Ryan didn't question her instinct. He simply tore down the poster, which crumbled at his touch, to reveal a small wall safe hidden behind. Set into the wall, it had a simple tumbler lock.

"Better be something here—can't keep wasting

this," J.B. grumbled as he repeated his previous procedure with an even smaller blob of plas-ex.

The explosion sounded louder in the enclosed space as they retreated to outside the door. When the plaster dust had settled, Ryan could see that the door of the safe was hanging loosely from its hinges, and that the plaster surrounding had powdered in the blast. Advancing to the safe, Ryan used the long barrel of the Steyr to maneuver the door open, mindful of any booby traps that may not have been knocked out by the initial blast.

The door creaked and fell off the hinge. Peering inside, Ryan could see nothing but a small, spiral-bound notebook. Taking it out gingerly, he could feel that the pages weren't of paper, but rather of some kind of plastic that was as thin as paper.

He put the book on the desk and opened it. The pages were typed, which made it easier to read.

"What does it say, lover?" Krysty asked, peering over his shoulder.

"Makes no sense to me," Ryan said simply, shaking his head. "I can see the words, but what they're supposed to mean..."

"Let me see." Mildred took the book from him and began to read.

Obviously, it made some kind of sense to her, as she began to flick through the pages, referring back and forth, and nodding to herself from time to time.

"Fireblast!" Ryan exclaimed after a few minutes, the tension getting to him. "Are you just going to stand there until we all get old and die, or are you going to tell us what it says?"

Mildred gave Ryan a withering look. "The psycho

who wrote this was clever, but mad. It kind of makes sense, but I need to read it through to get the gist. So lay off for a minute, eh?''

Ryan grinned in apology. Mildred grinned back and returned to the text.

Finally, she put the book down.

"Oh, boy, you're going to love this," she began. "These guys had nothing to do directly with the U.S. military, which means that this redoubt isn't, strictly speaking, the same as the others we've come across. But—and this is a big but—they were part of a secret order that was partly funded by some black operations within the U.S. government."

"Who gives shit now?" Jak interrupted.

"Yeah, that bit may all be ancient history, but it does explain why this is different from other redoubts. It was built using official plans and official money that had been siphoned off from official budgets. Strange, really, but I used to kind of think back in the old days that people who talked about that sort of thing happening were all nuts. Guess I was wrong and they were right, for all the good it did them."

"Nice story, but still no nearer to telling me why it's so important now," J.B. mused.

"Ah, I think I may have an idea," Doc interrupted. "Would I be right in assuming that some of that old whitecoat paranoia was therefore justified, and that the men behind this redoubt—and doubtless others like it—were more powerful than even their paymasters would suppose? After all, those laser rifles…"

He paused, waiting for the import of this to sink in. J.B. gestured. "Okay, go on, Millie."

"Why, thank you, John," the doctor answered with

a sardonic edge to her voice. "According to this journal, this order, the Illuminated Ones, was in possession of knowledge that foretold the end of the world, and were hoodwinking the U.S. government. All the while they were supposed to be developing new tech and providing an extra bolt-hole for some government higher-ups, they were working on their main plan, which was to find the secret world at the center of the earth."

"Crazies," Jak spit, turning away.

Doc allowed himself a chuckle. "Of course, it does all fit, does it not, my dear Dr. Wyeth? Even when I was a young man, there were secret societies devoted to the accumulation of arcane knowledge, power and wealth, led by men who believed themselves better, and somehow 'illuminated' by secret truths. And men talked about secret entrances to hidden worlds at the center of the earth, and of gateways to enormous knowledge and wealth that lay to the north—"

"Like Trader's stories and legends?" Ryan asked. "Could that be all they were?"

"Stupes like him could make it so by going there, Dad," Dean answered, gesturing to the plaster-dusted skeleton on the carpet.

"It's a fair point, lover," Krysty added.

Ryan allowed himself a smile, and was about to answer when Mildred cut him short.

"There's a couple of things I haven't mentioned yet. Important things."

"And they are?"

"Firstly, this journal ends about fifty years after skydark. This guy decided to stay behind when some made the jump to another gateway."

"What? Then there may be—"

"Hang on, Ryan, I haven't finished yet. Some made a jump, and others decided to move up top. He couldn't face the change, so—" she let the comment hang, with just a glance at the skeleton "—so I guess there may be a colony waiting for us up top."

The one-eyed warrior shrugged. "It's possible, sure. But this also means that they must have had another base, better equipped, right? They wouldn't just jump at random. Not if they'd been here that long."

"That's a reasonable assumption," Mildred agreed. "So maybe we should make sure we can get back in here when we've taken a look outside, see all we can see."

Krysty nodded her agreement, although the way her hair was moving closely around her neck and shoulders suggested a deep-seated unease at developments. "Mebbe their jump was to the mythical base in the north—the promised lands."

"That is a lot of supposition, and it's possibly joining dots to form an abstract picture," Doc mused, "but it'll do for fitting the pieces together until something better comes along."

But J.B. had spotted the hesitancy in Mildred's voice. "Why do we need to make sure we leave a way back in? If the main door is in as good condition as the rest of the redoubt..."

"That's the problem, John. These crazies were so keen on their center-of-the-earth theory that they made their redoubts deeper than any we've ever come across. Deep enough to protect it from quakes nearer the surface that have affected other redoubts. That's why this is in good repair still. But..."

"But it means it's a whole lot longer of a way up, and there's no knowing what we may find, right?" Ryan fixed his steely blue eye on Mildred.

"Right. And if the way is blocked, then we've got big trouble. We either risk a quick jump and God knows where this redoubt is linked to, or we stay here and gradually suffocate as the air gets poorer."

"Shit choice," Ryan said simply. "Guess we'll just have to find a way out."

Chapter Three

The Armorer was restless as they made their way through the darkened corridors of the redoubt toward the elevator shafts and stairwells that led to the surface.

"If there are still survivors up there, then they may be able to tell us about this so-called promised land...if they don't try to chill us first," he added with a wry inevitability.

"Erewhon," Mildred muttered.

J.B. gave her a questioning look.

"Sorry, John," she answered him. "It's just the name that journal gave it."

"An apt name," Doc interjected dreamily. "A source of much pride to an ancient philosopher who should have known better. Would Samuel Butler smile at his Erewhon Eden being used for something that may be so apt?"

Dean shot Doc a quizzical stare. "What does all that mean?"

Doc smiled. "Erewhon, nowhere...just change a few letters. It could all be so apt."

They came out into a loading bay about forty feet square and ill lit by the one remaining, flickering light. It was dustier than the rest of the corridors, and the temperature dropped a few degrees in the wide concrete expanse.

Directly in front of them were two large elevator bays, with the tempered-steel alloy doors closed. Small gatherings of dirt and dust on the floor swirled slightly in a faint draft, and collected at the point where the supposedly airtight door met. It didn't encourage a belief in the working condition of the elevators.

"Could be that just the seals have broken down," Ryan muttered, hunkering down to feel the dirt, and to judge the draft.

Krysty joined him. "Not good," she whispered, almost to herself. "This isn't just surface dirt—this is rock dust."

Ryan stood, noting that his own sense of unease was mirrored in the way Krysty's hair had tightened to her skull. The one-eyed warrior examined the comp panels that had controlled the elevator. They were dead, blank screens failing to register any signs of life no matter how many buttons he pressed.

"Guess it's the stairs and maintenance shafts, then," J.B. drawled, watching Ryan. "Good exercise."

Ryan smiled. "Guess so. Gonna be a hell of a climb, though."

"Why?" Jak asked.

"These people were obsessed with getting deep into the earth, and this is much deeper than the usual redoubt. So we're going to have to climb farther," Mildred explained.

"So the sooner we get started the better, I guess," Dean said, looking around to find the access door to the emergency stairwells that were used to access a redoubt's maintenance ducts.

The unassuming entrance was hidden in the dark shadows of the bay, and wasn't on the centralized comp mainframe for the redoubt. This had been a measure to insure that parts of the redoubt could be accessed by engineers in cases where the mainframe had gone haywire and caused a malfunction that jammed the sec doors or elevators. So each door accessing the shafts on every level was notable only for having no sec lock, but a large lever lock.

For Ryan and his people, trying to get out, this became irritating, as they couldn't just tap in a code, but had to blast the lock from the door and waste valuable plas-ex or ammo. J.B. complained bitterly to himself as he used yet more of the valuable explosive to blow the door. He had hoped that the armory would replenish his stocks, but was still sorely disappointed by what they had found.

The door blew, swinging noisily on dry hinges.

Coming forward to the dark hole that the stairwell formed, Ryan peered upward, his good eye trying to focus through the stinging dust. Form took shape in the blackness.

"Still some kind of stairs or ramp, and it looks intact for as far as I can see. We'll spread out and take it at twenty-yard intervals. J.B., you're last. I'll go first."

With that, Ryan stepped into the darkness.

IT WAS crushingly claustrophobic in the service shaft. There was no way of seeing which way was up and which down; there was no way of telling where the ceiling lay, and how far in front there was actually a floor left. Ryan kept a hand out to his left, his fin-

gertips brushing the side of the stairwell shaft so that
he had some kind of bearing. To his right may have
been a wall or a sheer drop as he continued upward.

The air was fresher, suggesting that somewhere
above them was access to the surface that was letting
in air untreated by the redoubt's defective condition-
ing plant. The problem with this was that a gap or
hole letting in untreated air suggested that there had
been a landslide of some kind. That in turn suggested
the unpleasant thought that the shaft may be unstable.

In the enclosed dark, Ryan could hear his combat
boots on the concrete, coming down in measured
tread, with only the occasional skittering of small
stones, concrete chips and gravel beneath his feet. Behind him, he could hear Krysty, treading delicately on
the concrete, measuring each step for danger. Her sil-
ver-tipped cowboy boots made a higher note on the
sounding board of the concrete. Her breathing, like
his, was slow and measured.

Jak was inaudible, despite being third in line and
only forty yards behind Ryan in the enclosed darkness. The albino had uncanny hunting instincts, and
was able to move in silence amid the most impossible
conditions.

Doc, in the middle, was even more audible than
Krysty. Despite his tenacious strength, the battering
of time travel and torture had told heavily on Doc's
reserves of stamina and the way in which he could
cope with such obstacles. His feet shuffled, his
swordstick tapping rhythmically on the concrete floor.
His breathing was regular, but hard and rasping.

Dean, behind Doc, was out of hearing range, but
Ryan could feel his son's impatience, lest Doc slow

too much and leave the party falling too far behind. With Mildred bringing up the rear, Ryan knew he could rely on her to be on hand to help Doc, and that J.B. would keep things together.

So far, Ryan had resisted the urge to either call out to his people or to use one of the precious flares that he carried. Like so much other salvaged tech, the flares were inclined to be erratic when set off, and sometimes could fail to ignite…or would explode with enough force to take off the hand of whoever tried to ignite them.

"Listen up," he said in a low tone that he hoped would carry sufficiently to the back of the strung-out group. "I'm going to light a flare, see what the fire-blasted hell is in front of us. So no one jump when the lights go on."

He had been unwilling to raise his voice. Since entering the service shaft and stairwell they had all maintained silence, broken only by the odd whispered word of warning to the immediate follower if there was an obstruction on the path that could cause injury, a raised piece of concrete that could turn an unwary ankle and hold them all up. Without a recce of the shaft ahead, there was no way of knowing if a sudden noise would set off a collapse of some kind. So they had all kept quiet. But the risk of startled exclamations and shouts when the flare went off was a greater risk than Ryan's hoarse cry.

"You okay, lover?" Krysty whispered.

Ryan nodded, forgetting the dark. "Just about. But we need to see what's ahead."

He took the flare from the canvas bag that was slung on the opposite side to his Steyr. The flare spluttered twice, small sparks illuminating Ryan's concerned, concentrated visage, before seeming to die off. Then, when he was almost at the point of giving up, it suddenly hissed and sputtered into life, throwing a phosphorus glare around the shaft.

Looking back over his shoulder, Ryan could see his companions in a line behind him, all adjusting their eyes to the sudden light. He could also see the way in which the shaft was constructed. Reinforced-concrete beams supported the roof and lined the walls at regular intervals. Also regular, but falling in between the beams, was a series of graduated steps, each forming a platform of about twenty-five feet in length, some of which were irregularly raised.

"Most ingenious," Doc murmured on observing this, taking the brief opportunity to halt for a moment's rest. "Not steps, but neither a ramp. The slightest movement of the earth will merely alter the one platform, rather than stress and crack a complete ramp or break a fixed staircase."

Ryan looked at his wrist chron. They had been progressing up for nearly an hour. The incline was gradual, and the shaft had a slight bend to it. Looking ahead, he could see that the platforms were a little more uneven, suggesting earth disturbance. But all the columns appeared to be intact. He noted that the width of the tunnel was less than he had supposed, and it would have been possible for him to stand in the middle with both arms extended to touch the sides.

From the elapsed time and the gradation of the tunnel, he suspected that they still had a long way to go.

"Okay, now we know where we're going," he said, almost to himself. "Let's go."

A flare would last twenty minutes, the last five showing a fading light, so Ryan knew that they had been walking for over fifteen minutes when they came to a sharp corner, the first they had encountered.

But even by the fading light he could see that it wasn't a constructed corner. The earth had savagely taken the shaft and bent it to its own will.

"Problems," he said over his shoulder, trying to make his voice carry without raising it. "We've got an earth move."

As he said it, he was aware of the platform beneath his feet moving. It was a slight movement, but growing with every second. The concrete platform was tilting on loosened earth, the angle of tilt increasing the momentum in a dangerous equation.

"Fireblast!" he yelled, the flare falling from his grip as he slid on the platform, a thin coating of moss from the seepage of damp earth causing his heavy combat boots to lose their firm hold as the angle increased.

Ryan tilted his muscular frame to the bend of the earth, not fighting the momentum but rolling with it, using it to adjust his own equilibrium. As the shaft tilted and rolled in his vision, he saw that the others were also encountering similar problems. Krysty had been slammed into the wall of the shaft, and was fighting to regain both footing and the breath that had been driven from her body. Behind her, Jak was down, but already springing to his feet. Doc was down, and beyond him there was darkness, filled with the rumble of moving earth and the crunch and whine of breaking concrete and twisting metal as the support rods in the columns bent beneath the pressure of the moving rock and earth.

And then, as suddenly as it had started, it ceased. Ryan stood silent and still, straining every nerve to detect any further movement. By the fading light, he could see Krysty, propped against the near wall of the shaft.

She caught his glance and briefly shook her head. With her razor-sharp mutie sense, she was the likeliest to detect any further danger in the depths of the earth.

Doc looked up, not yet daring to clamber to his feet.

"Safe?" he whispered. It seemed uncannily loud in the silence following the miniquake.

Ryan nodded, moving slowly to pick up the spluttering and dying flare, and moving with an infinite care back to where Krysty stood.

"Go back and check," he said quietly. Krysty assented, and they both crept back to Jak, who was standing perfectly still, feeling for the slightest movement through the balls of his feet. As they approached, the albino looked at them, the flare illuminating his red eyes so that they glowed like coals.

"We move, not it adjust us," he murmured, indicating that the resettled earth should be still for some time. The three of them went back to Doc, who was gingerly picking himself up and dusting himself down. Without a word, Doc fell in behind them and muttered an oath to himself when he saw that a wall of concrete, earth and rock cut them off from the others.

"Hope they behind, not in," Jak said simply.

IT WAS PITCH-BLACK, and Mildred clung to the concrete floor, aware that she was at some crazy angle where her feet were above her head and her hands were pressing against the angle where the floor and wall now met.

The dust and dirt that filled the air clogged her nose and mouth. "John," she spluttered through a mouthful of earth, "are you okay?"

"In one piece," the Armorer replied quietly. "How about you?"

"Everything works and nothing hurts...much," she replied with a smile no one could see. "Damned quake's got me almost upside down, but other than that..."

"I'm coming forward," J.B. replied. And then there was silence for a short while, broken only by the distant shuffle of earth on concrete. J.B.'s voice broke again. "I must be near you. Things seem to have died down, and it's all pretty solid. There's a ten-foot raise in front of me, but enough of a gap to get through."

While Mildred tentatively picked her way around the steeply angled shaft until she was once again upright, she could hear J.B. ascend to the top of the platform and the scrape of his boots against the concrete as he felt his way down to floor level.

"Millie, where are you?" he whispered, only feet from her. She reached out to embrace him, and they silently thanked fate that each was, so far, okay. Finally, he said, "We need to get forward, find the others. Think we can risk a flare?"

"Uh-uh...too risky until we know how much air

we've got. If we're in a pocket, then the flare could use it too quickly.''

"Okay, let's find out," J.B. said simply, passing her and tentatively moving forward. He went only a few yards before reaching a wall of rock and earth.

"Shit, we're cut off back here."

"And no way of knowing how deep that wall of rock is," Mildred added, almost to herself.

DEAN KNEW that he had been unconscious, but had no idea for how long. He only knew that his mouth tasted bitter, and his head was ringing as he raised it.

Slowly, allowing himself time to adjust to the crazy angle of the floor and for his balance to assert itself over the waves of nausea that washed past him as he sat upright, he took in his surroundings. There was no light, and he waited in silence for his eyes to adjust to the residual light.

But there was no residual light.

Dean fought back the sudden surprise and panic, and tried to think logically. He was still alive, and although the fall and subsequent unconsciousness had left his body aching, there was no damage that would impair him. On his hands and knees, moving slowly to keep any disturbance to a minimum, Dean explored the limits of his enclosed world. It was only a couple of yards each way around, and the roof was too low to enable him to stand straight when he attempted to rise to his feet.

The extent of his problem hit him squarely. He now knew he was cut off from all his companions, and what was more he had no way of knowing which direction was forward, which direction actually led to the unblocked passage or back to the redoubt, or even if there was a way out.

For a second, the black despair of loneliness threatened to engulf him, and hot salt tears pricked at the back of his eyes. If he managed to get out, was there any guarantee that he would find his father alive, or Krysty or Doc or…?

Cursing himself for being weak at a moment when he needed strength, the Cawdor blood began to tell. A steely resolve settled on Dean, and he shifted onto his knees, picking one end of the enclosure at which to begin his attempts to burrow out. Extending one arm upward, he felt once more the concrete passage support that was keeping the roof in place. His fingers feeling along gently, he could trace stress lines and fracture contours in the concrete where it had been twisted in the tunnel fall. In places he could reach into the column where the concrete had broken away and the cold metal of the steel reinforcing rod was bared.

A tentative push showed him that the roof support, such as it was, was firm enough for the moment. Firm enough for him to start disturbing the earth and rock, moving it away from the pile that had formed at one end of the enclosure.

It had never occurred to Dean that any kind of earthmoving work depended so much on being able to see what he was doing. As he moved the loose earth around clumps of rock, he found himself cursing repeatedly as shifting rocks crushed his fingers, and every time he made some small headway into the rockpile he felt other loose rocks tumble in to fill it— rocks he would have shored up if he could see them.

He had no idea how deep the fall went; it was something that he couldn't even think about. It could have fallen all the way to the top of the shaft, in which case he would run out of air long before he had the chance to make any progress. But there was nothing else he could do. So he concentrated on the matter at hand.

SWEAT RAN in rivulets down Mildred's face and neck. She could feel it down her back, gathering in a cold pool in the hollow at the base of her spine. She had stripped down to her undershirt, her clothes bundled beside her in the angle where wall met floor. She felt as though she had been shifting rock and dirt for all her life, and still she seemed to be making no headway. The atmosphere was already fetid and rank, and she was glad for the small flow of cleaner air coming through the gap where J.B. had climbed from his part of the fall.

Loose earth gathered at her feet, while large rocks were passed back to the Armorer, who disposed of them at the back of the enclave, piling them carefully. He would have liked to heft some of the smaller ones over the gap and into the space behind, but couldn't risk one loose rock landing in such a way as to trigger a minor slide.

They worked in silence, to preserve air and energy, and because they had to concentrate intently on the task at hand. Neither wanted to think about the possibility of the rocks building up behind them before they broke through, and their making for themselves an even smaller, tighter prison.

J.B.'s head was filled with random thoughts of the

past, or early days traveling with the Trader, of meeting Ryan and of the friends they had lost along the way. Now to be lost himself? He dismissed that as he took another rock from Mildred.

Mildred was remembering when she was a girl, scared of the dark and locked in the basement at her father's Baptist church. She had only been there an hour after the door had closed behind her while she was exploring. How old was she then, about six? It had been so boring and so cold until she was discovered. She could do with that cold now, and someone like her father to just come along and open a door that would let them out.

BY THE LIGHT of the flare, it was easier for Ryan and Jak to remove rocks and brush falling dirt out of the way. Krysty and Doc took the rocks as they were removed from the earth fall, piling them at the sides of the shaft so that they still left a clear path.

With light and more air, Jak and Ryan were working at speed, forming the beginnings of a tunnel. Jak used the flatter slabs of rock to shore up the two-foot-high tunnel, enough for a crawl space if little else. They were working on limited time for themselves as much as anyone who was left on the other side of the landslide: there could be another miniquake at any time, triggered by their activity in the shaft.

Jak suddenly froze. "Stop," he hissed. "Listen."

Ryan also froze, straining every fiber of his being to pick up whatever Jak had heard. The albino's face was rapt, his eyes narrowed, his teeth biting into his bottom lip with an intense concentration that was beginning to draw blood.

Krysty and Doc exchanged a look, both standing expectantly, feeling useless at that moment.

It was there again: Jak briefly looked at Ryan and nodded once, then again, in time to the noise.

A smile flickered at the corners of Ryan's dust-caked lips. Faintly, so faint that it was almost impossible to hear, came the rhythmic scraping sound of rock being moved.

"Still alive," Jak stated baldly, "and trying to get through."

DEAN FELT exhausted, and was on the verge of giving up. Not with frustration, but simply because it seemed to have been going on forever. Deprived of all other sense, there was just the darkness, the heat, the stench and the rocks. He felt as though he were moving automatically, not even knowing what he was doing or why.

He moved another slab of rock, which jammed against one that was sticking out of the mass at an angle. The stones grated on each other, and Dean pulled at them, powdering small fragments that he breathed in with the increasingly bad air, feeling it scour his nasal passages and bite into his throat. Even to cough was too much effort, and he choked down the bile that the reflex of coughing brought up. He maneuvered the stone from side to side, trying to lever it clear.

The blackness was becoming all-encompassing. It wasn't just lack of light. It was lack of sound, lack of feeling, lack of everything.

Dean began to slide once more into unconsciousness.

"STOPPED...get moving," Jak said, snapping back into action with renewed energy. His sinewy limbs twisted around rocks, digging out earth with his bare hands to grip the rocks and pull them loose, but still making sure that he shored up the small tunnel as he went along.

Ryan didn't waste time on a reply, but joined the wiry albino in his task. Ryan's hands were larger, his arms thicker, but he worked just as determinedly to loosen the rocks and tunnel deeper.

Behind them, Krysty and Doc cleared the rocks and dirt that they left in their wake as their progress increased rapidly. No one spoke, but they all knew that the cessation of the noise was a bad sign. It could only mean that whoever was digging had either reached the point of exhaustion or had become unconscious.

And either option was bad.

MILDRED WAS LIKE a machine. She could no longer think about what she was doing, just act purely on instinct. And instinct was telling her that what she had to do to survive was keep digging out those rocks and dirt, keep shoring up that space she was making, keep passing it back to J.B.

The Armorer was also acting like an automaton. His spectacles—useless in such a situation—were secure in his pocket for when he would need them. His fedora was jammed on the back of his head, his close-cropped hair underneath wet with sweat. His clothes stuck to him with a paste of perspiration and dust that would have felt uncomfortable if he had been able to spare the attention to focus on this. But there was no part of him that could afford to focus on anything other than collecting and disposing of rocks.

Mildred kept burrowing until something jolted her out of the routine she had established. Something that took a moment to register.

She was picking at loose soil, and a warm draft came through that dirt. Then she was picking at nothing....

"John, we're through. It's empty...." Her voice was nothing more than a pained croak, but in the silence it was enough to penetrate the Armorer's consciousness.

"Millie, keep going...got to get there," he returned, suddenly aware of how dry and cracked his own throat seemed.

Jolted back to a form of consciousness, Mildred redoubled her efforts and had soon made a hole large enough for herself to crawl through. She had a bad feeling as soon as she was through, and coughed at the poor air in the new enclave. She crawled a few feet farther to allow J.B. to follow, pushing her clothes and their blasters before him.

"It's too hot. Must be a hollow in the slide," she whispered. Grasping before her, she felt a leg in the darkness. "Oh, sweet God," she wailed, continuing to feel up the leg until she came to the torso, "Dean?"

"Is he alive?" J.B. managed to husk.

Mildred could feel his chest rise and fall in shallow breath. She nodded, then managed to croak "Yes" when she realized that J.B. couldn't see her.

But how could they go on? What lay in front of them?

"FASTER," Jak murmured, his mouth set in a thin, determined line.

"Not too fast—bring it all down on us," Ryan reminded him, feeling tightly enclosed in the dark tunnel. Jak was a couple of feet ahead, passing rocks down his body and packing the walls and ceiling. He was full length, and Ryan knew almost the whole length of his own body was in the tunnel. So they had to have burrowed through at least three yards of earth and rock.

"Nearly there," Jak snapped back. "Earth loose..."

MILDRED HEARD the movement of the rocks and earth grow louder, and climbed over Dean to where the rock that had defeated him stood, jammed in the tunnel entrance he had made.

"Pull him back, John," she whispered, and as the Armorer pulled Dean's prone body back from under her, she began to work at the rock. The rocks and earth around it began to loosen as the opposite side of the rock moved. She used the way in which it had wedged to swing it around and shore up dirt that was beginning to fall from the roof of the small tunnel.

The earth fell away slowly from one side while she clawed at it from the other. A residual light from the other side of the tunnel, almost unbelievably bright in the total darkness she had been forced to work in, backlit the white hair and scarred pale features of Jak Lauren.

Mildred almost cried with joy to see him. The flicker of a smile even flitted briefly across the albino's features. It was driven away as he remembered how precarious their position was at that moment.

"Quick, not last long," he breathed.

Mildred nodded and began to enlarge the hole where the tunnels met. Soon it was large enough for Jak to crawl through.

"Come," Mildred gasped, "Dean's unconscious."

As she backed out of the tunnel, Jak crawled through. He was completely blind in the total blackness, but felt Dean's limp body, and slithered back into the tunnel, dragging the prone boy after him.

Ryan scrambled back out of the tunnel, having heard Mildred and realizing that he would be of better use at the tunnel mouth to help bring his son into the open shaft.

As Jak appeared, pulling the still unconscious Dean, Ryan suppressed the fear that his son was dead...but not enough for Krysty not to notice and shoot him a worried glance.

Mildred crawled through, drawing the cleaner air in great gulps through her tortured throat. J.B. brought up the rear, and lay gasping for breath as Mildred immediately checked Dean, ignoring her own condition.

"He'll be okay," she told Ryan in short gasps as she drank greedily from the canteen of water he offered her. "Just needs to recover from the heat and the air—get some oxygen into him."

Even as she spoke, Dean was stirring slightly. Krysty was resting him in a reclining posture against her, and Doc held the boy's head, gently tipping water to his lips.

"Take it easy, my dear boy," Doc whispered. "The worst is over."

"Mebbe," Ryan said softly, overhearing Doc, "but we need to get moving quickly, no matter how tired we are. We can't risk staying here."

"Take turns carrying Dean until recovered enough walk alone," Jak offered.

Ryan nodded. "Me and you first to give J.B. and Mildred a chance to recoup their strength."

The albino nodded and turned away, looking at the sudden bend in the shaft.

"Hope not hit another slide," he said quietly.

Chapter Four

"Dark night! This explains a lot," J.B. said breathlessly, wiping his spectacles on his shirt.

Ryan whistled softly. "Seems stupe to go all the way up just to go all the way down, but I guess mebbe that's the only way for it to be."

Jak was sitting with his legs dangling over the precipice. "We okay, but how Doc?"

Doc made an expression of distaste. "I think that after the trials of the past few hours, this will be a mere bagatelle."

They had finally reached the top of the shaft after several hours' climb, lengthened because of their weariness in dealing with the landslide. Although all of them would have liked to have rested, Ryan was certain that the only viable course of action was to keep moving. The others knew he was right, even though J.B. and Mildred were almost unconscious as they walked, and Dean was carried for the first hour by a relay of Ryan and Jak, and then Krysty and Doc, the latter breathing heavily the whole way, but refusing to give in to his own weariness until Dean was able to stand unaided.

Ryan's decision to keep moving was vindicated by the number of partial earthslides and movements that they had to traverse as they made their way up the shaft. It was no surprise that the elevators had long since been decommissioned by the change in geography, as the shaft, which had previously been fairly straight, began to bend at ridiculous angles, so much so that at times they felt they were turning back on themselves. The concrete platforms that formed the steps had moved to angles that sometimes entailed a climb of several feet to get over the top, followed by a drop to where the level had fallen on the other side. It became harder to discern their depth and when they were likely to surface. They could only tell when the tunnel began to lighten, and the hole formed at the top of the shaft became visible.

Eventually, with aching muscles that had begun to weaken to jelly, they saw the top of the shaft widen, and after two more scrambles over bizarrely angled platforms, they found themselves at the mouth of the shaft.

This had to have been the way that the survivors of the redoubt had taken some fifty years before, as the growth of mutated plant and vegetation around the mouth of the shaft was thick and heavily spread, suggesting that it had been established sometime, and therefore the earth movements had occurred during the period when the Illuminated Ones were still in the redoubt.

It was only when they came out of the mouth of the shaft and looked around that they could appreciate what had occurred.

They found themselves some fifty feet above the surrounding country, with the mouth of the shaft facing a sheer drop on one side, and a seventy degree descent on the other among some verdant foliage that almost choked the hillside. The shrubs and plants formed an unbroken carpet, hiding whatever mutated horrors might be found ground level.

It seemed obvious that in the time directly after skydark, when the Deathlands was formed in the upheaval and devastation, this part of the country had suffered severe tremors and quakes that had lifted up a part of the ground that, by chance, contained the gateway to the redoubt. The sec doors to what had once been the entrance were probably hidden and decayed in the lush vegetation beneath. The maintenance and emergency shaft had only been protected and preserved by the concrete platforms of the graduated steps.

They now took the opportunity to rest and recuperate before pressing on. Although it would be easy for them to be spotted from the lower levels, they also had a clear view of any potential enemy themselves. It would be impossible for anyone—except perhaps Jak—to move through the forest below without causing disturbance. The territory beyond the sheer drop was more sparsely vegetated, with the remains of a two-lane blacktop road about three miles to the east, with a ruined gas station and diner sitting on it like a toy. Anyone moving on the terrain would be as visible to them as they would be on top of the hill.

"So which way you reckon we move, lover?" Krysty asked Ryan as the one-eyed man stood on the edge of the drop, scanning the horizon.

"Guess we go down the rock face. It won't be easy, but it'll be less risky than going down into that forest," he said. "What do you say, J.B.?"

The Armorer shrugged. "I don't reckon either of

them, but seeing as we can't go back, either, I guess there isn't much choice.''

"Better danger seen than not seen," Jak added.

"I take your point, gentlemen," Mildred said slowly, "but do you think all of us are up to it right now?"

"Madam, I shall endeavor as always to do my best. I can ask no more nor no less of myself." Doc bridled.

"Relax, you old coot, I wasn't particularly thinking of you," Mildred answered. "I'm not too sure about myself at the moment, and even more so about Dean."

"I'll be fine," Dean spit. "You can save your worry."

"Don't be a fool, boy," Ryan snapped harshly. "Mildred's right to a degree. You've been unconscious and haven't had a chance to recover. If you're concussed, then it could be a tricky descent."

"I'll be fine, Dad. What are we going to do, wait here forever 'cause I've had a sore head or Jak needs a bandage on a grazed knee or—?"

"That's enough," Krysty said softly. "If you stumble, we all do, remember?"

Dean stood and stared for a moment, biting his tongue. Then his temper subsided, and he had to agree. "Yeah, you're right. But I'll be okay. I just won't be stupe about it."

"Just as a matter of interest, where would you say we were... I mean in general geographic terms?" Doc broke the awkwardness by changing the subject. He knew the cloud cover would prevent J.B. from taking a reading with his minisextant.

"My guess is to the north, probably more eastern than central, judging by that forest," Ryan replied, indicating the slope to their rear.

"I would have thought so, too," Doc mused. "I wonder if that means the Iluminated Ones had their bases within more than just mat-trans distance to the so-called Erewhon?"

Ryan pondered on that for a few moments. "You mean like within a fairly easy wag distance, in case they needed to do it over the surface? If the mat-trans failed and they were surface safe?"

Doc nodded. "It's a thought, is it not? After all, it would fit with what little we know from the journal and also from the surrounding area."

Ryan nodded. "Then we try and head north along that old road when we reach it. Head for the building first, see if there's anything there to salvage."

"Sounds good to me," J.B. muttered. "Just got to get down there first..." As he spoke, he looked up to the sky. The dark, purple-tinged chem clouds overhead began to discharge a fine spray of rain that began to soak through.

"Great, that's all we need," Dean said, hunching against the rain.

"Feels fresh after all that dust," Mildred said absently.

They all spent a few moments absorbing the rain, resting up with their thoughts before they began the descent.

It was Doc who first noticed it. After scratching absently at an itch on his cheek, he rubbed the tips of his fingers together with a bemused expression.

"What is it?" Ryan asked, his sharp eye catching Doc's gesture.

"I think it may be time for us to move," Doc said with a distracted air. "My dear Dr. Wyeth, would you do me the honor of rubbing your fingers together?"

"What?" Mildred gave Doc a puzzled stare. Then, seeing the seriousness of his expression, she rubbed the index and middle fingers of her left hand together. The texture of the skin on her fingertips was softened, almost soapy. As she rubbed, the skin peeled painlessly away.

She felt her face, where the rain was gently falling. There was the same soapy texture.

"A mild acidic solution, if I surmise correctly," Doc said.

Mildred nodded, then said to Ryan, "We need to get going. It's a way to that roadhouse, and we need the shelter. Too much of this rain and it'll peel our skins off."

Ryan nodded, tentatively fingering his own face. "Then we go now," he said simply.

The descent down the sheer drop would be difficult for all of them. They had no equipment with which to facilitate the climb, and it would mean going down with nothing to link them together other than a thin nylon rope.

Looking over the edge, Doc raised an eyebrow. "Well, at least it gets an incline after about thirty feet, so that will be the worst over with," he said with a grin.

"That makes me feel a whole lot better," Mildred said sarcastically.

Linking themselves together with the rope, they began the descent. Jak went first, as he had an instinctive talent for the climb, and would hunt out the best hand- and footholds he could find for the others. He was followed by J.B. and Mildred. Krysty came next, with Dean following. In both pairings, the former was to keep a close watch on the latter, in case their weakness following the landslide experience was to affect their ability during the descent. And for this reason, Ryan left Doc to bring up the rear, covering the older man. So if Doc stumbled and lost his footing, then Ryan would be able to take the strain.

The descent began well. Jak found that the surface of the hill, although straight down, was pitted with enough outcrops to provide ample foot- and handholds. He crawled down the surface with ease, his hands and feet probing the surface for the largest pieces of jutting rock. Following in his wake, J.B. found the descent easier than he had feared.

Mildred and Krysty had been wary for different reasons. Mildred was worried that her weariness would take a toll and Krysty had thought about doing the climb without her boots, concerned that they were far from suitable for such a climb. Jak's choice of footholds took that into account, however. Dean followed behind Krysty with barely a sign that he was exhausted. He marshaled his concentration in a single-minded display worthy of the Cawdor name.

The one-eyed warrior noted this in his son as he followed on after, but suppressed his pride to concentrate on Doc.

Doc was finding the climb difficult, and the light rain seemed to be more irritating to him than to the others. He was far more tentative in feeling for the hand- and footholds, and a couple of times Ryan had felt the nylon rope tighten as Doc had either moved away and pulled on it, or else had stumbled and almost fallen, his weight straining against Ryan.

"Everything okay, Doc?" Ryan called.

Doc replied with difficulty, his breath coming short and his tone distracted. "I shall get by, my dear Ryan, but I'm not saying it'll be easy."

The rock face was bare of vegetation except for a few small patches of moss and one or two scrub trees that grew at awkward angles from fissures in the rock. One of these scrub trees was covered in sparse green foliage and appeared to house a nest of some kind. Always wary of the possibility of mutie birds, Jak had steered a path away from it, a path followed by the others in their descent.

But not Doc.

As he passed within a few feet of the scrub tree, Doc felt his foot slip on the small protrusion he rested it upon. It was his second such stumble in just a couple of moves, and he panicked momentarily. Flailing backward, his weight pulling against Ryan, he fell to his left. The nearest handhold was the scrub tree, and Doc grabbed for it gratefully.

Below him, Ryan was glad for the strength of the wire-thin nylon rope as he felt it strain along its short length as Doc teetered above him. He wasn't so pleased as he looked at the scrub tree.

"Good heavens!" Doc exclaimed as he steadied himself, his feet finding solid purchase beneath him, his balance regained. For the tree bent under his grip to reveal a bird's nest in the center. And in the nest were four jet-black chicks of a young age, their mouths open automatically for food at the movement of their nest. Their voices broke the quiet of the air with harsh, strident cries that belied their small size. He peered over them, momentarily enchanted and forgetting his precarious position.

As one, they snapped at his face with strident cries, panic and fear of attack overtaking their desire to feed.

The loud cries were echoed by a deeper, much more strident call. Doc looked up, and the only impression he received was of a black shape swooping down on him at great speed. He barely had time to raise an arm to protect himself before the bird was upon him, screeching loudly and pecking at him with a beak as hard as the rocks to which Doc clung.

Doc hugged in close to the rocks, his face contorted in a rictus of pain as the flesh of his hand, clinging to the scrub, was ripped and torn by the slashing cross of the bird's beak, the stench of its body and the shiny black glare of its feathers filling his vision as the rhythmic beating of its wings and the hideous eardrum-splitting screech of its anger filled his ears.

"Fireblast! Move away from the bastard, Doc," Ryan yelled as he drew the SIG-Sauer from its holster and tried to aim at the bird. It was mutated somewhere along its lineage from hawk, but the beak had developed into a honed knife-edge slashing machine. Its dark eyes gleamed dull hatred as it bobbed and weaved around Doc, hovering close to him, its ten-foot wingspan obscuring the man's huddled form. Ryan bobbed and weaved like the bird, trying to line up a shot that wouldn't risk hitting Doc, but it was proving impossible.

Below the one-eyed warrior, Dean, Krysty and Mildred had all drawn their blasters. All were good target pistols, but the bird was saving itself by the sheer ferocity of its attack, staying too close to its prey for them to risk loosing a shot without hitting Doc.

At the bottom of the rope, J.B. and Jak exchanged a hurried glance.

"Too close for a shot," the Armorer yelled.

Jak nodded his understanding, and was already scrambling up the rock face, the rope pulling tight against J.B. as the albino passed him. From the patched and ragged camou jacket, Jak palmed one of the lethal and razor-sharp leaf-bladed knives with which he was so deadly. Taking aim, he let fly with a throw that propelled the knife straight and true for the flapping creature's vital organs.

Jak was astonished to see the knife hit the black hawk's feathers and bounce harmlessly away. The bird didn't even seem to notice the knife's impact.

"Hot pipe! The mutie must have armor for feathers," Dean exclaimed.

"Figures," Mildred said. "If it rains like this, it'd be a protection against the acid."

"Nice theory, Mildred, but it doesn't help Doc," Ryan shouted down to her, still trying to get in a clean shot at the bird. "Doc'll have to try and deal with this himself."

Which was something Doc was attempting. His hand had almost gone numb on the scrub from the overload of nerve damage and pain he was feeling. He felt his frock-coat sleeve ripped by the iron-hard beak, and the similarly armored claws plucked at his pants, tearing through to the flesh beneath. He knew that unless he acted swiftly, he would be forced to let go of the scrub, let his other arm fall and leave his face and eyes vulnerable to attack.

He had to chance all on one throw of the dice. Doc had not, in his youth, been a gambling man, recognizing the innate losing chance stacked against the fates. But since arriving in the Deathlands, he had learned that sometimes the long odds were the only ones.

Like now...

The bird's attack had been insistent and concentrated, yet not truly effective. Something at the back of Doc's mind told him that, sooner or later, the bird would have to fly away from him or change the angle of its attack in an attempt to penetrate his feeble defenses. When that happened, then he would have the briefest of moments in which to launch his own attack, or for his companions to come to his defense. Yet he knew he couldn't leave it to them, as they may be undergoing the same trial as himself.

This was something he had to do alone. And it had to be soon. He prayed that his chance would come soon.

As Doc's mind raced to formulate some plan of action, the black hawk screeched once more. But was that a note of irritation or frustration he could hear in its cry?

His moment had come. The bird, tired of mounting a seemingly ineffective attack, had drawn back in order to change the angle at which it attacked the prone figure. As it hovered just a few feet away from him, shining black wings flapping loudly and remorselessly in the air, blocking the sun, Doc used his few seconds' respite in which to act.

Still keeping his handhold on the scrub—for in truth his shredded flesh was too numb to move with any speed—Doc moved the arm that had been flung protectively across his face.

It seemed to him that it moved in slow motion, but with a relentless inevitability. He didn't take his eyes from the bird as it hovered, and could see in the glittering dark eyes the recognition that he had made himself vulnerable to it. It wheeled in the air, rotating its body to swoop back and attack the unprotected face.

All the while, Doc's free arm moved across his body to the LeMat, which he kept in his belt. The heavy double-barreled percussion pistol came up in his hand, leveled at the bird as it flew toward him.

The black creature filled his vision, the heavy dark feathers gleaming in the light and rain with an oily, almost metallic sheen. The screech of the bird's cries were almost symphonic, so close to Doc that he could hear strange and wonderful voices in the cacophony that filled his ears. The razor-sharp, armored beak opened, exposing the red maw and fetid breath that was close enough to hit Doc in hot waves as it cried out. Underneath the bird's body, its claws were raised, ready to grip, tear and rend.

It took an almost arrogant patience to wait until the barrels of the LeMat were nearly touching the beak as it closed in, a perfect grasp of timing as his strained arm muscles were trembling, causing the pistol to waver slightly. Just a moment too soon, and some of the shot may have missed the bird. A moment too late, and the talons would have caused serious—perhaps fatal—injury before he had discharged his shot.

But Doc's timing was perfect. As the pistol touched the tip of the beak, his fingers tightened, gripping the stock of the pistol and squeezing the trigger. First one barrel, then the other, in succession so rapid that it almost sounded as one shot. A shot muffled by the explosion's enclosure in the bird's mouth.

Ball and grape at enormous velocity discharged into the maw of the mutie bird. Although its outer feathers, and possibly the skin underneath, had become hardened and mutated to protect itself against the acid rains of the area, the inside of its body was still soft and fleshy. Even the armored beak could prove no protection against ball and grape at such close range.

The bird screeched a high, almost inaudible note that was choked short as its throat disappeared in a spray of tangled flesh, blood and feather. The beak was ripped into sharp ribbons that whipped up into the glittering eyes, tearing them as it had torn at Doc and all its prey. The eyes, perhaps, registered surprise at its own natural advantage being turned against itself. But it was only brief, as life had already begun to flicker and die as the brain was pulped and mashed by shot that ricocheted around the skull, breaking through the top and spreading fine splinters of bone and feather into the air.

For a split second, the rain became red, and the bird hovered at the apex of its flight, the body hanging in the air, bereft of a head. For the beak had become detached from the skull, which itself had imploded into thousands of fragments.

The silence after the muffled explosion and the high-pitched cry was heavy and oppressive for that fraction of a second, broken only when the bird fell heavily, plummeting toward the bottom of the sheer rock face, hitting the incline where it began only a few feet from Jak. The weight of the bird pulled it to earth with increasing velocity, breaking the once fearsome body upon the rocks.

While the others were still watching the bird fall, Ryan was edging toward Doc.

"Doc," he said softly, "you ready to move?"

Doc looked at Ryan.

"I fear that I may still be paralyzed by fear, my dear... Oh God, I'm so sorry, my friend, but I fear your name has temporarily escaped me." Tears welled in the old man's eyes as he pushed the LeMat into his belt.

"Don't worry about it, Doc," Ryan soothed, "it'll soon come back. You've done the hard part. Now, let's get out of this rain."

"Yes, I fear that it may be a great mistake to stay out in the rain. One could always catch pneumonia."

Although still trembling, Doc was able to descend from the rock face with a greater ease than any of the others would have thought possible, perhaps because there was still enough adrenaline flowing in his veins to give him the extra strength and sureness of foot needed to make the descent.

Ryan kept close to the old man, just to make sure that he was able to make the descent, and was relieved when they were all on the flat earth.

The corpse of the mutie hawk, already crawling

with insects, caught his eye. "Did I do that?" he asked absently. "I seem to recall—"

"I wouldn't worry about that right now," Mildred said gently, taking Doc by the arm. "Right now we just need to get to shelter."

Covering the exposed areas of their flesh as best they could, they set out on the hike to the old road-house.

"Mebbe we would have been better staying in the shaft," Dean complained as they trudged across the bare terrain, with hardly any scrub to provide shelter between the bottom of the hill and their destination.

"Couldn't risk it, son," Ryan replied. "What if there had been another slide, either trapping us or forcing us out? Then we would have had to make the trek anyway. You don't like my calls? You try making them sometimes."

The one-eyed warrior didn't like having his decisions questioned, especially by his own son. But if the boy could learn why a certain call was made, then Ryan was prepared to accept the occasional complaint.

Besides which, the rain was getting harder, stinging his eye as it blew across the flat earth. It was more important to set a strong pace and reach the shelter of the roadhouse.

Chapter Five

The diner looked deserted, but looks could be deceiving. There had been no signs of life from the roadhouse while they were hiking across the three miles of plain between the hill and the two-lane blacktop, and certainly they had been in a position where they would have been open and easy prey if anyone in the building had wanted to mount an attack. Even so, there was no way that they were going to walk straight in without doing a recce first.

While the others adopted defensive positions as best they could on the arid plain around the old road, Ryan and Jak went forward to carry out a quick survey of the building.

Keeping low to the ground and fanning out to divide any possible fire, they approached the building from the side that had the fewest windows.

Ryan took the front. There were double glass doors, with the glass still intact. One of the long windows was broken, but the other was still in place. Ryan dived to the duckboarding veranda tacked on to the front of the building to give it an old-world look. He crawled along under one of the windows, SIG-Sauer in hand. He had left the Steyr with J.B.

He took the double doors at a roll, landing beneath a table that he flipped up with a hefty kick of his left foot. He was now in cover and able to survey the inside of the building.

Empty. And layered with undisturbed dust, enough to suggest that it was a long time since the diner had been in regular use.

"Jak?" he called.

"Clear out back." The albino slid through the kitchen door, the .357 Magnum Colt Python still in his fist, red eyes still darting side to side, aware of any movement in his peripheral vision.

Ryan rose to his feet. "Guess we're okay to rest up here, then."

He went to the side of the diner and opened the window. He could see the rest of the group, plainly visible despite their best attempts to seek cover in the sparse scrub. He gestured to them to come on, thankful that the diner hadn't been occupied. He judged that the weather had to be harsh in this part of the country, as the land was wind and rain blasted. The forest on the gentler slope of the hill could only have grown because the sheer rock face acted as a weather break.

Truly a rock and a hard place.

The others had now gained the safety of the diner, and were glad to be out of the rain, which had increased in volume from a gentle spray to a hard shower that beat on the duckboard exterior of the building.

"It's just as well this was here," Mildred said as she divested herself of the outer layer of her clothing. "I'd guess we've all had a few layers of skin softened. It's just a matter of how long we had until it started to peel."

"Or how long it'll take until it starts right now, unless we can wash it off," Krysty added, shrugging off her coat and pulling her hair back from her face. The sentient red tresses clung tightly to her, and not just because they were damp. They could sense the damage being caused by the rain.

"We have attained shelter. To hope for ambrosia and nectar would be too much, would it not?" Doc asked wearily, seating himself at a padded bench seat by the window. No one replied directly, and it wouldn't have mattered, as the old man was off in a reverie, distant from his friends.

"Mebbe not that, whatever means." Jak smiled slyly. "But one thing for sure—this place not that deserted."

Ryan furrowed his brow and cast a curious glance at Jak. "Meaning?"

"Someone use place sometime. Why else running water?"

"You're kidding," Mildred said. "That would be too much to hope for."

She headed past Jak for the kitchen area at the back of the diner, while J.B. called cautiously, "Watch what kind of water it is, Millie. If the supply is rainwater, well…"

Mildred poked her head from the kitchen door, good-natured annoyance puckering her features. "Give me some credit, John. Of course I'll test it first…on you, if you like."

As a joke, it wasn't even that funny. But the tension of the passing day needed some kind of diffusion, and Mildred had supplied the safety valve.

On examining the water supply, Mildred found that

a water-purification unit had been rigged in a storage tank that stood in an attached outhouse. It was a system cobbled together from pieces of salvage, but the filters appeared to have been changed recently, as there were only a few crystals attached to the copper pipes used to electrolyze the acid from the water.

Ryan agreed with Mildred that this suggested a ville somewhere near, and one that had a good working knowledge of predark tech. Certainly, someone with a good knowledge of chemistry had rigged the filtering system and kept a mains supply maintained from a nearby reservoir or river, which suggested a small pumping system of some kind. The water pressure was erratic, but constant enough to indicate good maintenance on the pump.

The positive aspect of this was clean water to drink, and also to shower. The rest rooms of the diner-roadhouse were supplied with showers, and the group took the opportunity to wash the acid rain from their skin. Once this had been done, Mildred tackled Doc's wounds. The deep scratches on his hands had ceased to bleed, but needed dressing. Searching the scavenged medical supplies in her med kit, Mildred found antiseptic and some bandages. Hoping that she would strike it lucky, she searched for the first-aid kit that all such diners would have carried by law before sky-dark. Cursing, she found that whoever used the diner had also used most of the first-aid kit, and there were only a few bandages left. The seal on the package had long since been broken, probably for several decades, as the adhesive on the small bandages was no longer of any use.

Doc was grateful for the bandages she could supply, and Ryan allowed the old man to rest while he organized watch. It was imperative that they take turns standing guard, as it was now apparent that the diner was in use as a way station, perhaps on a trading route.

It was while J.B. and Dean were on watch that the Armorer made his discovery.

The diner was lit by a small oil lamp that they had found in the kitchen, along with fuel to keep it going. There was a small generator, which again suggested that the roadhouse was in semiregular use, but it was empty, and they could find no fuel to run it.

The oil lamp was better. It enabled them to have just enough light to see what they were doing, without advertising their presence to the immediate area.

Dean took the kitchen and one side of the diner as his territory, while J.B. took the front and other side. They patrolled between the windows, keeping low and watching for movement outside. It wasn't difficult, as the terrain was so flat and open.

After a short while on watch, J.B. decided to poke around the area of the front diner where the others weren't sleeping. Although the front seemed to be in little use, judging from the way the dust and dirt seemed undisturbed, it seemed unlikely that, by the sheer law of averages, whoever used the kitchen and rest rooms didn't, at some point, use the front.

And if they used the front, then there was a chance that they may have inadvertently left behind some clue as to their origin or position in the terrain.

If there was such a thing, then it wasn't immediately obvious, and so the Armorer began a methodical search of the benches and tables of the diner.

Most of the seats were padded and covered in a PVC plastic that had originally been a bright orange check but had now faded to a dull pattern that was barely discernible. The covering was cracked in places, and it creaked when J.B. leaned on it or moved it to run his hand down the cracks between seats and cushioning.

But it was worth the effort. Down the back of one bench was a scrap of paper, much folded and worn. Taking it back to the light and straining his eyes, the Armorer could see that it was a hand-drawn map. It was crude, and with no indication of scale, but with ville names and travel routes written on it.

And just to help them, it even had their own location clearly marked.

"I MUST ADMIT this is surprising," Doc remarked the following morning after taking the map from Ryan. "I would have put us much farther east."

The one-eyed warrior nodded. According to the map, they were right in assuming that they had arrived to the north of the Deathlands, but were wrong in assuming that were still on the remains of the Eastern Seaboard. Although the lush vegetation they had seen on the gentler slope of the hill resembled the kind of growth they had seen to the east, they were in fact far to the west of the country, well on the way to what had once been Seattle.

It was an area of intense memory. Seattle was the area where Ryan and J.B. had traveled in a war wag to meet up once more with Trader, their old mentor, and his companion Abe. It was the area where Ryan and Trader had almost been ransomed into marrying the hideous daughters of a deranged baron before Abe and J.B. had rescued them.

And now they were back. On a different trail, and a long way down the line, Abe and Trader had gone from their lives once more.

"From the Illuminated Ones' point of view, it could still make sense to be based here," Mildred said. "In the old days, there were a lot of military bases along the line from here up through Canada to Alaska. The redoubt may only have been one in a chain. Besides which, it's near enough to Washington, without being too near...."

She left unspoken her point that the redoubt and surrounding area were still habitable, whereas the hole in the world that had once been the capital of the old United States was still too rad-blasted for anything other than mutie bacteria to dwell.

"So which ville do we head for?" Krysty asked. There were two on the map, equidistant from the diner.

"This one looks the better bet," J.B. said, pointing to a ville that was marked but wasn't named. From the scrawled lines, it looked as though the city was belowground, using the network of surviving tunnels and sewers that had proliferated before skydark.

"It's certainly where whoever owns this map comes from," Ryan mused, "and it looks like whoever they are is part of what's left of the Illuminated Ones."

He indicated the map. Around the edges were scrawled numerous slogans and words: "Kallisti = Kaos;" "The future lies in the hands of the hidden past;" "Dreams are reality;" "The sun people are the shining ones."

"If the 'sun people' are illuminated by that sun, then I suspect that may be right." Doc sighed. "Why do these philosophies always seek to be self-aggrandizing?"

Dean gave him a puzzled stare. "Doc, sometimes I wish you made more sense. But mebbe you can tell us what this ville means." He stabbed a finger at the other marked ville on the map—Samtvogel.

"That's not English, is it," Ryan stated rather than asked. Unlike most dwellers of the Deathlands, Ryan was at least aware that there were other lands outside of his own, and that there were other tongues.

"German," Mildred replied before Doc. "It means—"

"Velvet bird," Doc finished for her. "A most curious name...and with a most sinister edge."

"It certainly doesn't feel right," Krysty said, her hair weaving about her. "I'd opt for the underground ville any day. Doc's right, there's just something..." She tailed off.

"No ville's an easy option," J.B. said quietly. "Always trouble around every bend."

"Which is exactly why we should follow our gut instincts," Ryan said decisively. "We'll head for the ville that seems to be old Seattle."

THE NIGHT'S REST in the diner had restored their energy, and although it was disappointingly bereft of any food, it was still good to eat from a proper table, even if it was only self-heats. They spent some time checking their supplies and cleaning their blasters, then hit the blacktop, heading farther east for the outskirts of the ruins of Seattle.

A breeze blew across the arid plain, breaking the heat from the sun that beat down from a now cloudless sky. The blue was tinged with a pale orange glow, the remnants of the chem clouds that carried the acid rain.

It was good weather for such a trek: not too hot, but neither numbing with cold. The rain, hopefully, would stay away. It would take a sudden increase in the speed and intensity of the wind to bring chem clouds scudding from beyond the horizon, but there was no such thing in the Deathlands as even or predictable weather conditions.

JAK SLOWED, a frown crossing his scarred features.

"Hear that?"

Ryan turned from his position at the head of the line. "I hear nothing…yet. What is it?"

Jak concentrated. "Wag. Going fast."

J.B. looked around. "Dark night, we're sitting targets here."

Ryan looked around them. The Armorer was right. They were on the asphalt ribbon that stretched to the horizon in either direction. The hill from which they had descended was like an anthill in the distance behind them, and there was little around except sparse scrub and a few sickly trees, bent over and half-dead from the acid rains.

"Fireblast, where the fuck do we go?" he muttered.

As he scouted around for defensive cover, the wag came over the horizon, shimmering against the asphalt and seeming to hover above it as it careered toward them, the sun behind it making them squint against the glare to follow the wag's progress.

The nearest cover was a small stand of scrub bushes 150 yards to their left. A smaller group grew to the right.

"Split into two, divide their fire," Ryan snapped. "J.B., you take Mildred and Dean and that patch—" he indicated the smaller crop "—Krysty, Doc, Jak, over here..." With that he took off for the sparse cover, knowing that J.B. would already be halfway to his own patch.

The one-eyed warrior knew that he could trust J.B. to follow tactics close to his own. They had learned together under Trader, and knew the only way to handle a situation like this. Perhaps, if they were lucky, whoever was in the wag would pass by without stopping. There was no way they could actually have been missed, standing out against the empty road, or maybe the driver of the wag and his passengers would be friendly.

But the only thing it was wise to assume or expect was hostility. Anything other than a firefight would be a bonus.

Ryan hit the ground with the Steyr already unslung, settling the stock into his shoulder as he lined the sight against his eye. Without looking, he knew that Jak had his .357 ready, Doc had the LeMat poised and Krysty had the Smith & Wesson .38 in her hand.

On the other side of the road, J.B. had his Uzi set to rapidfire, while Dean and Mildred had their blasters ready for use.

The engine of the wag rattled, coughed and died.

On the last rattle, the rear exit door descended. It was a six-wheeled all-terrain vehicle, probably ex-military. It was armored, with opaque glass on the windshield and side doors, and nothing along the side. Instead of standard military colors, it was painted in red, blue and green swirls that offered no camouflage and just made it stand out in the arid, dull landscape. Not that there was anywhere to hide.

With a massed cry, six figures emerged from the rear of the wag. All were carrying rifles of the type J.B. had found in the redoubt armory, and were dressed in one-piece suits that fitted closely to their bodies. Although of a uniform design, the suits were of varying bright colors. That two of them were female was obvious from their body shape, but their faces were hidden behind the opaque glass shields of silver helmets.

They were unlike anything any of the companions had ever seen before, and the surprise this caused gave the anonymous attackers just the edge they needed to take the offensive.

The air crackled as pulses of laser light shot from the crystals at the end of the rifles, searing heat into the dirt and scrub that raised clouds of smoke and left small trails of fire.

The weaponry may have been impressive, but the attackers were poor shots. While the pulses of rapidly fired laser bursts ate into the dirt in front of them, both Ryan and J.B. opened fire. Taking the man nearest to him, the Armorer loosed a quick burst from the Uzi. It wasn't the optimum distance for accuracy with the weapon, but it was enough to tear into the man's orange suit at knee level, the material ripping and spraying red as blood spurted from entry wounds. He pitched forward, his high-pitched scream of agony muffled by his helmet and his rifle flying off to his right as he threw out his arms to cushion his fall.

Ryan opted for one of the middle two, a man in a dark blue suit and the tallest of the attackers. A head shot would have been the optimum for a quick kill, but the one-eyed warrior had no way of knowing if the opaque glass on the helmet was bulletproof. A chest shot would have been difficult because of the way the man was holding his laser rifle, so Ryan aimed lower, for the abdomen. He squeezed gently on the trigger, channeling all the tension and adrenaline into the perfect shot.

The blue figure stumbled backward, doubling over and dropping his rifle, his hands instinctively flying to his stomach as though to stem the flow of blood that spread across the material of his uniform, turning it red.

Of the remaining four, two dropped to their knees and shot a steady beam of laser fire that scorched up a trail of earth on either side of the blacktop, each headed for the scrub where the two defending parties were covered.

"Shit, time to move," J.B. exclaimed, knowing that the laser would at the very least set their scant cover alight, even if it didn't actually touch any of them.

Mildred was out of cover, rolling to the left of the scrub and coming to rest with her elbows braced on the ground, her left hand locked to her right at the wrist, steadying her aim as her finger began to move on the trigger. Three shots barked from her blaster. It was too swift for a perfect aim, but she was close enough to the moving targets to cause two on her side to cease their fire and duck while Dean and J.B. took the opportunity to leave the now burning scrub and assume firing positions.

The same was happening on the other side, except that it had become a race between Jak and Doc to see who could come up and fire first. Doc was surprisingly swift for such a frail-looking man. His deceptive strength was matched by a burst of speed that saw him roll and aim in a fraction of a second.

But the albino was quicker. Death had always been Jak's trade. Hunting animals or people, it amounted to the same thing. The Colt Python barked fractionally before the roar of the LeMat, causing the two attackers standing to their side of the road to dive haphazardly for cover that wasn't there.

Things were now equal, and also stalemated. With no cover for either side, it was a firefight that could only end in complete annihilation for one side. There was nowhere to run and hide as the laser rifles crackled their beams of intense light and heat, failing to find range because of the fire from the more conventional blasters.

There were more of Ryan's people firing, but they had the problem of reloading, while the laser rifles seemed to have an indefinite life.

Automatically, Jak and Krysty had fallen into firing alternately to allow each other and Ryan more loading time, also covering Doc while he reloaded the LeMat.

On the other side of the road, J.B. kept up short bursts of Uzi fire while Dean and Mildred alternated shots with their blasters.

"Time for a little change," the Armorer muttered to himself as he laid down the Uzi and extracted the M-4000 scattergun. J.B.'s favored shot from the blaster were barbed fléchettes that would cause considerable damage, even at this range.

Covered by Dean and Mildred, and pushing his fedora back on his head, J.B. lined up the M-4000 and let fly with the scattergun. The barbed metal charge spread out in the air, scratching the paint on the side of the wag, scraping the opaque glass on the helmets of the nearest two attackers and tearing into their flesh. The thin material of their uniforms was no defense against the charge, and both went down beneath the hail of hot barbed metal.

Whether they had been chilled was unimportant. It brought the brief and bloody firefight to a close as one remaining male attacker kept up a covering fire while the remaining woman hurriedly gathered the laser blasters, throwing them into the rear of the brightly colored armored wag. That done, she climbed in and helped pull in the man whose knees had been ripped to shreds, and who had been attempting throughout the firefight to edge toward cover.

The man covering their retreat edged toward the rear door, pausing only while the woman assisted one of those wounded by the fléchettes to struggle into the wag.

With one last covering blast, the man climbed into the wag, the door slamming shut as the engine coughed into life. The wag shot forward enough to complete a tight turn before screeching past them and back down the blacktop the way it had come, disappearing toward the horizon.

Ryan and J.B., on their respective sides of the road, had already signaled the firing to stop, and the retreat had been carried out with only the bare minimum of cover to stop the laser blaster taking accurate aim. It was pointless to waste valuable ammo on a retreating force.

The companions regrouped on the blacktop, looking down at the corpses of the chilled attackers.

"What do you make of that?" Ryan asked.

"Not see sec like that before," Jak said, gesturing at the corpses.

"Or blasters like that. They're impressive when they work," J.B. added. "No idea of how to shoot in a firefight, though."

"Perhaps just as well in the circumstances," Doc added. "Interesting that they should take such care to recover their arms, do you not think?"

Krysty looked down the road, where the wag had vanished over the horizon. "They came from the way we were headed," she said quietly.

Dean pursed his lips, shaking his head. "Hope they don't come from the ville we're headed for, then."

"You hold that thought, son," Ryan said. "Because we've got to press on, see what we find."

Chapter Six

The map found by J.B. in the diner showed them that the remains of the blacktop was the main route from the redoubt to the remnants of Seattle. With the sparse vegetation surrounding, Ryan felt uneasy that his people would be exposed and in the open as they followed the route. On the other hand, at least it would be easy to see any other traveling parties.

They continued the route in silence, the clear sky an orange blue that shimmered under the rays of the sun as it beat down on them. What would be better—the acid rain and a cooler temperature, or the humid heat of the blazing sun? Ryan thought.

He watched with concern as Doc seemed to wilt visibly in the heat, his overstressed body finding the blazing heat hard to handle.

Dean and Jak dropped back in order to help Doc, with J.B. bringing up the rear and not allowing the party to straggle too much. They were still tight enough to adopt defensive positions with speed, if required.

But so far the route march had been uneventful.

Over the past half mile, the level of plant life, cover and vegetation was growing thicker and more verdant, the previously empty horizon becoming crowded with the skeletal remains of buildings. They were now overrun with mutated growths, bizarrely colored flowering plants with thick, toughened stems growing up around the concrete. Ryan went over the advantages and disadvantages. The cover would protect them from the elements and hide them from any potential enemies, but it would also hold unknown hazards and hide any potential enemies from them.

Casting his icy blue eye to the melting heat of the sun, feeling the sweat run down his forehead from his soaking hair, he reckoned that right then the shelter from the sun was worth any amount of hazard. Besides, the fact that they were reaching the ruins meant that they were approaching the outskirts of Seattle, and their destination.

"Does the map give us any sign of how the hell we get into the tunnels and old subways?" Mildred asked in a harsh, cracked voice, forcing every word through her dry vocal cords. They had been unwilling to use water from their canteens except at specified intervals, conserving the valuable water they had obtained from the ruined diner. Conserving it for Doc, if he needed more than the others.

The old man was leaning heavily on his lion's-head swordstick, the silver glinting in the sun.

"I must confess, I shall be glad to attain shelter," he croaked.

Krysty reached out to Ryan for the map. "Can I look at it?" she asked.

The one-eyed warrior handed over the map, sensing that she wanted to try to feel any danger that may lie on the path ahead. He would never understand her mutie sensibilities, but he trusted them implicitly.

Krysty took the map from him and studied the bare markings of the terrain. The ville of Samtvogel stood alone and to the southwest of the city ruins as they approached it; the unnamed ville built beneath old Seattle stood in front, the entrance hidden somewhere amongst the undergrowth and concrete.

Krysty returned Ryan's intent gaze in a similar fashion. Her hair, already close to her skull, plastered by sweat in the glare of the sun, clung even closer.

"There's something…. It's not right now, but there is going to be a problem. Gaia! I wish this wasn't so clouded."

Krysty handed the map back. "I just think we need to be more on guard than ever."

THE FIRST DANGER came all too soon.

Once they had penetrated the outer growths of the city, it became apparent that the surface was uninhabited. It was also apparent that the thickness of the vegetation, mixed with the concrete debris and remains of old Seattle, would make it imperative that they send a scout to find a route and spot any immediate dangers. Ryan had noticed that Doc was finding the going hard, despite his best efforts to keep pace, and the line was straggling and dangerously loose, with J.B. dropping too far back for safety.

Ryan halted them on a street corner, where the remains of an apartment building was all that stood visible and identifiable in the foliage. The thick green plants were multicolored at their heads, but all had the same thick green stems, the size of Ryan's arm, with sticky follicles that secreted a sweet smelling sap. It was a milky white at the tips of the hairs, and all the companions were cautious to avoid contact with the stems, in case the sap was in some way toxic to the skin.

The way had been fairly easy up until this point, as the remains of old roads and sidewalks were still visible, and hadn't been infested with the thick-stemmed plants, instead being covered by a carpet of what appeared to be a creeping vine of some kind. It had a sentience within it, and a couple of times the tendrils responded to the way Doc's swordstick came down, the smaller point concentrating the weight it carried enough to cause the tendrils to rear and try to grasp at the cane, wrapping themselves around its length.

The building on the street corner still had three floors upright, even though the rubble from the wrecked upper floors spilled across one part of the intersection, cutting it off from an easy access. The lobby of the building was intact, the plate-glass doors standing open, miraculously in one piece, although pitted with small stones that had fused to the glass, and a web of minute cracks that connected the stones.

"We'll rest up here," Ryan announced as they gathered. "We need to recce the surrounding area before we go any farther. It's getting thicker out there."

"And more humid and sweet smelling," Mildred added. "We really need to find out how thick those mother plants get, because we can't risk what might be in that sap."

"Want me recce?" Jak asked, knowing already that Ryan had selected him.

The one-eyed man nodded. "Take a look at the map, try and get us in the right direction if possible."

"Always route if look hard enough," Jak said with

a grin. He took the map from Ryan and studied it. Jak couldn't read well, but a diagram or map was a different matter. From his earliest days hunting on swamps and bayous down in Louisiana, Jak had learned to look at a diagram as he would a spore on a tree. The fact that there was little, if any, writing on the map made it easier for him to absorb.

He handed the paper back to Ryan. "Hope not hide entrance too good," he said with a twinkle in his eye.

Ryan laughed. There wasn't an entrance constructed in the whole of the Deathlands that Jak Lauren couldn't find.

When the albino had slipped through the doors and disappeared noiselessly into the vegetation, Ryan and the rest of the companions made themselves as comfortable as possible in the lobby of the building. It wasn't difficult, as much of the furniture had been left intact. Only the elements that had penetrated this far, and the brave tendrils of plant life that had ventured into the less welcoming atmosphere, had made any effect.

There were three large leather sofas scattered across the rich carpeting, now overlaid with mildew and growths of moss. The leather had a layer of dusty, almost verdigris-like spore, which J.B., Dean and Mildred cleared from each one. Otherwise, they were probably as comfortable as they had been before skydark.

Doc settled his weary frame on one of them, reclining until his head rested against one arm.

"Wake me when young Jak returns, my dear Ryan. I fear I must rest...." His voice was already drifting off to sleep.

"Not before I check those wounds," Mildred muttered, moving across to him to run a medical eye over Doc's dressings. The wounds hadn't been that deep, but when any antiseptic procedures were at a premium, Mildred could never be too sure.

The wounds weren't infected, and Doc was asleep before she had finished.

"I think we all need that," Krysty said, noting that Ryan himself looked weary.

"I'll take first watch, Dad," Dean added.

The one-eyed man assented, and they rested while Dean and Mildred took the first watch.

JAK SKIPPED across the roots of stunted trees and over the beds of creeping vines with scarcely an impression, and no sound at all. Despite his heavy boots, he was able to distribute his weight in such a way that he left no sign of his passing…or at least, no sign to anyone other than one as skilled in the arts of tracking as himself.

The details of the map were in his head, and he applied them to the landscape around. As he moved farther into the forest, the thick-stemmed plants were joined in the landscape by small, stunted trees with no height but trunks at least three times the thickness of any other tree Jak had ever seen. Their gnarled and twisted roots broke ground regularly, surfacing beneath the creepers to form an ankle-breaking obstacle should an unsuspecting foot catch in them.

It was impossible at times in this part of the old ville to tell where the buildings began and ended. What hadn't been destroyed in the nukecaust or earth movement had since been taken down and crumbled by the inevitable forward march of the forest, the mutie heart of postskydark nature claiming back what man had destroyed.

Jak scaled one of the trees. It rose no more than eight feet from the ground, but by standing on the topmost branch, which was thick and sturdy in relation to the trunk and so could easily support the slender albino, Jak was able to see through the dense growth of stalks, and also through the multicolored heads that spread their sweet yet pungent scent across the air.

It was while he was balanced on this branch that he saw them. Although, to be accurate, he heard them before sighting them....

There was little noise in the forest. It seemed that any animal life found it hard to survive in the conditions, and so there were only insects and a few small birds. Their chatter and high-pitched noises were soon cut out of his hearing by Jak's attuned ears. They were still registering, but were disregarded as he searched for other sounds.

Like the humming...no, not humming, a chanting of some kind. Jak could make out sounds formed into words of some kind, but not in a language that he could recognize. There was a variety of male and female voices; this he could tell by the differing frequencies.

Jak scanned the horizon, drawing close into the large oval leaves on the branch as he did so, instinctively using as much cover as possible, even though it was unlikely that they would be aware of his presence. It was proving hard to locate their direction, as the trees and plants acted against each other, the wood becoming a sound dampener, and yet the plants and their flowers acting as sounding boards, amplifying and distorting the sound as the party approached, making its true direction difficult to determine.

Jak's instincts told him to keep his attention focused on the direction from which he thought it had originally come, so he turned back that way and carefully scanned the horizon. His eyesight was slightly impaired by his lack of pigmentation, but his other senses more than compensated for this by being ultrasensitive, finely honed by his years of hunting and stalking.

It didn't take him long to locate them. They were crashing through the trees and brush with little regard for stealth, chanting loudly. They numbered twelve in all, six groups of two with a pole strung between them. Their clothing was a multicolored collection of old rags, dyed brilliant purples, oranges, pinks and yellows, which mirrored the plants around. They had probably found a way of extracting the color from the flowers and using it as a dye. They had obviously been hunting, as they had something strung from the poles, something just a little too obscured by their own bodies for Jak to make it out. Something that looked as if it were an animal. The alarm bells sounded in Jak's brain. How could they have been hunting an animal when all his senses screamed that there was no animal life in this forest?

Jak assessed their direction. They were headed for the outskirts of the old ville of Seattle, and presumably out to the other ville, the one with the stupe name…and there was only one route out, one which would take them right past Jak's companions.

The albino slipped down the tree. He had seen enough to judge the party. That they had been hunting suggested knives or blasters. This made them a danger, one he had to warn his companions about before the party reached the old apartment building.

JAK HAD a good start on the hunting party, and was faster. He was back at the ruined apartment block in next to no time, and outlined what he had seen.

"Sounds like these aren't from the ville we want," J.B. said.

Ryan agreed. "They don't sound like the bastards we met on the way, and they're headed the wrong direction."

"Think they're from the other ville?" Dean asked.

"Possibly. Best thing is to take cover, let them pass. Watch them. No point wasting ammo on a firefight that might bring more forces down on us from who knows where."

The lobby of the old apartment building sheltered them well from the path through the old street, as the pitted and scarred glass was opaque, and the most accessible path through the forest undergrowth was some yards from the glass doors. Still, Ryan was concerned that the oncoming party of hunters may spot signs of the companions passing, so he ordered the companions onto the second floor of the building, going ahead to check that the stairwell was safe, and that enough of the floor on the first level was intact and stable enough to support their weight. The windows on that level were blown out, but the foliage entwined around the building was thick enough to provide them with cover as they observed the passing hunting party.

Jak slipped out the front of the building to check for any obvious signs of their passing and entering the ruined building. He wouldn't have time to completely cover their tracks, but as this was a war party returning home, he felt fairly sure that covering the most visible signs of progress would suffice.

While Jak did that, Ryan took the old stairwell beside the apartment building's elevators. It was sturdy, and still firm beneath his testing feet. Krysty and Dean followed, with Mildred, Doc and J.B. at the rear.

On the first floor, there were five apartments. In their time, they were fairly spacious and comfortable. But now they were covered in creeping vines, powdered with mildew and fungi spores, the fabrics and wooden furniture having long since capitulated to the humidity and fungi. Only the metal frames and remnants of old tech such as long since defunct TVs and stereos stood relatively unscathed. They were strange reminders of the days before skydark in an environment nature was otherwise successfully reclaiming.

Ryan opened each door carefully, partly in case there was some hidden intruder, either mutie, man or animal, or in case the floor gave way beneath him.

"These old buildings were made with concrete floors, so we should be all right," Mildred remarked, "unlike those poor bastards." And she gestured toward the remains of two people that were lying half on the rotting bed, and half on the floor of one apartment room.

Ryan was looking for an apartment whose rooms

overlooked the only route the hunting party could take through the undergrowth. It was important that the rooms be one apartment, and therefore adjoining. He was unwilling to spread his forces over two apartments, with a solid unbroken wall between them and no easy means of communication should a firefight break out.

The third one they came to was the one they wanted. What had once been a spare and stylishly furnished lounge was linked to a bedroom with a sunken pit for the long since rotted bed by a sliding door that splintered almost to powder with just the slightest pressure from J.B., the runners having long since seized up with rust and the clogging spore of fungi. A creeping vine had encroached along the door, and as the splintered remains ripped the long stems, they shuddered and coiled as though in pain.

Krysty also shuddered. "I'll be glad when we're through this jungle. Sentient plant life is the worst kind of mutie I can imagine," she almost whispered.

Ryan and Dean had meanwhile been checking out the windows, and their position onto the old road beneath. Ryan checked the large and wide bay-window area in the lounge, while Dean took the deeper bedroom window, which had less width.

"Listen," he said as he joined the party in the lounge, "they're getting near. Weird noise," he added, looking bemused. "You'd think they want to be heard."

The companions maintained silence, listening to the distant chant, the higher, keening voices carrying farther through the forest. Suddenly, J.B. whirled, the Uzi falling easily to hand and into a firing position.

The safety was off, and his finger was pressuring the trigger, on a hair.

Jak appeared in the doorway. "Me," he said simply. "Covered tracks."

"Dark night," the Armorer breathed, "I nearly chilled you, Jak!"

Jak grinned like a white wolf. "Hearing better than think," he said. "Near now," he added.

Ryan assented. "Time to take formation. What about the cover, Dean?"

"Some big stems and leaves over the window, but it goes low and that's bad."

"Okay, you and Doc take in there, and keep well back. J.B., you and me take one side of this, Krysty and Mildred the other."

"Me?" Jak asked.

"Take the stairwell. It's the only way up, so if they see us they'll have to come that way. One man can cover it for now, and someone will join you if a firefight starts."

"Not firefight." Jak shook his head. "They carry knives, but no blasters."

"Sure?"

The albino nodded.

Ryan smiled grimly, his mouth a tight line. "That'll make it easier if it does blow up." The chanting was louder now, and the sound of the hunting party's movement through the forest could be heard clearly. Ryan's voice dropped to a whisper. "Assume positions."

Jak disappeared into the hallway, heading for the stairwell. Ryan and J.B. took up position at the window, with the one-eyed warrior using the cover of the plant life to assume an upright posture, while the Armorer took a lower position. On the opposite side of the window, Mildred and Krysty took up positions mirroring the men. In the bedroom, with less cover, Doc and Dean took each side of the long window, shielding themselves with the wall at the expense of reducing their field of vision.

Beneath, the chanting grew louder, the procession of the hunting party coming into view.

"Bastards," Dean breathed, his jaw dropping and bile rising in his throat. He had to breathe hard to stop himself from being violently sick as the party came fully into view.

Doc, who was on the blind side of the window, risked peering around. He withdrew his head rapidly, not wanting to believe what he saw.

"Truly," he whispered to himself, "if there is a God, he has forsaken this place...."

In the lounge, shielded by the plants, the four companions exchanged looks that registered a mixture of anger and disgust. They had seen many things in their travels, experienced many kinds of degradation and horror. But this was somehow among the worst.

The hunting party beneath was now in full view. Their ragged clothes, wrapped around them like robes rather than worn, were multicolored and dyed from the flowering plants, as Jak had surmised. He had been correct in observing that none of the six below carried blasters, just long knives that were a mix of hand-hewed blades wrapped onto wooden hafts with twine and a couple of old knives, rusty but still honed enough to provide a jagged sawing edge.

As they approached, the companions could see that

the hunters were muties, each with his own particular traits. One had a vestigial arm growing from his chest, the tiny, half-formed fingers on the end clenching and unclenching in time with his step. Another had a completely bald head that had dewlapped layers of skin that sunk over his one eye, which was located near the center of his head. The dewlap was covered in open sores. A third shuffled on a stumped foot that had a thickened pad of calloused skin where the toes turned under. The fourth was enormously barrel-chested, with a thin, tapering waist and sticklike legs that had straining whipcords of muscle supporting his weight and balance. The fifth was unevenly made, with his head sinking into his body at an obtuse angle.

But it was the one at the front who seemed the most mutated. In many ways, he was a perfectly muscled specimen, with flowing blond hair, a chiseled jawline and the high keening voice that cut across the others. His eyes glowed with an insane, messianic light, and he strode evenly on legs that were strong, with well-muscled calves. His torso, however, was an immediate and grotesque reminder of his mutie heritage: for in the center of his chest, poking through the saffron-and-yellow robes he wore, was the head of another body, small and stunted, that grew from his stomach. The eyes on the head of the small ''twin'' looked around with a similar gleam to that of their ''owner.'' By his bearing, as well as his position, this mutie was the leader of the party, setting a fairly swift pace at the head of the first pair.

They walked in a ragged file, in three pairs. Each pair had a pole suspended between them, the pole dipping and swaying as the catch that hung from it took the weight of the singing kill, jogged into motion by the carriers' uneven footfalls.

Except that *kill* was the wrong word. The catch was still alive...at least some of the catch was still alive, while some of it had died on the journey.

Two children were suspended on each pole. There were three boys and three girls, a pair per pole. They were still alive, but dying rapidly in agony and pain because they hadn't been tied to the pole.

They had been impaled.

The front carrier of each pair held a pole end that was sharpened to a point and dripping in blood and bodily fluids. The sharpened end had obviously been inserted through the rectum of each child, and passed through the body to come out of the mouth. How they had managed to impale two children on each of the long, swaying poles was something that none of the companions cared to consider at that moment. Possibly, they had been drugged or sedated in some way.

It didn't matter. All that mattered was that the children had been impaled while alive, their internal organs ripped and bones crushed while they were still alive, and some of them were still alive now, suffering unimaginable pain as they died slowly while being taken to wherever the mutie hunters came from— probably the ville marked on the map as Samtvogel.

Mildred raised her ZKR, sighting at the leading mutie, her teeth clenched to prevent tears rolling down her face, and to prevent herself from crying out in rage and horror. Krysty felt Mildred move, despite being unable to tear her eyes away from the procession beneath. Krysty reached down and stayed Mildred's hand.

"Not our fight…not now," she whispered.

The procession passed from view, seemingly unaware of the observers above them. They continued on the road out of the old ville.

As they passed, the companions relaxed their guard, J.B. slipping out to bring Jak back from his guard on the stairwell. The albino eyed them impassively as Mildred told him what they had seen.

"Good Krysty stop you," he said simply. "Not fight if not need."

Ryan agreed. "Although I would've loved to have chilled those fireblasted fuckers just for the hell of it," he added.

Doc shook his head sadly. "Much as it saddens me to say it, I fear Jak is correct. You made the right decision, Ryan, my boy. Who knows what perversity the noise of a firefight would have brought out of the woodwork."

"There'll be time enough for them later, if we come across them again," Ryan spit, biting on his disgust. "Now we need to find a way into the underground ville, see if they're the people who attacked us or if we can ally with them."

JAK SCOUTED ahead, then returned to tell them that their path into the forest was now clear. Checking weapons, they assembled in the old lobby and moved out. Ryan and Jak took the lead, the albino leading them through the path he had scouted.

Ryan had to admit that Jak had done a fine job. The way through the thick undergrowth and the hidden and treacherous rubble was easier than he had expected, and he was relieved by the way that Doc was able to tackle the terrain. The rest had allowed the old man to recuperate his sometimes surprising reserves of strength, and the old man's outrage at what he had seen had added vigor to his step.

They proceeded with nothing to impede them for over an hour by Ryan's wrist chron, making good distance and coming to the area on the map where the first of the underground tunnels was sketched in.

"What exactly are we looking for, lover?" Krysty asked.

"Hard to say," the one-eyed man replied, studying the map. "It could be an old subway, or mebbe a sewer. Could be something leading from a basement of one of these old buildings," he added, indicating the ruins around them. They were now entering Seattle proper, and in the distance the remains of the needle could be seen, still precariously defying the elements, jagged and crumbling against the currently still skies.

"So how do we know what to look for?" Mildred interjected, her mind still distracted by the hunting party.

"Signs of disturbance, mebbe regular use," Dean mused. "If this ville is underground, then I guess they try and keep it as sealed off as possible, with just one or two ways in and out."

"Exactly," his father agreed. "So if we can find some signs of life, then we're heading right."

Jak had been scouting the way ahead while they stopped to examine the map, as they had reached an area beyond his previous foray. J.B. kept watch.

"Jak's back," the Armorer said softly as Jak whistled to alert them.

The albino reached them, appearing noiselessly in their path. "Found way in," he breathed. "But sec men headed here. Armed."

Ryan cursed. "If they're after the muties, then they'll be trigger-happy. Take cover until they're past. Keep alert, but no firing unless necessary. This is their land, and they know it too well."

Ryan was stating the obvious, but it didn't hurt to reinforce this in his companion's minds. Without needing instruction, they split into two separate groups, one taking each side of the trail they had been following.

Jak and Dean took one side, with Mildred and Doc, while Ryan, Krysty and J.B. took the other, mindful that they were a man short on their side.

They were safe in cover and stilled when they heard the sec team approach. The sec men were making no attempt to hide their approach, and the conversation that could be overheard soon revealed why.

"Those mutie fuckers. I say we should wipe them out once and for all," one sec man muttered savagely. He was a large, bearlike man with straining muscles, flowing white hair and beard. He carried a battered Heckler & Koch like Ryan's old and once favored blaster. The one-eyed man noted this from cover, knowing how effective the H&K could be, especially in the relatively confined clearing of the track.

"You know Alien wouldn't hold with that," drawled another, a rangy man with receding sandy hair and a Lee Enfield .303 in his hand, carried with a casual air that suggested speed when surprised.

"Damned Alien," the bear growled. "Harvey

knows what I mean. We can't afford to lose kids like that.''

"We can't afford to lose anyone, Jake," a third sec man said, this one younger than the others, seemingly sluggish. He was fat, with a belly that spilled over his belt, and had a blaster that looked from a distance to be a Colt Detective Special.

The fourth sec man wore a plaid shirt and had long, silver-gray hair that belied his youthful face. Carrying a Sharps rifle over his shoulder, he had so far been silent but now he spoke in slow measured tones. He sounded more thoughtful than the others, and had a reasoned edge to his voice.

"Seems to me there's no way to stop the muties. The Sunchildren have always been a problem, but their pesthole ville is too exposed to mount a good attack without them seeing us coming from a long way off. No good to us to have too many men chilled wiping them out. They don't often trouble us, right? They only sacrifice once a year, and it's only the dumb-ass kids that lets themselves be swiped. Just the casualties of living.''

The bearlike man glared at the silver-haired sec man. "We get them back, and I'll let that stand, Downey. We lose them, then you 'n' me gonna come to blows...Harvey or no Harvey.''

"Meaning?''

"You know what I mean. It's a shit code to live by, letting our young get taken and not giving a fuck.''

"I didn't say I didn't give a fuck. Just that you have to accept shit if you live in it. We win, we lose.''

The four sec men passed by where the companions had hidden themselves, blasters ready.

Ryan was relieved that the sec men hadn't seen them and there had been no need to fight. From their dress, they weren't allied to those who had attacked them on the blacktop, and perhaps they would know who those weird people were. And certainly he knew that his friends wouldn't be averse to joining a party headed for the mutie ville of Samtvogel. But not now. To reveal themselves would be to invite a firefight. They would stay hidden, then progress to the ville. The arrival of the sec men was fortunate, as it would allow them to track an entrance to the underground ville that much more easily.

On the other side of the path, Jak tensed. Only four sec men, with none behind? He knew that he had seen double that number. He raised the Colt Python, ready to use it.

"Don't," warned a voice behind him as he felt cold metal against his neck.

A whistle sounded from behind Ryan, and the sec men on the path whirled and hit the forest floor, ignoring the curling creepers as their blasters jumped to hand in ready positions, trained on the foliage in front of them—the area where the companions were hiding.

Ryan fell to one side, rolling as he hit the branches and plant stems, coming around with the SIG-Sauer in his hand.

He came face-to-face with a snub-nosed Colt Magnum Carry, the small-barreled blaster chambered for six rounds of .357 Magnum, despite its size.

The rangy man holding it in an outstretched hand

smiled, his uneven yellow teeth showing in almost a snarl.

"I wouldn't, my friend. You're good, but this is our land."

Chapter Seven

"Well now, let's get you all out here in what passes for the open in this pesthole of a forest. Let's see what we've got here."

With this, the rangy sec man gestured with his blaster, ushering Ryan onto the path through the undergrowth. The one-eyed warrior tensed his muscles as he rose, his hand wavering toward the panga still on his thigh, judging if he could reach swiftly the SIG-Sauer that he had been forced to discard on the carpet of creeper vine.

The sec man grinned. It was a slow, lazy grin that started at the corners of his mouth and spread across his face without ever touching the eyes.

"You could try, my friend, but you'd only get another empty hole through the center of that thick skull," he drawled.

Ryan judged the distances, then relaxed visibly. It would be volunteering for the farm, and he would wait for a better chance. He cursed his unwillingness on this journey to head straight into a firefight. His attempts to move stealthily and avoid wasting both time and ammo had led them into this.

Ryan stepped slowly backward, out into the center of the path. Jak, Dean, Mildred and Doc were already standing there, stripped of their weapons. As Ryan emerged, he saw from the corner of his eye that J.B.

and Krysty were also emerging backward, their hands in the open.

"That was a fine job of ambush, friend," he said slowly. "Never heard you coming. Did you, Jak?"

The albino nodded.

"You're not so bad yourself, Cyclops," the sec man replied. "We knew you were there, but not how you figured we were coming...unless it was that mutie scum," he added, directing a venomous glare at Jak.

Jak's blazing red eyes returned the look, not moving but saving it for a time when he could even the score.

The four sec men who had passed them were now on their feet, blasters raised but easy. There would be no nervous trigger fingers here, only carefully considered blasting.

The sec man who had his blaster trained on Ryan was one of four who had swept around behind the two groups as they waited in the undergrowth. His companion was a small, wizened man with nut-brown skin, and a 9 mm Walther PPK was trained steadily on J.B. and Krysty. Covering the others were two sec men who looked like twins, both with shoulder-length matted dreadlocks and coffee-colored skin, small glazed brown eyes unwavering. Both had beards to cover their pockmarked skin. They were intent on keeping their charges well covered.

"Don't know shit 'bout whose these fuckers are, Harv, but they ain't Sunchildren," one of them said in a high-pitched voice. It sounded out of place in his burly frame.

"Shouldn't say that, bro," the other replied in an

equally high voice. "That mutie shit can be all-fire clever, and this dude sure is mutie," he added, indicating Jak.

The sec man covering Ryan, who was obviously the man called Harvey, and sec chief, laughed mirthlessly. "Don't think they're anything to do with the Sunchildren," he replied.

Then he directed his attention to Ryan. "You'll have to excuse the boys there, but Ant and Dee lost their balls to the mutie fuckers when they were just kids. Being twins, they would have been better for sacrifice. It's only 'cause they're such feisty fuckers that they escaped—nearly unscathed."

"Hate that shit, though," one of the twins muttered.

Doc cleared his throat noisily. "If you'll excuse me, gentlemen, that would seem an eminently reasonable point of view. I wouldn't be averse to chilling a few of those scum-suckers myself," he said quietly.

"You?" One of the twins laughed, his voice rising to a screech. "Old man, you couldn't fart your way out of a vine leaf!" He prodded at Doc with the barrel of his blaster, a dirty and grease-covered shotgun that even J.B. couldn't recognize in its seemingly poor condition.

In relieving the party of their blasters, the sec men had been slack enough to leave Ryan his panga, J.B. his Tekna knife, and Doc his lion's-head swordstick, making the mistake of assuming it was to aid his walking. A mistake the twin was to regret, as Doc stepped back, sweeping the big sec man's feet from beneath him with the stick and then drawing the sword in one fluid motion, the speed of which took the sec men by surprise.

"Could I not?" Doc asked softly, the point of the sword pressing into the grounded man's throat.

Ryan tensed, sensing the sudden increase in tension around him. The blasters of the sec men rose just a fraction, fingers almost audibly tightening their grip. Harvey's smile vanished, to be replaced in a fraction of a second by a roaring laugh.

"I'll be damned," he roared. "Can't remember the last time Dee was bested like that, let 'lone by someone like him," he added, indicating Doc with a nod of the head. "Guess you people are as hot as I thought." The laugh vanished, and his tone dropped almost to a whisper. "So tell me why I shouldn't just chill you all right now."

"Because it'll waste your time. You want to go after those fuckers who've got your kids," Ryan replied.

"Good answer. But to chill you will take just a few seconds."

Ryan smiled, slow and with a vulpine grace. "You sure about that?"

Harvey shook his head. "No. Tell you what, Cyclops, I don't reckon on you being part of that scum. I'll worry about why you're here later. Give you a straight choice—a firefight now, or help us track that scum and mebbe not get chilled later. Sound fair?"

"No," Ryan answered slowly, his gaze traveling over his friends and the gathered sec men. "But I don't see that we've got a say."

"Knew you'd see it my way," Harvey said.

"Just as well. Take you anytime," Jak said softly, but with an underlying menace.

Harvey eyed the albino speculatively. "You know, mutie, I reckon you're just about mean enough to pull it off. Which is why I want you with us rather than against us."

"Feel good 'bout that?" Jak asked in the same tone. "How you know we not turn?"

"Would you, Cyclops?" the sec chief asked Ryan.

"Mebbe. Mebbe not right now," the one-eyed warrior replied carefully.

"Mebbe when not look," Jak added.

Harvey gave a rueful grin. "I really like your spirit, especially as the odds are less than even."

"Usually that way," Jak said, his red eyes unwavering on the sec chief.

Harvey considered that. "You people got a lot of balls. Just mebbe we'll get along fine. But we've got unfinished business. With us?" He waited until Ryan, casting his eye around his companions, nodded assent. "Good," the sec chief murmured quietly, almost to himself.

Under his direction, with a guard still covering them, the companions retrieved their blasters from where they had been forced to let them drop, and the party assembled on the path. Under Harvey's lead, with Ryan and Jak close behind, a sec blaster still half-raised toward them as a deterrent, they set out at a rapid pace.

"They've got some lead on you," Ryan told Harvey, continuing with what they had seen and when. The sec man listened in silence.

Finally, he said, "Those poor kids'll be chill meat

by now anyway, Cyclops. But the least we can do is give the poor lil' fuckers a decent burial. Not to be burned and eaten by that mutie shit…no offense,'' he added, nodding toward Jak.

"No," the albino answered in a neutral tone belied by his expression.

"Tell us what you know of this ville Samtvogel," Doc said to the leading sec man.

Harvey turned sharply. "How do you know about that, old man?"

Ryan told him they were outlanders looking for a better life, and as they traveled toward Seattle they came across a deserted diner, neglecting to mention the attacking party from the war wag. That could come later. He then produced the map.

"Shit," Harvey breathed, "if I ever find out which fuckwit left that to be found. You'll have gathered that the old place is a staging post for us," he continued, "So you know where we're going."

"Only as a name on a map," Ryan replied.

Harvey paused, walking in silence for some time, Ryan waiting patiently for an answer. By now they were out of the old ville and onto the blacktop, leaving the heavy forest behind and headed out to the scrub.

It wasn't until they had cut away from the blacktop and were headed across the bare and rough terrain, with the setting sun lending a coolness to the previously humid heat, that Harvey outlined what his people knew of the Sunchildren and Samtvogel.

The Sunchildren were a band of inbred muties descended from a predark cult led by a man named Sunchild, who believed that the nukes were a cleansing fire from the gods and that they should make their base in the wilderness, ready for the Judgment Day, when the gods would come to deliver them. They had, according to the legend that he had tortured from a captured mutie, welcomed the times of the dark, looking upon their mutations as a blessing from the gods, adapting their bodies for the new world to come.

The gods demanded sacrifices of children, the new lives replenishing the energies of the gods. The eating of flesh transferred that energy to the cultists. As they had become more mutated and inbred with each succeeding generation, so their lust for flesh had grown to the point where the current Sunchild was a drooling idiot whose only joy was the snatching of children from the underground ville, which Harvey revealed was called Raw.

He then went on to explain that his ville was run by a baron named Alien, and consisted of some survivors from the old ville of Seattle along with the descendants of people called the Illuminated Ones, who had emerged from an underground installation which they believed had been destroyed by a bomb after they left.

Listening, each of the companions wondered if the bomb had been in charge of the suicide they had found with the journal, but all elected to stay silent on the matter for now.

"...and they do say that there are other Illuminated Ones out there somewhere. Been some weird shit seen around here from time to time, which is why I'm so pissed at whoever left that mother map in the way station. We don't want our ville left exposed like that." He paused. "Of course, Cyclops, if you and your people had seen some weird shit on your way toward us, you'd tell me now, wouldn't you?''

Ryan fixed the sec chief with a steely blue glare.

"No, of course you wouldn't," Harvey murmured. "You're far too smart for that."

THE SACRIFICIAL FIRES lit the sky a brilliant white and orange, shining like a small sun in the blackness of the descended night. The ville itself was a collection of old ranch houses in a small valley, the original buildings in a state of disrepair and ruin, daubed a myriad of colors that flickered in the firelight. Around the ruined houses were shacks constructed of metal, wood and any raw materials that could have been found, pulled together rather than constructed, in a haphazard and flimsy fashion. And scattered among the shacks were tents made of rags and blankets strung over poles, offering scant protection to the muties who inhabited them.

The ridges of the valley were fenced off with rusty barbed wire strung around the dusty, unstable rock, stretching around for a distance of two miles. At irregular intervals were dead birds, hawks like the one that attacked Doc Tanner, mutated birds that resembled woodpeckers with grotesquely enlarged and toughened beaks, even some creatures that may, once in their genetic history, have been chickens—impaled on the wire and in varying states of decay and corruption.

The party of eight sec men and the seven companions had walked straight to the head of the valley, with little attempt at concealment.

"Interesting idea of decoration they've got," Ryan

remarked. "And an interesting idea of not being seen that you've got."

"Yeah, where are their sec forces?" J.B. added, peering into the gloom and voicing the unease felt by the others.

"Ain't got any sec forces. They don't need them," Harvey answered, poking at one of the bird corpses with the snubbed barrel of his blaster. The rotten carcass fell off the wire and landed in the dust. "The only thing that wants to come anywhere near this pesthole is the wildlife. Come to that, even that ain't so keen."

"Why don't you wipe them out once and for all, if they're such a problem?" Mildred asked.

Harvey shrugged. "We've got other things to do. Besides, they don't bother us much, and that's all we ask. Guess we just don't like visitors."

Doc eyed the sec chief speculatively. Now why would that be? he wondered. On reflection, he decided to save that question for another time.

Krysty had other ideas. She had kept silent for some time, but there was something about the sec chief that made her hair crawl close to her neck.

"Why don't you like visitors?" she asked. "Why do you keep the entrance to your ville so well hidden you don't even mark it on your own maps?"

"Privacy," Harvey said shortly. "It's a rare thing, and we prize it."

"Especially if you have something to hide."

Harvey's eyes momentarily blazed, but Krysty didn't flinch under his glare. She could feel his men tense around them, and saw from the periphery of her vision both Ryan and J.B. tense also, expecting trouble.

The sec chief won the struggle to control his temper and said quietly. "Our business is our business. Mebbe you'll find out later...if we want. Meantime, we've got work to do."

The fifteen-strong party looked down at the ville of Samtvogel. The inhabitants, clearly and unmistakably visible against the light of the fires and the dull colors of the valley, were moving slowly toward the center of the ville, which was a circular courtyard between the two largest ranch houses in the valley. It was here that the fire blazed. Standing between the two houses, and completely blocking one entrance to the yard, was a squat object, painted in a multiplicity of colors and standing malevolently over the unfolding scene.

"What's that?" Doc asked, gesturing with his stick.

"Who knows?" the sec chief answered in a bored tone. "Some kind of totem left over from the old days. I'll bet as how most of the mutie scum are so dumb they don't even realize it's there, let alone what it is."

"Perhaps..." Doc replied in a faraway tone that made Ryan look at him sharply.

There was no time for the one-eyed warrior to ask Doc what was on his mind, as Ant spotted something in the melee below.

"There they are... Shit, what a bunch of sick fucks," he whispered, pointing to the center of the ville.

The multicolored muties, chanting tonelessly and incessantly, had taken the three poles and upended

them, so that the corpses of the children sat one on
another, sinking down the poles into heaps of dead
flesh. Some of the muties were laying kindling around
the feet of the bottom children.

No one could tear their gaze away, wanting to, but
unwilling to believe what they were seeing and needing confirmation.

"Those are our dead," Harvey whispered, "and
they ain't gonna burn them."

"So how do we attack?" J.B. asked. He wanted to
ask why it was so important to get back some chilled
kids, risking their own necks for nothing, but figured
at that point it was more practical to figure out how
they could mount the attack and get out in one piece.

"The way I see it is like this," Harvey said after
pausing to gaze around the circumference of the valley edge.

JAK SLID DOWN the loose stones and patches of scree
that constituted the sides of the valley. He knew that
it would appear pitch-black in the area immediately
outside of the gathering of huts, shacks, old ranch
houses and ragged tents that made up the ville of
Samtvogel. The intense light of the fire would only
carry so far, and mutie eyes wouldn't be able to adjust
to the sudden change in light levels. As his flowing
white hair and pale skin shone out against the dark
of his camou clothing and the dark earth, he was
pleased about this.

The raucous chanting, growing in volume and intensity as the ceremony approached, also served to
mask the sound his party made while descending the
sides of the valley. With the looseness of the earth, it

was impossible for even Jak to maintain a complete silence. For the people with him, however, it seemed to be a case of how much noise they could make.

"Don't see why we couldn't just march in," grunted the small, nut-brown and wizened figure who slid down beside the albino, slowing his descent so that he was level with Jak. He managed to blend in with the landscape, only the whites of his hazel eyes shining in the dark. His name was Blake.

"You'd like them to have any inkling we're coming?" came a laconic voice from behind, indicated only by the flickering firelight that caught his spectacles. J.B. was slowing his descent with solid footfalls, reasoning that any noise he made was more than masked by the chanting. "We walk in and announce ourselves, just makes things harder," he added.

Blake grunted noncommittally.

There was one main track in and out of the ville. It took the shallowest incline out of the valley, and consisted of beaten earth and the remnants of a bitumen road. Two poles, once probably part of a sign hanging over the road, or perhaps a gate system, stood stark against the bare earth around.

The surrounding incline took a sharp turn upward, until at the rear of the ville it formed an almost vertical wall. This made it easy for Harvey to split the group into two separate parties and assign one to take each side of the valley. Jak, J.B. and Blake were joined by Mildred, Ant and Dee and Doc. The latter was picking his way down with infinite care, and the others waited for him to join them.

"Old man's too slow if you ask me," Blake grumbled.

"Wouldn't say that," Ant replied, his twin nodding agreement. "He can move fast enough when need be."

"Why, thank you, kind sir," Doc answered, settling himself beside the others. "When do we move?"

"Harvey signal," Jak told him.

ON THE OTHER SIDE of the valley, Harvey and Downey picked their way down to a spot about twenty yards from the first ranch house. Dean and Krysty followed, joined by the rangy sec man with receding hair, who was named Rankine. They were a few yards in front of the next pack, with Ryan behind the bearlike Jake and the fat sec man, whose name was Bodie. For his size, Bodie was surprisingly nimble, and the one-eyed warrior noted this, in case he should ever come up against the sec man. His reason for taking the rear position was partly to keep a watch on the Raw sec men, partly to keep an overall view on Harvey's tactics.

If Samtvogel had no sec forces or no blasters, then an attack from the sides, using the contrast between the dark hillside and the bright light of the ceremonial fires, should stand a good chance of success. Ryan had attempted a quick head count of the Sunchildren, and although there was too much movement for him to be certain, there seemed to be about seventy-five to eighty of them—five to one. Not good odds generally, but the blasters would even that up considerably.

Hit hard, hit fast, attain the target and retreat. The theory was sound, although the logic of carrying out the attack just to win back some chilled flesh was skewed. Better to do that than face the firefight in the forest, though. The odds were marginally better, and this could make them some progress toward their ultimate goal.

The one-eyed man joined the rest of the party, and they sat for a second watching the obscene celebrations beneath. One mutie, in a flowing and tattered robe dyed in many colors, had taken the center of the arena and seemed to be leading the chanting. The sound changed, a high keening note of blood lust now entering the massed voices.

"Think the others are in position?" Downey asked. His question was directed at his chief, but it was Dean who answered.

"With Jak leading, they'll have been waiting for us and getting bored," he whispered.

Harvey spared the youth a grim smile. "Hope you're right, boy, 'cause it's chilling time."

The assembled party readied their blasters, checking that chambers were full, magazines loaded, without even consciously thinking.

Harvey took a flare from the small leather bag he wore attached to his belt. He cast a glance over the seven people around him, eyes dwelling for a moment on Krysty—Raw women didn't join sec attacks, and he was still of two minds about Krysty and Mildred— before he nodded, almost to himself, and lit the flare. Standing, he threw it high into the air, describing a parabola that let it fall onto the roof of the semi-derelict ranch house, landing sputtering on the flat surface.

Harvey hollered, psyching himself up, and launched himself forward.

ON THE OTHER SIDE of the valley, J.B. was the first to react, rising as he saw the flare arc through the darkness, like a shooting star on the edges of the firelight.

"Go," he yelled simply, barking out the word.

Mildred was close behind him, with Jak streaking down the slope at an angle, spreading the line of attack. Ant and Dee took position between Jak and the Armorer, while Doc and Blake moved off to the other side, the seven warriors fanning out to dilute and confuse any concerted attempt at defense.

While they did this, Harvey was followed by Downey down the slope, while Ryan and Krysty moved off to form the farthest point of the line, with Bodie, Rankine, Dean and Jake taking the points in between.

On both sides, the attacking parties held fire until they could be sure of making all their shots count. Harvey's men carried only one blaster each, and of the companions, only J.B. and Ryan had more than the one blaster. J.B. had the Uzi in his hands, set to fire short, controlled bursts; Ryan grasped his SIG-Sauer, with his Steyr in reserve, while the Armorer had his M-4000 to fall back on. At the back of his mind, he considered it would be a useful weapon to scatter the crowds in front of the ceremonial fires.

Despite the raised voices and the inevitable noise of a sudden run down loose ground, neither party seemed to draw attention from the Sunchildren. There were very few of them at the edges of the ville, the majority of them now converging on the central arena, where the three poles of impaled children were now surrounded by kindling that was being doused in some kind of foul-smelling oil.

The muties were chanting louder and more intensely, with the keening edge growing higher and more desperate. On the belts of leather and material that kept their robes together, their blades glinted in the firelight.

The party led by Harvey arrived at the bottom of the hill and into the bowl of the valley. Harvey and Downey flattened themselves against the back of the ranch house; Ryan and Krysty took shelter behind a shack, while the others used some of the tents as cover, keeping low.

It was here that Ryan made the first chill.

The one-eyed man trod stealthily around the side of the shack that was sheltering himself and Krysty, measuring his footfall while the redhead kept him covered. Although his senses were on triple red, he was fairly sure that the shack was empty as all the muties seemed to have gathered in the center of the ville.

He didn't reckon on those that were too ill to make the ceremony.

Time seemed to freeze and then move with a painful slowness as he stepped past the opening at the front of the shack, only to feel a hand snake out and grab at his ankle. It took him by surprise as he had seen nothing from the periphery of his vision. The hand came from his blind side, emerging from the corner of an eye where there existed only an empty socket.

The grip was feeble, but exuded an uncanny

strength when Ryan twisted, trying to free his boot while also turning to see what had taken hold of him.

The arm was wizened and covered in open sores, blistered and bleeding. It had crude tattoo marks all the way up to the elbow, in some spiraling and arcane design. As Ryan pulled harder, a face appeared in the dim light of the ville's outer reaches. It was a parody of a human face, with no chin, a formless nose and eyes that were aligned at a forty-degree angle across the forehead. The mouth was a toothless, gaping maw, opening with a dull croak that threatened to get louder with each breath.

Ryan didn't want to risk a shot from the SIG-Sauer, alerting the chanting Sunchildren, so he drew the panga from its thigh sheath and sliced down through the night air. The momentum of the razor-sharp blade carried it deep into the skull of the mutie, driving through the softened bone of the skull and cleaving clean through to the palate.

It was just a pity that the momentum stopped before the panga blade tore into the larynx, as the mutie let out a high-pitched and piercing scream as it died. A scream that cut through even the loudness of the chanting.

The scream was followed by an eerie silence as Ryan felt the grip loosen on his boot, freeing him.

SUNCHILD, THE CHOSEN, hereditary leader of the ville, stopped in midchant, arms raised. The muties gathered at the foot of the poles, about to ignite the kindling and fire the sacrifices, looked at their leader, a questioning look spreading across their dull visages.

Sunchild, raised in a stagnant genetic pool altered

only by mutation, was little more than a drooling idiot, but a drooling idiot with a strong sly streak running through him, and a cold ruthlessness unhindered by any intelligence or thoughts of morality.

If there were intruders, he would add them to the sacrifice, and the gods would gorge on energy, as would his people. He turned and caught sight of a flash of white hair and red eyes burning in a pale face, a flash that was followed by the roar of a blaster and a burning sensation across his shoulder.

He screamed, and his people were suddenly galvanized from their frozen stupor, the chanting beginning again in earnest as they turned back to face the surrounding ville, blades coming to hand.

As soon as the silence hit, Jak took one look at Ant and Dee.

"Something's fucked up," Ant whispered.

Jak nodded. "Hit fuckers fast."

Before the sec men had a chance to register what was happening, Jak streaked forward from cover, skipping nimbly over the detritus of the ville, spread out between the shacks and tents, making for the central arena where the Sunchildren were gathered. J.B. was on his tail, moving on a path that would take him into the center. Mildred was close behind, dropping to one knee at the side of a shack and leveling her ZKR, taking aim to pick off the first mutie to move.

Doc once again took the sec men by surprise, his long thin legs taking him on a path that cut between two tents, the heavy LeMat percussion pistol ready to discharge into the throng of the multicolored enemy.

"Damn, boys, we're gonna miss the fun," Blake

complained, taking off in pursuit. The twins exchanged glances before raising their shotguns and following.

By the time they had taken their first step, Sunchild himself had already seen Jak, and taken the slug from the Colt Python .357 in the shoulder, the grazing blow taking a chunk of bloody flesh from the top of his shoulder joint and sending him spinning as the momentum of the slug drove him around in a circle before collapsing.

"THAT'S FUCKED things," Bodie breathed as Ryan withdrew his panga from the now chilled mutie and returned it to its sheath as he turned, raising the SIG-Sauer to the first of the muties that came toward the group, following the direction of the cry.

The roar of Jak's blaster and the scream of Sunchild momentarily halted the onrush, and some of the muties turned, their chanting stopping.

"Now!" Harvey screamed, coming from cover. He and Downey started to fire, picking their targets and watching the muties fall as every slug hit home. Bodie, Jake and Rankine also came from cover, firing as they advanced, taking steady steps with each discharge, cutting through the muties.

Ryan and Krysty were also cutting a strong swath, each shell from the SIG-Sauer and the Smith & Wesson counting not just for one mutie down, but also for another two or three turning in panic or confusion.

On the other side of the arena, J.B. was chopping down the muties with ease, the short, controlled blasts of the Uzi taking out two or three at a time. In the confusion, he couldn't tell whether they were chilled or merely injured, but that was unimportant. He and Jak were through to the center, where he shouldered the Uzi while Jak holstered his Python. The wounded behind them were now the responsibility of Doc, Mildred and the sec men.

The Armorer and Jak cleared away the kindling with hands and feet, working at the poles to loosen their grip in the ground, ignoring the smell and sight of the children before them.

"Dark night," the Armorer breathed, "how the fuck did they get them in here?"

"Who cares? How get out?" Jak gasped, sinews straining as he worked at a pole.

"Jak, watch out!" was yelled from behind him. The albino whirled in time to see a purple-clad mutie, snarling with an unreasoning hatred, throw himself forward with a bayonet blade grasped in his fist. The albino stepped to one side, parrying the mutie's arm and watching him fall.

The mutie came to his feet in a roll, ready to spring forward once more. Jak was in the process of drawing his Python when he heard a deafening roar beside him, and the mutie's midsection dissolved into ribbons of blood, flesh, intestine and splintered bone as the grapeshot from the LeMat tore into him.

Doc lowered the blaster beside Jak. "Come, lad, let us get these poor children's corpses unstaked."

Jak turned. Three of the stakes were now lying flat, with Dean and J.B. both laboring on two of the remaining three while the sec men from Raw kept them covered.

There was no sign of the other group.

"FIREBLAST! Where are they coming from?" Ryan yelled above the roar of the chanting and of blaster-fire.

"They heard us first, lover, so we've got the lion's share," Krysty replied over the clashing noise. She could see the other party freeing the stakes and holding their ground.

And as suddenly as it had started, they were through to the center themselves, with Harvey and Downey close behind.

"Where's Dean?" Ryan yelled to the sec chief, losing sight of his son. Harvey shrugged.

Rankine was pinned down by three muties, his Lee Enfield .303 having been knocked from his grasp by a thrown rock. While Jake and Bodie were in front of him and plowed on regardless, Dean was close enough to spot the three muties descend. They were too close to Rankine for the youngster to risk a shot, so he holstered his Browning Hi-Power and flew at them. A high kick caught one at the point of his jaw-bone, just beneath the ear, shattering the bone and driving shards of it into his brain.

The second mutie was grabbed by the hair, his head pulled back and a straight-handed chop to the throat taking him out.

Rankine was able to deal with the third mutie himself, grasping fingers reaching the barrel of the Lee Enfield. Pulling it into his grip and grasping tighter, he swung it so that the stock crashed across the mutie's nose, bloodying his face and throwing him backward.

"Thanks, kid," the sandy-haired sec man puffed as he struggled upright.

"Thank me if we get out of here," Dean returned with one eye on the surrounding crowd of muties. Some of them had started to fight one another, confusion and blood lust clouding any reason they possessed.

Rankine and Dean joined the others in the center. Dean joined Mildred in positioning one stake on their shoulders. Rankine and Jake took another, while Ant and Dee took a third.

"Form a circle, fire out when need be, and we head for the main road," Harvey said. "I know these fuckers. Once we get out of the light, they'll be too scared to follow."

"Hope so," Ryan said shortly. The odds still bothered him. As did the fact that Doc seemed to be choosing the wrong time to get distracted, staring at the painted totem.

Doc turned to the one-eyed man. "If—when—we get out, then I fear I shall have something of import to discuss," he said with a worried frown.

"Worry me later," Ryan returned. "This is gonna be a bitch."

It was about to get worse. The sound of a blaster discharging cut through the chanting and yells of the muties.

"I thought you said they didn't have blasters!" J.B. yelled at Harvey.

Chapter Eight

It was Sunchild himself who had the blaster. Where he had found it was something none of them could ever know—the fact that he had no idea how to use it was undeniable.

The mutie leader appeared in the middle of the crowd, the scarlet of his blood blending with the colors on his robes, running together in a mess of red as it flowed from the wound in his shoulder. Whatever else, the mutie leader had immense reserves of strength and stamina. He waved the blaster in the air, yelling in a fury even more incoherent than the chanting he had previously led.

It was hard to see in the glare of the firelight, but it looked like a long-barreled blaster, possibly a .44 Colt Peacemaker. The Armorer strained his eyes to tell, wanting to know how many shots the mutie would have left. Especially as he had just discharged the second round.

None of the party had seen where the first shot was directed, but it was an even bet that it was as random as the second, which fired off at an oblique angle, stopped by the soft flesh of a mutie with only one arm, the other showing just a few fingers flapping at the shoulder.

Now the mutie had no arms, its only true limb

blown off at the elbow by the heavy lead slug, ripping sinew, flesh and bone at such short range.

The companions and sec men encircled the poles, facing out. What had been difficult before was now shaping up to be a deadly proposition.

"You said they didn't have blasters," Ryan stated flatly. "Our entire attack was based on that…but they do."

Harvey shook his head, momentarily thrown. "Never seen the bastards use them before. Didn't even know that they had them," he whispered.

"Seems certain they don't know how to use them," J.B. snapped, "so mebbe we'd better get going before they do."

Harvey nodded. "We keep tight, lay down a covering fire, staggering shots to preserve ammo. But first I think we need to carve ourselves a little path."

The uncertainty that had plagued his voice a few moments before was now gone as the sec man's tactical brain clicked into gear, going through the permutations of what was possible in this situation.

From the leather bag at his belt he produced an old gren. He pulled the pin and lobbed the bomb overarm toward the road out of the ville. Ryan noticed that a few of the muties automatically followed the path of the gren as its dark shape arced in the light, their inbred idiocy responding to stimulus, even in the middle of a battle.

The sec men laid down a volley of fire, driving the muties back, while Harvey counted carefully, hissing the numbers between his teeth, until he screamed, "Now!"

He hit the ground hard. The sec men around him

did likewise. The companions took only a split second between them to realize what Harvey had been counting, and followed.

The gren exploded, either on impact with the ground or else in the air directly above. It was hard to tell, as it landed somewhere to the rear of the pressing crowd of mutie Sunchildren. Shrapnel from the gren spread out in all directions, and the air was suddenly filled with shrill screams as those at the rear of the crowd were either hit by the white-hot metal or thrown forward by the concussion of the blast.

There was more confusion among the ville dwellers, and a few more shots were loosed. J.B.'s experienced ears picked up that it was more than one blaster...a Peacemaker, probably Sunchild's, as he had suspected, and a Walther PPK, like the one carried by Blake. So there were at least two. The Armorer surmised that the blasters had been picked up from sec men claimed in raids by the Sunchildren in the past. It was obvious that they had no idea or experience of blasters, and probably only used them now because of the injury to their leader.

But even a blaster in the hands of an incompetent idiot was a threat. The sooner they moved out, the better.

"We go now, yeah?" he yelled as he scrambled to his feet.

"Head out!" Harvey returned.

The party scrambled to its feet, the circle of sec laying down fire that kept the Sunchildren at bay. They had pressed forward from the back, and those at the front were seeking to move back, away from the blasterfire. The result was that the muties had got themselves into a tangle of limbs and falling bodies on either side of a clear pathway. For, as Harvey had figured, the forward force of the gren explosion had parted them, driving them to one side of the point on the dirt road where the gren had landed.

In fact, this was the major obstacle that confronted the party on the way out. There was a large hole in the road where the gren had dug out a gouge of earth, and the pole carriers had to negotiate the treacherous sliding earth at the sides of the earthen indent.

Once past that, the resistance they encountered became almost negligible. As Harvey had told them, the confused and cretinous Sunchildren had preferred to stay in the light, only a few thrown blades and the odd stray shot following them, and causing no danger.

The incline out of the valley was wearing on those carrying the poles, and once they were in open country, with just a faint, angry buzz of sound from the ville of Samtvogel all to remind them it was there, the party swapped over. Ryan and Harvey took one pole, and the lead on the route back.

It was quiet, and they traveled in silence, all the companions wondering silently why it was so important to recover the chilled corpses. Harvey and his sec men kept an uneasy silence, unwilling to say anything in front of the strangers.

Doc was keeping pace with the frontrunners of Ryan and Harvey, cradling his LeMat and keeping an eye out for anything that moved across the arid plain. He seemed to be deep in thought, deeper than any of the others.

Finally, he turned to the one-eyed warrior.

"Ryan, my dear friend and leader, there is something I shall have to share with you,'' he said insistently.

Ryan shot him a warning look, fixing him with his steely eye. Doc appeared to notice and take heed, for his tone changed noticeably.

"It is, ah, a personal matter, and perhaps now is not the time...but certainly I shall need to converse with you on something that is causing me much alarm.''

The old man moved away, with a backward glance at Harvey that made the sec man curious. Downey, keeping guard in a similar parallel position to Harvey as Doc was to Ryan, also noted the old man's behavior, and made note to himself to keep an eye on the crazy old man—who perhaps wasn't as crazy as he seemed.

THEY MADE easy progress through the edges of old Seattle, past the apartment building and through the forest, Harvey and his sec men leading them on a path that only a thorough working knowledge of the territory could reveal. They went farther into the forest than Ryan and his people had penetrated before their first encounter with the sec force.

Here, the many-colored flowering plants decreased in favor of the mutated and stunted trees, which grew from the mounds of rubble. The creeping vines were more prevalent, flowering white and sweet smelling, the flowers open even at night. The tilted buildings, standing firm yet looking precarious on mounds of moved earth, their structures yielding slowly to gravity. Varieties of vine crawled across the spaces between buildings, forming a ceiling of green, sentient plant life that kept that part of the forest in perpetual twilight.

"Not much farther." Harvey spoke suddenly, his voice surprising in the silence engendered by their journey. It was a response to a question he had felt had been unspoken for some time. "You wouldn't have found the entrance, even with the map," he continued with a note of pride creeping into his voice. "We're real careful to keep ourselves hidden. You never know what's around...."

Or what they had to hide, Mildred thought. There was something that was nagging at the back of her mind about the corpses, and why they needed to be retrieved. She tried to steal a look at them as she walked beside the pole carried by Bodie and Rankine. But the chilled corpses were too distorted by the manner of their chilling, and the way in which they were hanging, for her to get a good look without somehow stopping the party and causing suspicion.

Doc wouldn't be the only one with something to say to Ryan, she mused.

Her musings were cut short by their arrival at a hidden entrance to the ville of Raw.

"Pull up here, people," Harvey commanded for the benefit of the companions.

The one-eyed warrior looked around. It seemed as though they had arrived on an old street corner that was marked by three derelict and overgrown buildings and a stand of mutated trees growing out of the rubble where once a fourth had stood. The creeper was thick beneath their feet, and he couldn't see how they could get beneath it easily.

"Over here," Downey said with a sly smile, moving to the small copse of trees. The companions followed him, to find that the silver-haired sec man was reaching into the bole of a tree. He contorted his face with effort, tugging at something within.

A section of ground to one side of the copse shuddered and began to move upward, hinged at one side so that it flipped over. Leading off from the opening was a flight of stone steps, roughly hewed from rock and concrete blocks that had been primitively mortared together.

"After you," Downey said, indicating the opening.

Jak grinned admiringly. "Nice hide."

Harvey grunted as he and Ryan led the way down. "Takes us down to an old basement, tunneled through to an old mail subway line. But it's kept to a simple winch system so's we can use it if we lose what power we have."

"You've got power, fuel?" Ryan asked, wondering if this was part of the hidden stores of the Illuminated Ones.

"Some. We do some trading, sometimes. Most of our power is wood, oil from the plants for lamps and stuff. The creepers're really good for that. Any real power is used by the tech people...." He trailed off, seemingly unwilling to continue, aware that he may already have said too much. He was spared any questions by a sec man appearing from the shadows at the bottom of the stairs.

Ryan started at the sudden appearance, shifting the pole weight to one shoulder while his now free hand snaked down to the holstered SIG-Sauer.

"It's okay, Cyclops, he's one of mine," Harvey stated laconically, feeling Ryan's weight shift to his rear and guessing what the one-eyed warrior's move would be.

"You got them back," the sec man said in a flat voice, still hidden by shadow. He had a blaster in his hands that Ryan could tell was an Uzi from the shape and the way he was holding it. As he stepped out, Ryan could see that his eyes were blue, and his hair long and blond, framing a face that was lean with a hard, cold harshness.

Ryan marked him down as dangerous. He wasn't an enemy yet, but caution was always a necessity.

"Chilled, but at least we can give them a decent send-off," Harvey replied.

"Jenna will be way pissed," the blond sec man said, shaking his head before stepping back into the shadows and letting the group pass with only a word of greeting to his fellow sec men, and a look of suspicion for the companions.

"Jenna?" Ryan asked as they proceeded down empty, winding tunnels dimly lit by oil lamps.

"Baron's wife. Some say the real power. Now I wouldn't be the one to spread that, Cyclops, but I would pay heed if it reached my ears."

Ryan said nothing, not sure if the sec chief was giving him a warning or a threat.

The lights grew more regular and brighter as they progressed through the tunnels, which were obviously a serviceable entrance into the heart of Raw. As they walked along the rail tracks of the old mail line, they found that there were more and more signs of habitation: small shacks sprung up along the way, with a few small fires outside them and children running and playing. Children who, in the darkness up above, would have been sleeping. But here there was no day and night, only the perpetual half light of the lamps. In many ways, this was no different from if they had lived in the twilit forest up above.

"Hey, Jak, notice anything?" Dean whispered to the albino as they entered another, more heavily populated zone of the ville.

"Mebbe," Jak replied carefully, with one eye on the sec men surrounding them.

"A lot of these people look the same?" Dean continued, forgetting the proximity of the sec force with whom they had hunted.

"People all same anyway," Jak said pointedly, flashing a warning glance at the young Cawdor.

"Yeah, mebbe," Dean said slowly, too lost in thought to be noticing Jak's true meaning.

"Nice ville you got," the Armorer said, taking in the surroundings. "Good guard system—especially the tunnel complex."

"Yeah, we like to keep it tight and safe," Harvey answered, warming to a theme close to his heart. "There's a shitload of tunnels and basements in this old ville, but we keep ourselves pretty much to one sector, making sure that the others always have a watch on. There's not many folks about these parts, but we like to keep ourselves to ourselves."

"Yeah, so you've said before," Krysty replied, trying to keep the note of suspicion out of her voice. But she couldn't stop the curls of her hair coiling tight to her throat and collarbone.

They continued through the populated area. Some basements leading off of the tunnels had been converted wholesale into living units, or areas where vital survival trades were practiced. There was a cobbler and blacksmith, an area that seemed to act as a communal kitchen and dining area for at least that sector, and an armory. J.B. caught this in passing, and could see that there were two women at work dismantling and cleaning blasters. There were boxes lining the walls, and the smell of oil and cordite hung in the air around the cordoned-off area.

"We don't have as many blasters as some villes, stranger, but we like to keep them in good working order. You never know when you may need them, right?" Bodie murmured to the Armorer, a hint of warning in his voice.

J.B., taking it for now, said nothing.

Looking around, Ryan could see that they had quite a crowd following them, and other people appeared from tunnels leading off their route as word spread that they had returned with the chilled young.

By the time they reached the central hall, they had a crowd behind them that had to have constituted most of the ville.

"Just how many people you got under here?" Ryan asked Harvey, casting a look over his shoulder.

"Two-fifty, mebbe three hundred," the sec chief replied. "Not much mutie business, either. We get enough people traveling through to keep us pretty mixed in the old gene pool."

Ryan's eye narrowed, even though he said nothing. It was more than a little unusual to find such a knowledge of genetics expressed so casually in any ville in the Deathlands, let alone one that was relatively isolated.

They came to a halt in the center of the large room.

It was circular, draped in somberly colored swathes of old material that lent it a shadowy, dusty air. At the far end a long wooden table, with high-backed chairs, stood on a small dais, imposing over the rest of the arena. The hall itself had to have been part of a deep foundation, as it had a rough earthen floor, yet the walls visible through the gaps in the drapes were of concrete. Through one such gap, Ryan could see the ragged edge of a floor that had been torn down— or had fallen—at some point in the past. That accounted for the surprisingly high and impressive ceiling.

The sec party put the poles down in the center of the hall. Harvey's sec men stepped back from the bundles of chilled and stinking flesh; Ryan's people did likewise. Casting a glance over his shoulder, Jak saw that the rear of the hall was now full of ville dwellers, yet there was an eerie silence among them, with not even any sobs to break that silence.

"What now?" Ryan asked Harvey, noting Jak's unease.

The sec chief said nothing, but gestured toward the table and the high-backed chairs.

Two people had somehow slipped into the room from some secret entrance. One was a large, thickset man who was just under six feet, and looked like his muscular frame was beginning to run to fat. He wheezed slightly under his long, flowing gray hair and long gray beard, but his eyes were still sharp, moving with a deliberate slowness over the chilled children and then over the outsiders among the sec group.

Krysty shivered, a wave of nausea sweeping over

her. Her hair coiled tight, then sprung loose, and for a moment she thought that she may pass out. She slowed her breathing, willing the wave of nausea to pass. What, she wondered, had caused that? It wasn't the old man, so it had to have been...

Glittering, raven-black eyes bored into her. Krysty felt the wave begin to swell once more and fought back, fighting at the tendrils of fear that began to wrap themselves around her mind. Her mind! That was what was happening: the woman accompanying the baron was attempting to reach into her mind. Krysty could feel that same doomie, feelie instinct that she herself possessed to a small degree: the woman in front had sensed that in her, but had a stronger ability and was trying to gauge Krysty's strength.

The flame-haired woman fought back mentally with all the willpower she possessed, closing off sections of her mind as she felt the tendrils of the other touch them. She used every trick she had learned from her mother.

"Krysty, are you okay?" Mildred whispered urgently. Standing just to the rear of her, the older woman had noted with alarm the sudden tension in her friend's body, and the minute muscular contortions as Krysty's mental struggle was reflected in microcosm.

The raven-eyed woman standing beside the baron abruptly looked away as she saw Mildred lean toward Krysty, and the link was broken.

Krysty suppressed a gasp, and whispered over her shoulder, "Okay now. I'll tell you later."

The ville's baron sat on the highest of the chairs, the woman seating herself at his right hand. She looked younger, with long raven hair to match her eyes, and sharp features that would have been classically beautiful if not for the hint of something sadistic around those eyes. She appeared to be temperamentally opposed to the baron, who now spoke.

"So, Harv, you couldn't bring them back alive this time," he said softly, with a warmth and sadness in his voice.

"'Fraid not, Alien," the sec chief replied. "Bastards have got blasters, too. Good thing we ran into these here folks. Cyclops here is a good fighter. So're his people."

"Really?" the woman said in a voice that was silky, but with a biting undertone that hinted at sarcasm. "Not up to the job yourself, then?"

"Stop riding him, Jenna," the baron said softly, with a hint of indulgence in his voice. "Harv usually does okay. Averages means we lose a few."

It wasn't lost on Ryan or any of his companions who the real power and ruthlessness may be in the ville of Raw. For Krysty, this was particularly alarming, she needed to get the others where they could talk.

But not yet. While she pondered this, the baron confirmed what they had already gathered. He introduced himself as Alien, and the woman as his wife, Jenna. Her smile on being introduced was cold and saurian. She came out from behind the table, stepping delicately past the pile of chilled flesh on the floor, and walked among the sec party, examining the newcomers.

She stopped when she was in front of Mildred. "Interesting," she said to herself, then louder,

"We've never had a black here. It'll be interesting to talk. How many of your sort survived skydark, I wonder? Have you little communities?"

Mildred was less than inclined to discuss her past, let alone her racial origins. It was all she could do to stop from punching the lights out of the baron's wife. From the corner of her eye, she caught J.B.'s warning glance.

"I was on my own when I joined my friends," she said shortly, through gritted teeth. "It's a long story."

"Well, later, then," Jenna replied, losing interest. "Are we going to cremate now, dear?" she asked, turning to the baron. "The poor things will start to stink us out otherwise."

"Good point, my dear," Alien replied indulgently.

To the companions, he said, "Please, after the ceremony you must join us. I want to know more about you."

He turned to Harvey. "Get the fires ready."

The sec man nodded and directed his party to activities they obviously knew too well for their liking.

"We'll help," Dean said suddenly, moving in front of Rankine to help Bodie lift one of the poles.

Dean was the only one of the companions to offer, and in fact the only one who could now, as the sec men had the poles under their control. Ryan noted with interest the look of alarm that crossed Harvey's face as he looked at Jenna, and the flash of anger that crossed hers. Alien, on the other hand, seemed oblivious to this exchange.

"Thank you, son," was all the baron said. In the face of this, Harvey had little option other than to let

Dean continue, although it seemed to make him considerably jumpy.

The sec men, with Dean, made off the way they had come, the crowd parting to let them pass.

They took the first junction and headed off for some time. The atmosphere grew hotter, and Dean felt the sweat bead on him, his clothes begin to cling.

"What's that?" he gasped, the hot air searing his lungs.

"Furnace," Bodie replied in a short breath, the fat sec man also feeling the heat.

They arrived at the furnace room, a system of old boilers looted from the remains of aboveground and linked together to form a system of lighting and hot water. By the careful use of a piping system, it was feasible to run the boilers at a high temperature and yet use very little fuel. They used the trees from the forest above as wood, and it seemed that the wood fibers were densely packed in the mutie stumps...

Dean was aware that Harvey's lecture was intended to distract him from the task of taking the chilled children from the poles and placing them in the fires. This was done via a metal palette that led into an oven probably taken from a predark crematorium.

Dean would have looked on the sec man's lecture as an attempt to distract him from the horror in front of him if not for the fact that the sec chief had to surely have been aware after the raid that Dean had seen such things before. The youngster thus reasoned that it was a distraction for something he wasn't supposed to see. But what?

Dean had his suspicions and feigned interest while the sec men took the corpses from the poles. It wasn't an easy or pleasant task, as the poles were impaled through the entirety of each body, and it took a considerable effort to pull the poles from the corpses. Several times, the sec men stopped to vomit, and at those moments Dean was glad for Harvey's distraction, even if that wasn't his original intention.

When the corpses were all removed, the six of them were laid on the palette, and Dean took the opportunity to help Jake and Bodie push the palette into the fires.

For the first time, laid out as they were on the metal surface, Dean was able to get a good look at the bodies. All of the children had blond hair and blue eyes.

It struck a chord, something he had learned at the Brody school. Something his father and Mildred had talked about from predark days.

It was that something that had made him want to accompany the sec men here, to confirm what had been bugging him the whole way back, when the corpses had been too dark, too distorted, too contorted to view properly.

Blond hair. Blue eyes.

The image of the corpses disappearing and charring in fire was somehow horribly familiar.

Chapter Nine

"So you have been inside the place of legend," the guff and amiable baron said with a twinkle. "Never held with the way all those old stories were turned to myths. Old tech is what led us to skydark. Why be so crazy about something that got us into shit like this?"

Ryan indicated a certain degree of agreement. "Thing is, Baron, it's not what happened then...it's what we can do with it now if we can get our hands on it. If a baron like yourself had access to it."

The one-eyed man left the phrase hanging in the air as he took a bite from the cooked bird's leg that he held. They were now all seated at the long table, Alien and Jenna holding court while Harvey and Downey sat with them. On the other side of the table were lined the companions, Dean having returned with the sec men from the furnaces and so far holding his tongue on what he had seen.

Alien had dismissed his people from the hall after the corpses of the children had been taken away, and they had returned to their homes within the tunnels in a manner that suggested Alien didn't need force or the heavy hand of a sec force to rule. He had ordered food to be brought to the table, and when it had arrived had bid the others to join him.

After nothing but self-heats for some while, it was

a relief to have fresh food, even if the forest environment aboveground made them feel dubious about some of the vegetables. Doc also made a point of avoiding the meat, wondering if it was the kind of hawk that had attacked him.

Ryan's point hung in the air for some time, the baron chewing thoughtfully before answering.

"I'll tell you this," he said finally, "for we've nothing to hide here. Some of us are the descendants of those who came out of the underground base. It doesn't matter shit now, but there was a disagreement down there between those who wanted to make a new life, and those who thought there still might be a way to set up predark systems of government that could link up so-called alternative communities...least, that's what they called them. But alternative to what? How can it be an alternative when what there was before just ain't there anymore?

"So they went their separate ways. Some ended up here, along with some people they'd picked up along the way. Sunchildren weren't much of a problem, but the forest was. So when they found the tunnels and basements could be linked up, I guess it was almost second nature to get tunneling, 'specially after living underground for so long anyways. The rest, well, guess we try to keep ourselves to ourselves, live peaceful and get richer."

"Everyone would like that," the Armorer interjected, "but it's not that easy."

"It is here," Alien said, fixing J.B. with a friendly but rock-steady stare. "It is because we make it so."

There was an undertone that made Ryan cast a glance in the direction of the sec men. Both Harvey and Downey were seemingly unconcerned, but the one-eyed warrior noted that both had shifted their weight as they were seated, so that it would be easier for them to reach their blasters.

Jak had also spotted that, and by instinct had moved his own body weight so that he could move with speed and reach his concealed leaf-bladed knives with ease.

Before there was any chance for tension to break the surface, Doc leaned over the table. He addressed his question to the baron, but his eyes were on Jenna as he spoke.

"The question still remains unanswered. Is there any of the poisonous old tech still on the premises, the rancid remnants of a bygone and perhaps best forgotten age? Some relic of that pernicious evil known as the Totality Concept?"

Alien scratched at his beard. "I don't know what you mean by that, old man, but we do have some pieces that we try to get going. It's all useful if it can be made to work."

"Then I would be most grateful if you would let me and my companions view it at some point for interest's sake," Doc remarked, sitting back.

"Mebbe," the baron answered noncommittally.

But Alien's answer wasn't important. Doc had already discovered what he wanted to know, and watching him the others also drew their own conclusions. Doc hadn't idly brought up the name of the Totality Concept, the umbrella under which many government black operations had been carried out before skydark. He had spoken the name in the hopes of eliciting some kind of reaction.

The baron hadn't recognized the name at all, and had seemed genuine in his bemusement at the use of the term. But then, Doc hadn't been watching the baron: his eyes had been kept firmly on Jenna. And he had seen her sharp features harden as the words were spoken. The raven eyes had fixed on him, met his full on and tried to fathom his intent.

There was old tech here. Old tech related to secret government projects of the past. And maybe there was something that would link this ville to the main body of the Illuminated Ones, and the place in the north they were searching for.

THE FIRST INTIMATION that they may be in for a rocky ride came later that night, when Harvey and Downey led them—at Alien's behest—to the quarters where they would sleep while they were staying in Raw. The baron had assumed they would stay with an open-ended invitation that could be construed as either friendly or a threat: there was a possibility that he had no intention of letting them leave.

Once they were alone in the comfortable quarters, they discussed what they had seen. Krysty's feeling that she had encountered another mutie with seeing power was echoed by the unease felt by both Doc and Mildred. And when Dean told them of what he had seen at the furnace, Mildred was quick to add this to the way Jenna had dismissively talked of her as a black.

It seemed certain that the real problem would be Jenna rather than Alien. How much did the baron's wife sway him, and how much of the loyalty of the sec force belonged to her rather than her husband?

"If there is old tech from the whitecoats, and she has her hands on it, then I shudder to think…" Doc mused, shaking his head and causing his mane of white hair to cloud his features.

"Play along for now, find out the real score, then get the hell out," J.B. said, polishing his spectacles.

"It's the only way," Ryan agreed. "Besides, I don't see as we have other options at the moment. Until we know the layout here, we can't break for it. And they're not putting us under immediate danger. If they felt like that, then we would have bought the farm by now."

"That woman, though…" Krysty shuddered.

Jak was pacing the floor. "Closed in. Feel like in trap here. Nowhere run."

Ryan agreed. "But that's why we need to bide our time. Mebbe scout around."

"Mebbe," the albino whispered.

ALTHOUGH THERE WAS no differentiation between day and night this far belowground, there did appear to be some consensus on what constituted day and night, as it wasn't too long before the tunnels and basements that comprised the ville subsided into a silence broken only by the insomniac, and those whose tasks kept them working through the night.

The companions had fallen to sleep, the rigours of the past twenty-four hours having taken their toll. Ryan and Krysty were entwined beneath blankets, and Mildred and J.B. also slept close together. Doc was mumbling in his sleep, whimpering and turning in a turmoil of nightmare.

But at least he was sleeping, Dean wasn't. Not any

longer. A gentle rustling, a soft padded footfall was enough to wake the light-sleeping youth.

Dean didn't move. If this was an intruder, then the young Cawdor wouldn't give himself away. He allowed his eyes to adjust to the poor light, letting darkness form substance and shape.

"Jak?" he whispered, as the shape became recognizable.

"Quiet," the albino returned, his voice little more than a breath.

Dean silently and swiftly rose from his bed. "What are you doing?"

His eyes adjusted to the dark, and the pale face and white hair of Jak Lauren were almost incandescent in the lack of proper light. With his dark camou clothing, it seemed as though Jak were nothing more than a disembodied head.

"Take look around...safer then," the albino teen replied, his eyes as sharp and red as twin fires in the ice of his face. His scarred visage was expressionless.

"Think we've got something to fear?" Dean queried.

Jak shrugged, but his eyes told another tale.

"Me, too," Dean said simply. "You want to go on your own?"

Jak nodded. "This time."

He knew that he would be quicker, quieter, safer without the less experienced youth; but he would never say so. However, for all his exuberance, Dean knew his own limitations in some areas, and so just assented.

"Be careful. I know, I didn't have to say it," he whispered as he returned to his bed.

But Jak was already gone.

RAW STANK WORSE than any another ville that Jak had seen since leaving the bayous. It was partly a stale, old smell left over from the predark days, when parts of the ville had been old sewer tunnels for Seattle. The ingrained ordure in the brick and concrete had survived the nukecaust, and would probably survive the end of the rest of the world. Jak's sensitive nose was clogged by this smell above all others, and he just figured that the inhabitants of the ville were used to it.

There were other elements to the smell. Sweat and blood, urine and feces, birth and death: all were collected together with no real outlet. On top of that, the smell of cordite; of the grease used to keep blasters in working order; the sickly sweet smell of the dyes used on cloth; the tannery and the blacksmith; old food and rotten vegetable matter, and something else…

It was a smell that Jak recognized too well. The sweet-and-sour smell of human flesh, roasted and charred. That had to come from the furnaces, from the disposal of the chilled children that they had helped return to the ville. And yet, Jak was puzzled. If the furnaces had a proper outlet for their smoke, as they surely had to if the ville wasn't to be permanently smoked out, then why did this smell linger so long? The other smells staying around he could figure: the air was fresh if not clean, so there had to be some ventilation shafts down here. But the furnace needed to have had a direct outlet built for it.

So why the smell? More than that, it didn't have the other elements that Jak would expect. There was no wood smoke mingled with it, and he remembered Dean telling them briefly that the furnace was wood fired. There had been something else the young Cawdor had wanted to say, but he had held his tongue.

Jak was naturally suspicious and cautious. It couldn't even be called second nature, as it was so much a part of him. It was why he was alive despite the things he had seen and lived through; it was why he was here now, and not some pile of bleached bones picked clean by scavengers.

It was why every nerve and fiber in his body was screaming at him that there was something very wrong in the ville of Raw.

This feeling, mixed with the claustrophobia he was beginning to feel beneath the ground, had driven him out to explore the tunnel system that comprised the ville. He wanted to know how the ville was constructed and get advance notice of any little surprises that Alien may have waiting for them...not that he distrusted the baron that much. There were no alarms ringing in his brain when he saw him. His wife was another matter.

Jak was used to redoubts. They were deep underground, but the rooms were generally large, well constructed and were connected by corridors that were also expansive. Another thing about redoubts was that they were all constructed along fairly similar lines, so that it was easy to get a general picture of the layout.

Raw was different. As a patchwork of cellars and basements, service tunnels and railways and sewers, it worked as a winding and labyrinthine construction of tunnels and rooms, some spacious but most constricted. Narrow so that you couldn't go more than two abreast, or low so that you had to stoop, they were connected by makeshift shafts and stairways that had been hacked out at strange angles. Sometimes it seemed that you were going back on yourself when you were still going forward. There were sharp angles and blind corners; niches where ambushers could hide, and great stretches where there was no cover. And there was little light. This was perhaps less of a problem for Jak than for the others. His eyes were sensitive to light, and he could register the lower levels much better than any of his companions. Even so, in places it was still too dark for him to feel that he could proceed without the utmost caution.

It was quiet now. Most of the inhabitants of Raw were asleep. He passed curtained-off partitions where the sounds of snoring and deep breathing could be heard. Once, he paused as he heard the sounds of moving bodies. He continued on only when he realized it was a couple taking the rare opportunity to make love, the woman's small cries reassuring him that the inhabitants weren't ready to jump out and attack him.

The living quarters of the ville seemed to be similar in every section he visited. Like the quarters they had been given by the baron, the private areas were little more than holes in the walls of the tunnels, small anterooms and sectioned basements that were protected from the run of the tunnels by a few scraps of material or a few pieces of old boarding. Not for security, but only for the lowest level of privacy. There was probably nothing to steal, as it didn't look like a rich ville.

But it wasn't poor. The people weren't ragged, the food seemed plentiful and everyone had been clean. There was a communal shower system where the companions and the sec men had cleaned up after eating and before retiring. And the baron had hinted that they had some old tech.

There appeared to be no particular hang-up from the baron or from the ville dwellers about personal possessions. Things that people would buy the farm for elsewhere didn't even seem to be a matter of interest here. There was space, and privacy seemed assured by these flimsy defenses.

It was so alien to Jak and the others that it worried him more. Everyone seemed peaceful and happy, yet that smell was driving him crazy as he tried to reconcile it, to trace it.

Because he was sure now that it wasn't the furnaces that caused the lingering odor.

Jak had no idea where he was in the ville. There had been so many spiraling and strangely constructed connecting passages that he was disoriented. But he knew he was leaving the furnaces to the rear of him as there had been a minute change in the temperature. As he moved through the ville, Jak noted the pipes that took heat and water to the different areas, the hot water dispensed from taps let from the pipes at regular intervals. These pipes were at the mercy of the pumping system, and the farther he got from the furnaces, the cooler the pipes became as the water pressure lowered, pushing the heated water less and less.

He had passed close to the furnaces at one point, feeling the heat increase as the system worked to its optimum. But here the pipes were more sluggish, the air around cooler. And yet the smell of charred flesh was fresher and stronger.

Raw had a secret, one that promised to be a triple-red threat for Jak and his companions.

The narrow and low tunnels connecting the different sections of the ville made Jak feel hemmed in and made his nerves jangle. There was nowhere for him to hide, and no routes for a quick escape if he was discovered. The tunnels were either long with nothing leading off except at either end, or else they had the small, partitioned living units that were full of potential enemies.

This tunnel had nothing. Nothing except the closed door that stood at the end of the corridor formed by the low enclosure.

Jak felt the pit of his stomach grow cold. It was the first time he had seen a door during the whole of his exploration.

The albino stopped in his tracks and hunkered down against the wall, keeping each end of the tunnel under watch. So far in his exploration he hadn't come across any sec men. Come to think of it, he hadn't even heard any moving about within the ville. Could it be that there were no sec men within the underground ville itself, but only stationed at the farthest reaches, to protect the hidden entrances from intruders?

If so, then there was a very good chance that Jak would come across some sec men very soon. From the drop in temperature, and the extent of tunnel he had traveled without seeing any living quarters, he was pretty sure that he had to have hit one of those extreme reaches of the ville.

Given time, he could find his way back to the sleeping quarters the companions had been allotted. But did he have time? With no wrist chron to measure how long he had been exploring, he had only his instinct—blunted by the lack of natural daylight—to aid him. This told him that he had been roaming the ville for several hours, and he wouldn't have time to find his way back before the inhabitants were generally awake and questions would be asked. Even if he had seen nothing, any sec chief worth his salt would assume that Jak had discovered any secrets that may be hidden.

So, with retreat and perhaps another night's exploration denied, Jak figured he may as well press on. Whatever was behind the door ahead, he would need to know if he and his companions were to make it through their stay in Raw in one piece.

IT WAS the general rise in background noise that awakened Ryan. The people of Raw in the partitioned units around were getting up and beginning to go about their daily business. Their muted voices and shufflings were enough to disturb the light sleep that had kept the one-eyed warrior alive for so long.

He opened his good eye, the light from outside the curtain filtering through in the artificial morning. Just as the lights were dimmed when night came around, so the ville dwellers' lamps and the lighting that lined the tunnels had beckoned the dawn of the new day. The lamplighter shuffled past their curtained partition, tunelessly humming some dirge to himself.

Ryan gently disentangled himself from the arms of the still sleeping Krysty, moving his body from under her where she had lain across him. She murmured to herself and opened her eyes sleepily.

"Morning?" she husked, her voice dry and clogged from sleep.

"What passes for it," Ryan replied, rising from the bed. The sounds of his own rising had caused the others to stir, and Ryan made a quick head count, a reflex that he couldn't prevent.

He was glad he had done it. "Where's Jak?" he asked quietly.

JAK LAUREN PADDED down the tunnel. Despite his heavy combat boots, his footfalls were quieter than the echo of someone else's footfalls. As he reached the door, he cast a wary eye around the lintel. There were no alarms or booby traps that were visible. Extending a hand, he traced around the lintel with his fingertips, barely touching the edges. There were no wires of any kind.

The door was made of beaten metal, the hammer blows that had shaped the old sheets into a flat door still visible, the welded edges rough. There was a lock set into the door beneath an old wooden lever handle. The fact that it was a wooden handle reassured him that there was little chance of the handle itself being electrified.

Jak brushed the handle with his fingertips. Nothing happened, so he took a tentative hold of it, and gently started to depress the lever.

It was then that the sound of someone approaching reached out to him. They were still some way off, but in the silence of the tunnel, broken only by the shallow sound of his own breath, it was loud enough for

Jak's sensitive hearing to discern that whoever it may be was approaching him slowly, with a shuffling walk that suggested lameness. The newcomer was also singing to himself and stopping every few yards.

Jak doubted that it was a sec man. It sounded too slapdash and without stealth. Someone carrying out routine tasks within the ville, without doubt. But still someone who may be armed and who could raise an alarm. Outside, Jak would have taken no chances and chilled whoever it was. But in here, where could he hide the body? And whoever it was would, as a routine worker, be missed.

There was nowhere to hide in the tunnel, not even to position himself so that he could ambush the newcomer. He would have to try to get through this door and hope that he could deal with whatever was on the other side.

The trouble was, when he depressed the lever, nothing happened. The door stayed fast. He pushed at it, gritting his teeth as he exerted pressure yet tried to control that effort so that the door wouldn't suddenly explode inward with a noise that would only attract the attention he was trying to avoid.

The door refused to move.

The shuffling and humming were getting closer.

Jak cursed to himself. The smell of sweet, burned human flesh filled his nasal cavities as he leaned up against the door, and through the thick soundproofing of the metal he could just about discern some quiet whimpering and shuffling.

He was no doomie, but he had a bad, bad feeling about whatever was hidden behind the door.

That would have to wait until later, though. Right

now, he had to get back to his friends without being seen. And with the shuffling growing louder, approaching the bend at the far end of the tunnel, that was going to prove difficult.

Jak looked at the walls and ceiling of the passage that stretched in front of him. There was nowhere really to hide.

Except maybe…

"LOOK, DAD, what was I supposed to do?" Dean asked in an exasperated tone that matched his father's. "I asked Jak if he wanted me to go with him and he said no."

"I would have expected you to stop him, not offer to go with him," Ryan rejoined. "Fireblast it to hell, you know that we don't move in these situation without knowing what each other's doing. Why do you think we survive like we do? We operate as a team."

"You were all asleep," Dean replied, "and Jak was going no matter what. Am I supposed to wake you all for a discussion?"

Ryan glowered at his son. He knew that in the same circumstances he would have offered to go with Jak. Two on a scouting party stood a better chance of returning and reporting than one. Yet they had to keep some kind of discipline together.

"Okay," he said finally, "it would have been better with two of you out there watching each other's backs than just Jak on his own. But it would have been better if he'd done it tonight, when we could all be in on it."

"It's Jak you need to tell that to," Dean replied softly.

The two Cawdors—father and son—held steady their gaze, neither willing to step down. The tension between them was heightened by the fact that they had to keep their voices low, only too well aware that it would be easy for anyone passing by to overhear them. Their barely reined-in anger was amplified by this, and their inability to let fly with their anger at each other. Eventually, it was Doc who interjected and broke the deadlock.

"Be that as it may, the main point surely is that Jak has not returned. And the question leading from that must be, why?"

"Only the first of a lot of questions, Doc," the Armorer said. He moved across to the curtain that partitioned them from the tunnel outside, where there were the sounds of people in transit. He pulled the material to one side, casually checking who was outside their unit, seemingly scratching himself idly and casually acknowledging those passersby who greeted him.

"No sec men watching over us," he muttered, drawing the curtain fully across and returning to the others.

"Right. First thing we need to do is try and find Jak. Is he in trouble? If not, what has he found that's stopping him returning?" Mildred sat on the edge of her bed and spoke softly but firmly.

"Why did he feel the need to do it?" Krysty added.

Doc favored her with an indulgent smile. "Surely you, of all people, don't need to ask such a question. One only has to look at you to see the bugs gnawing at the corners of your consciousness."

"Very picturesque, Doc," Mildred murmured.

"He's right, though," Krysty admitted. "It's that creepy Jenna. She's up to something, I'm sure."

"But does Alien know about it?" Dean mused. "It could make all the difference."

"Eventually," his father added. "Right now, our problem is Jak. And how we find him without arousing suspicion."

THE LAMPLIGHTER CAME around the sharp bend and shuffled along the tunnel toward the metal door. He paused at each of the small oil lamps that were hung at regular intervals along the walls, lighting each one in turn until the tunnel was lit with a dull yellow glow that reflected off the metal door.

He was still humming to himself as he turned and shuffled back. With the final lamp in this tunnel now safely lit, he had completed the day's work, and he could retire to his unit and sleep before it was time to eat. His leg was paining him, and he was grateful that this was his only job within the community.

And then it went black...

JAK PICKED HIMSELF up from the floor and looked at the lamplighter. He was unconscious and would remain that way for some time. When he came around, he would have no idea how he had come to pass out, and would probably worry that he had suffered some sort of fit. But that worry would die away as time passed, and there would be nothing to cause alarm either for himself or for the sec men. Which was exactly the way Jak wanted it.

He had taken advantage of the one piece of cover available to him: the ceiling. The water and heating pipes ran close to the top of the wall on one side of the tunnel, and on the other was a series of brackets that had, in the predark days, probably held steady a series of electric cables that had long since perished or been removed. The more recently placed brackets on which the lamps were hung ran below the level of pipes and the old bracket. This was crucial.

As the shuffling and humming neared the bend of the corridor, Jak had taken hold of the high brackets on one side of the tunnel and heaved himself up toward the ceiling, swinging his legs up with a tremendous kick and planting his feet above the level of the pipes so that his heels rested on the pipes themselves. The sweat of his effort plastering his brow, he had then swung one hand over, twisting his narrow and wiry frame so that he was able to turn completely and balance. Instead of facing the ceiling, with his back arched, he was now molded to it, facing down so that he could see whoever walked beneath.

He hoped that the ceiling was high enough, and the shadows deep enough, to mask him from whoever walked beneath.

He was lucky. The lamplighter was absorbed in his task, now nearly complete, and was content to light his lamps and retire. The thought of looking above him never even entered his head.

The lamplighter passed beneath, lighted the last lamp and turned to shuffle back. He walked underneath Jak without the slightest awareness that the albino, drawing slight and shallow breaths to keep as quiet as possible, was poised above him. As the lamplighter shuffled past, Jak dropped noiselessly behind him, timing the fall so that the edge of his out-

stretched hands chopped at the base of the lamplighter's neck, where the carotid artery passed along
by his collarbone.

The blow was swift and sure. The lamplighter fell
without even a sigh. Jak lifted himself from the
ground, checked that the man was still breathing, then
left him. The albino would have no qualms about
chilling the man if it was necessary, but to do so in
these circumstances would arouse more suspicion
than leaving him alive.

Jak moved off swiftly and silently.

"DARK NIGHT! Where in the rad-blasted hell have
you been?" J.B. barked as Jak appeared in front of
him.

"Time look around. Tell later," Jak said quickly,
taking the Armorer to one side. "Anyone miss me?"

"Apart from us, you mean?" J.B. said through gritted teeth, shaking his head to indicate a negative to
Jak's question.

They were in what seemed to be the center of the
ville, a small collection of tunnels with higher ceilings
and wider pathways than the majority of the settle-
ment. There were stalls laid out with goods, and units
where services were offered. No one appeared to live
in this section, which was occupied with the commerce of the ville—or what passed for commerce, as
no money seemed to change hands. When J.B. answered the solicitations of one vendor with the comment that he had little money, it was explained to him
that the ville worked on a communal system, and services and traders worked more as men in charge of
distribution than as merchants.

So with the inhabitants able to get what they wanted, the center of the ville was always full of people coming and going. Which made it difficult for J.B. to mask his surprise and anger when Jak suddenly appeared before him.

"Need talk. Something weird going on," Jak said in an undertone, mindful of those passing.

The Armorer assented. "We split up to try and find you—and not look like we were looking," he muttered. "Why did you take off like that?"

"Bad feelings. Not doomie, but sometimes..." Jak screwed up his face.

"Yeah, I know," J.B. agreed, anger dissipated by the look on the albino's face. "I know. Come on. Let's find the others."

They had only gone a few yards when Harvey and Bodie appeared before them, from out of the crowd surrounding a food stall.

"Well, hey there, white boy," Harvey greeted Jak, nodding at J.B. as afterthought. "So, what action's been going down, then?"

Chapter Ten

"Just taking a look around, seeing what's happening. Just the usual sort of thing," J.B. said with a deceptively laconic air. In fact, he was concentrating intensely on the body language of the two sec men. If either should make a move for his blaster, then the Armorer would be ready.

"Why not?" Bodie replied with an ease that couldn't be faked. "Guess if you're gonna be around for a while, then you may as well check it out, see where the action is." The fat sec man leaned forward with a leer and winked at them. "Fine gaudy house just off the main drag here. Don't get no trouble from the customers 'cause they always get value for money, you know?"

J.B. forced a smile. "I'll remember that. Right, Jak?"

"Sure."

Harvey narrowed his eyes. "Sure you're okay, Whitey? Y'all look kind of tired to me. Like you been up all night."

Jak shot him a look that questioned, but couldn't find the answer it sought. "Hard settle. Tossing all night," he said carefully.

Bodie gave a lecherous grin. "Sounds like you need that gaudy, boy."

J.B. laughed and slapped the sec man on the shoulder in a friendly manner, shaking his head. "Might just be right there, friend."

Harvey also laughed. It was even more false than the Armorer's. "Kind of like to stay and talk all day, but we got work to do, Bodie. Be seeing you," he finished as the fat sec man suddenly sobered and fell in behind his chief.

Jak and J.B. watched them disappear into the throng of ville dwellers.

"Think he know?" the albino queried.

"Sure as hell hope not. I'd trust that mud-sucker as far as I could spit him," J.B. murmured.

THE COMPANIONS ASSEMBLED once more at their allotted sleeping unit. While the combination of Mildred, Doc and Krysty had found little in their short search other than the fact that inhabitants of Raw were friendly if a little frightened of the outside world, Dean and Ryan had encountered the baron and his wife.

"She's the danger," Dean said softly, leaning against the wall and chewing the ball of his thumb. "Alien seems like a baron who wants the best for his people. But her... She asked where you were," he directed to Mildred, "and called you 'the black' again. I don't know if Alien even noticed, he's so under her spell. But the way she said it, I just keep thinking of the chilled," he finished.

Mildred said nothing. Krysty, on the other hand, turned to Ryan. She had plenty to say.

"We can't stay here. None of us are happy, and there's something about Jenna that makes me shiver when I even think about her. Gaia!" She shuddered.

"I don't know what she's up to here, but this time I don't want to know, either. I just want to get out."

The one-eyed warrior shook his head slowly. "I say we stay."

"Why?" J.B. asked. "Dark night, Ryan, after what Jak's told us, after what we all feel, why?"

The one-eyed man fixed the Armorer with a steady gaze. "Trust me, J.B. After everything, trust me. That bitch could be a problem, but there's something at stake here. The Illuminated Ones are one of the best leads we've ever come across. If Erewhon does still exist, it could be all that Trader spoke of. It could be the promised land. I can't just throw that dream away."

There was a short silence. Ryan was their leader, and the tacit agreement was that they follow his lead. But even at this risk?

Doc cleared his throat. "I believe Ryan may be correct. The risk may well be worth it. After all, does anyone know about friend Jak's nocturnal excursion? Does anyone suspect us of anything? On the contrary, everyone bar Jenna seems to like us. And frankly, she seems to dislike everyone except herself, so we are not alone in that."

Mildred pursed her lips and nodded, her beaded plaits moving in slow time around her head. "Damned if I don't think I'm going senile when I agree with this crazy old coot."

"J.B.?" Ryan asked.

The Armorer held steady, then said, "Dark night, yeah, for a while, mebbe. But if everyone is spooked, then it's time to go. Even you."

"Okay," Ryan assented. "Even me."

IT WAS DIFFICULT for Ryan to know where to begin. Somehow he needed to broach the subject with the baron, yet at the same time he figured that he would need to build his trust. But how could any of them do that when there seemed nothing to do?

Raw was run on strict communal lines. Everyone had a task, and everyone carried it out. Offers of help were politely but firmly refused by the ville dwellers, none of whom seemed concerned with getting to know the outlanders. Not from any sense of hostility or xenophobia—rather, it was because they were busy and happy in their tasks. Even when the Armorer dropped by the armory and offered to help, examining the store of blasters and grens and passing compliments on their condition, as well as dropping snippets of knowledge to encourage a dialogue, he was politely but firmly turned away. It was frustrating for J.B., who, if nothing else, had looked forward to killing time on his great love.

Alien had the community running like a well-oiled machine. No one other than the sec forces carried blasters inside the tunnels—no one other than the companions, that was, who still carried theirs about their person. There seemed to be no fights or feuds, and everyone the companions spoke to offered generous praise for Alien.

Yet it wasn't the fullsome and hollow praise of fear. It was a genuine love for a baron who tried to do his best for his people. Even Krysty, still spooked by the constant doomie feelings from Jenna that she could feel snaking like tendrils throughout the ville, came to warm to the large baron, whose twinkling eyes made him like some idyllic leader from myth.

"We aren't the Illuminated Ones, but we are from them," he told Ryan once more. "Some of those ideas and ideals came down to me from my family, and from those who taught me. I just try to put them into action. If this Erewhon place does actually exist, then mebbe it'll be like us with much more riches. Mebbe not. Mebbe they got lost somewhere along the way, which is what my family taught me. I don't know if I want us to know."

The one-eyed warrior found this frustrating, but yielded to the baron's obvious sincerity.

Nonetheless, after three days of idling around the ville, discovering nothing of any import and finding nothing to usefully pass their time, even Ryan found himself tiring of life underground.

"Face it, we're not going to learn anything from them," Mildred said as they held a meeting in the privacy of their unit. "Perhaps because there isn't actually anything to learn."

Ryan assented. "Dammit, I thought we were really onto something here. But the longer we hang around, the more we're tempting Jenna. She doesn't like us here, and she may come up with something if we don't go."

"So we check our equipment and head out?" J.B. prompted.

Ryan nodded. "I'll see Alien when the lights go up tomorrow. Tell him thanks, but we've got to be going. He's a good man, but I think he'll be glad to see the back of us."

"Harvey certainly will," Dean interjected. "The other guys are okay, but he's nervous with us around."

"I wonder why that should be," Doc mused. He had dropped out of the conversation to such a degree that the others thought he had drifted into sleep. "If Alien has nothing to hide, which I do not believe he has, then why would his sec chief be so jumpy around us?"

"Like always hiding something," Jak added.

"That's been bugging me, too," Ryan finished, "but that's between him and the baron and whoever else. Not us. Not now."

But his voice lacked conviction.

THE CHANCE to make a peace and farewell with Alien didn't occur. It was superseded by a far more pressing matter.

The lights outside the sleeping unit were still dim, so it was still officially night when Mildred and Dean were both jolted awake by the sound of running feet echoing through the tunnels.

"What—" Mildred murmured, rising.

"Shh," Jak hissed. The albino had heard the noise before the others, partly because he found it almost impossible to sleep in the underground ville. He was already stationed at the flimsy partition, keeping watch.

By now, the feet had passed on their way to Harvey's quarters. The echo had died as they approached, revealing that there were two sec men running close together. One was Rankine, and as he passed without noticing Jak, the albino saw that the sec man's face was grim and set.

"Trouble. From outside," Jak added. "Rankine smelt forest."

"Didn't notice they had patrols out there," Ryan mused. "Mebbe the children being chilled has spooked them. Something's certainly spooked Rankine."

"So do we wait for them to come to us?" J.B. asked. "'Cause if there's an attack—"

"Then we stand and fight," Ryan finished. "We'll wait."

Not that they had to wait for long. Almost as soon as they had fully risen and armed themselves, Bodie appeared in the entrance to the unit. He paused, taken aback by their readiness.

"Alien wants to see you," he panted, short of breath from having run. "Now."

They followed the fat sec man through the tunnels until they reached the main hall. The tunnels were alive with ville dwellers on their way to and from the armory, taking up blasters that some of them looked uncomfortable handling. For J.B., this was a bad sign. If you didn't feel happy with a blaster, then you shouldn't be given one, lest you end up being more of a danger to yourself than the enemy.

When they reached the hall, Alien was seated at the table, with Harvey standing in front, leaning over the table and jabbing at a map while talking in low undertones. Jenna was with them, and looked past the sec chief to where Bodie led the companions.

"Ryan Cawdor, if there is a time for you to repay our hospitality, then it's now," the baron said swiftly, not standing on ceremony. "Tell him, Harvey."

The sec man acknowledged the one-eyed warrior with a brief nod, swinging the map around on the table so that Ryan's party could see it clearly.

"We post two-man sentry teams at four compass points in a one-mile radius around the entrances to the ville," he began by way of explanation. "Nothing much happens, but you can't be too careful. I've been expecting something since we took back the children, but this is nasty. Rankine and Wilson took the southeast point here—" he jabbed at the map "—which is right in line with Samtvogel. That fucker Sunchild wasn't chilled when Four-eyes there shot him, and he's madder then hell. Used his mutie blood to get some stickies under his control, and a group of stickies and Sunchildren are headed this way."

"Got stickies here? What like?" Jak asked hurriedly. The mutie stickies shared some characteristics that were common, but as time went on there were generations that became more mutated, in strange and bizarre ways.

"Fuck it, Whitey. Stickie's a stickie to me. You muties may be able to tell each other apart, but I can't. Just know they're coming."

Jak's face grew whiter at the insult, but he stored his hatred for later.

"Okay, so we know the Sunchildren may all be armed after the raid, but we can assume the stickies won't be. Where the fuck do they come from?" Ryan continued, trying to figure where the stickie community would be, and thanking their luck that they had avoided them on their way to the ville.

"Does it matter where? Just chill the fuckers," Jenna muttered.

"Mebbe. But if we know where they come from, we can be ready for any second wave," J.B. said softly, in a voice like that of an adult explaining something to a stupe child. He ignored Jenna's look of pure hatred and continued, ''The last thing we want is to be taken by surprise.''

''Surprise is that there are any,'' Harvey answered. ''Must be a nomad band looking for a new land. I haven't seen any around here since I was a kid.''

''Let's hope they haven't left any at Samtvogel, then,'' Ryan said. ''So what's your plan?''

Harvey gestured at the map. ''Meet them here and here. Pin them from both sides, with outreaching parties in case they're running little surprises for us, figuring we'll do that. Mebbe they won't know they've been spotted, and we'll get lucky. Thing is, my boys aren't that many, and the rest of the folks here ain't really fighters. We could use some help.''

Ryan nodded. He could see that the request came directly from the baron, and was sticking in the sec chief's craw even as he asked. He confined agreement to a nod, not wanting to aggravate the situation by further comment. Besides which, time was short.

''Thank you, Ryan,'' Alien said simply. ''I'll be with you as this threat hits Raw. We leave immediately.''

HARVEY LEFT five sec men in charge of the ville. Each sec man headed a section, Raw being divided into geographical segments. The armed inhabitants were under their section leader. This left Harvey in charge of twenty sec men, with Alien allowing Harvey—as sec chief—to head operations. Ryan and his people were assumed to be under Harvey's direction. They were content to do this unless it led them into unnecessary danger, where they each privately reserved the right to take appropriate action.

They marched through the tunnels at double speed, unable to run because the width of the passageways demanded a disciplined exit. As they marched, Harvey assigned parties of sec men, directing them on their courses of action when they broke surface. At one junction, the party divided into two, the second group of sec forces heading for another exit, the better to approach the pincer movement Harvey directed.

Ryan's party followed Harvey and Alien, heading for the exit by which they had first entered Raw.

When they broke surface, the humidity hit them like a wave. The air just below the surface was less fresh, but was cooler and not filled with the sickly sweet smell of the forest undergrowth. As the first sec team emerged, they took up guard positions until all were safely out of the exit and in a position of defense. The entrance to the ville was closed and disguised before Harvey mustered his forces.

Having filled them in fully on the plan he had earlier explained in detail to Ryan and his party, he deployed his forces, sending them out on a long, semicircular run that would intercept with the course the mutie war party was taking.

"You sure he's got that right?" J.B. whispered to Ryan before the parties split. "Reckon they will take the direct route?"

"Not much intelligence or tactical sense among them, and they'll probably want to take the most direct route," Ryan reasoned. "Figure Harvey's probably got it about right. Best to stay triple red on the run out, though. Just in case he's underestimated Sunchild himself—just like he thought he didn't have blasters.''

The Armorer agreed, pushing his fedora back and polishing his spectacles. ''Don't usually say this, but good luck. We may need it yet,'' he said, only too well aware that the forces they knew they could rely on—themselves—were to be split in two by Harvey's division of sec forces.

''Hey, Cyclops! You and the blaster boy stop yakking. We've got work to do,'' Harvey snapped at them.

Ryan's face set, hiding his anger. Harvey's ability to use his tongue harshly at the wrong moments would get him into serious trouble one day...but not today.

Not when there was a larger enemy.

THE MUTIE raiding party was making no attempt to disguise its progress, and Ryan was able to hear them from some distance. He was in an ambush party that included himself, Krysty, Jak and the baron. Downey, the silver-haired and snake-hipped sec man with the Sharps, was in charge, although he was suitably deferential to his baron. Alien had confessed to being no fighting man, and he was proving that by being more of an obstruction than a help, his bulk becoming easily snagged on the sharp spines running down the stems of some plants and tripping over tree roots hidden in the creepers that moved alarmingly around his heavy-footed tread.

There were nine other sec men in the party, and Blake was one of them. The wizened and dark sec man dropped back to help the baron struggle through the undergrowth. Jak fell back in line to assist the sec man.

"I hate to say this, Baron," Blake whispered, "but are you sure you're doing the right thing coming with us? I mean—"

"I'm your leader, and that means in times of trouble, as well as peace," Alien said hoarsely.

"Baron not much good if chilled," Jak commented pithily.

"Time to worry about that later," Downey whispered over his shoulder. "We're getting closer."

It was superfluous for him to mention that. The sound of the mutie raiding party was now loud, and its direction easy to trace. As Harvey had surmised, they were heading straight through the only viable path that led through the forest, beaten down by several generations of travelers to and from the sites of the underground ville's entrances. They were now trampling the undergrowth flat, the Sunchildren chanting and loosing shots into the air with no thought of stealth. Other, clumsy and high-pitched voices were mixed in with the chanting, arrhythmic and confused. These were unmistakably the stickies, carried along by the Sunchildren, hyped up to a fever pitch of destruction.

"How many of the fuckers?" one of the sec men asked.

"Can't see from here," Downey commented. "We need to get nearer if we can."

"Let me see," Jak whispered, moving forward. "Better chance on own."

Downey nodded consent, and Jak was gone, vanishing into the undergrowth in front of the group with barely a ripple of foliage, as though he had never been there.

The chanting grew painfully loud as Jak skipped across the creepers, dodging the raised tree roots and climbing up one of the stunted trees in order to raise himself higher, hoping to gain a better perspective.

He could see them, but not clearly enough. Leaping from one bough to another, he traversed three more trees before he could get a clear view of them.

He suppressed the urge to whistle. There were fifteen Sunchildren that he could count, plus twenty-eight—maybe thirty—stickies. It was hard to be accurate as they moved about in a milling, frenzied crowd.

This meant that the total sec force was outnumbered by more than two to one. Scanning the mutie party once more, Jak guessed that they had maybe a dozen blasters among them.

He was about to skip back into the forest from his position when something on the far side of the cleared path caught his eye. He showed himself a little more as he identified the waving branches as the movements of Dean, on the other side. The youngster had obviously had the same idea as Jak.

Their eyes met across the roof of foliage. Jak signaled ten to Dean, indicating that they should both attack after ten minutes tracking the party. Dean nodded, then was gone. Jak grinned, teeth drawn back in a predatory smile, then returned to his group.

"Well?" Downey asked as Jak came into view. When the albino had explained the position, he added, "Okay, we'll trail them and then go for it. If we take them from behind, it'll buy us that extra few fractions of a second.''

''Mebbe more,'' Ryan added. ''The stickies will be too freaked to react that quickly. Good call.''

''Thanks for the praise,'' Downey returned sarcastically.

As they moved off, Krysty noticed Alien casting a quizzical eye over the sec man, obviously bemused by his comment to Ryan a few moments before.

Her hair coiled tight, and she knew it had nothing to do with the current chase.

MILDRED FACED Harvey with anger blazing in her eyes.

''What the hell do you mean, leave it until they've made the first push? They'll be expecting us to go in ten and be backing them up. Why let them take the brunt?''

''Why not?'' Harvey replied calmly. ''I just say that we wait until the muties've got their attention focused one way, then hit the fuckers from the other way.''

''But without them knowing, there's no telling—''

''Listen, bitch,'' the sec chief snarled, ''who the fuck's in charge here?''

J.B. stepped forward and pulled Mildred back. ''Not now, Millie,'' he said, adding in a softer voice when the sec chief's attention was taken by one of his own men, ''Who says we do what the bastard says anyway?''

Mildred grasped the meaning behind the Armorer's words and gave the briefest gesture of agreement. Independently, Doc and Dean had come to the same conclusion.

"We can't let that happen," the youngster whispered to Doc.

The old man cradled his LeMat and said with mock sadness, "Ah, but these old weapons, and indeed the old men using them, can be a trifle erratic at times."

RYAN CHECKED his wrist chron and stole a glance at Alien. The Raw baron was stone-faced, any emotion he may feel about going into a firefight tightly reined in. By his side were Jak and Blake. The small, wizened sec man seemed to grow in stature as he felt the time for battle come near; he was breathing slowly and deeply, his eyes faraway and focused on what was to come.

Looking around, Ryan could see that the rest of the sec men were also readying themselves in their own way.

Beside him, Krysty was hunkered down, her Smith & Wesson blaster clenched in her hand, her fingers coiled around the barrel and through the trigger guard with a deceptive languor.

The flame-haired beauty turned to him. "Not now, but later...then we need to worry," she mouthed.

Ryan nodded, then checked his chron again. It was time. They had been following at a distance, observing the mutie raiding party. Two of the muties had fallen by the wayside already—one of the Sunchildren and a stickie—chilled by the random blaster shots from the hyped-up muties. Given a long enough approach to Raw, they could probably do a very good job of chilling themselves.

But there wasn't the distance. And now the time was up, and Harvey's men should also be ready. Ryan looked at Downey. The silver-maned sec man caught Ryan's eye and nodded.

"It's time," he said simply, throwing the comment over his shoulder. "Let's go get them."

And it began. Ryan sprang forward, the taut muscles on his thighs and the strong, powerful calf muscles propelling him forward in an explosive burst. He brought J.B.'s M-4000 across his chest, keeping a firm hold as he broke cover. Downey was beside him, moving over the ground as though he were hovering above it, snapping back the Sharps and chambering the first round ready for a mutie.

They broke cover in two waves, spread across a distance of only a few yards. Jak had moved through the ranks from his position beside the baron, the Python .357 in one fist, a leaf-bladed knife in the other. Blake was almost level with him, the small man showing a surprising turn of speed, the slim and elegant lines of his 9 mm Walther PPK seeming huge in his small hand. He trusted Jak totally, there having sprung between them an unspoken bond—the bond of two men who knew their job and were masters of their art.

Among the other sec men breaking cover was Jake, the huge bearlike man who dwarfed the Heckler & Koch he grasped, swinging it around as soon as he broke cover and had sighted the rear of the mutie party. He roared as his finger tightened on the trigger, loosing his anger and adrenaline in one blast.

First chill, however, went to Jak. A stickie at the rear of the party turned and lunged toward the ambush party. Not wasting a shot at this point, Jak's knife flashed through the space between them and connected with the stickie, slicing through the jellylike, pale flesh at the creature's throat and producing streams of thin, watery blood that ran down the creature's neck and chest.

The stickie stopped in midstride, confusion and pain written across its features, the blank eyes and sharp, needlelike teeth identifying it as a mutie even before its mottled, irradiated skin could be properly seen. He tried to scream, but a thin, pained keening was all that emerged, followed by a gurgle as it drowned on its own blood, falling forward as consciousness slipped away.

By the time the stickie hit the carpet of creepers across the forest floor, the majority of the ambush party had passed it and were in the middle of a firefight.

Downey and Ryan were side by side, the sec man snapping off shots from the Sharps that took out confused muties as they attempted to turn to face their attackers without careering into each other. Ryan targeted a densely packed area of mutie flesh with the M-4000 to cause the maximum impact.

"We fighting on our own, Downey?" the one-eyed warrior heard from beside him, interrupted by random burst of fire from an Uzi. It was a familiar sound, but an unfamiliar pattern, and Ryan guessed that it had been a long time since Alien had regularly used a blaster. And if they made it back alive, Harvey may have a few uncomfortable moments.

"That's a good question, Baron," the sec man replied, his tone still laid-back. "I'd sure as shit like to know the answer to that myself."

FROM THEIR COVER, the second ambush party saw Ryan and Downey emerge, saw Jak claim first blood, saw the heaving mass of muties turn to face the sec force.

"It'll be a massacre," breathed one of the sec men. "It must be four-to-one out there."

"Wait," Harvey said softly, a hard edge to his tone.

"No way," the Armorer muttered, readying the Uzi. From the corner of his eye, he saw that Mildred had already sighted one mutie from this range, possibly at the edge of target range, but her practiced eye gauged that it was just close enough for her to get a lethal shot. The Czech-made ZKR was a good blaster, with the high degree of accuracy demanded by its previous life as a competition weapon.

"Go, Millie," the Armorer breathed as his thin and wire-strong limbs shot him forward and out of the undergrowth. He heard Harvey curse at the same moment as the crack of Mildred's blaster resounded in his ears.

J.B. broke cover about fifty yards to the left of the other sec ambush party. He raised the Uzi and cut loose, the 9 mm rounds tearing at the exposed flesh of the Sunchildren and the stickies.

J.B. didn't know if the rest of the sec force had followed him, or if he faced the muties alone on this flank. Perhaps not quite alone. The roar of the ancient LeMat sounded near him, first once and then a second time in quick succession as Doc unleashed ball and shot, dispensing death and agony into another group of muties. The sound was followed swiftly by the crack of Dean's Browning Hi-Power as he picked off the most dangerous of the mutie party from this angle—those who were quick enough to turn and had avoided the rain of death from J.B. and Doc.

The Armorer sensed rather than saw Mildred appear from the foliage, adopting the same technique as Dean. They had the advantage of surprise on their side, which gave them the time to pick their targets as the slow-witted stickies and the confused Sunchildren had to adjust to the fact that they were being attacked from two directions.

More blasterfire rent the air as Harvey, now unable to hold back his men, led the rest of the ambush party into the fray.

Both ambush parties were attacking the muties from closer quarters now, and while handblasters were essential, it would have been madness to use the M-4000 and the LeMat at such close range. The risk of chilling their own forces would have been too great. So Doc produced his swordstick, the silver lion's head grasped tight while the razor-sharp blade carved through the masses.

Ryan unsheathed the panga on his thigh, and used it as though the mass of mutie flesh were just so much foliage that needed chopping out of the way, hacking through limbs and torsos that blurred so much that it was only the bright robes of the Sunchildren and the hideous suckered and splayed fingers of the stickies that told them apart.

On the other side of the rapidly thinning mutie war party, J.B. had his Tekna knife in hand, thrusting with

a cold and calculating precision, thinking not of the
lives he was taking, but only the ones he was preserving back at Raw.

In the middle of the throng, Jak's white hair
whirled around his head like a whip as, dervishlike,
he dealt death in close combat with the leaf-bladed
knives, a flick of the wrist carving swathes through
the war party, the Python safely holstered to enable
him to ply his deadly trade.

Despite their greater numbers, and the fact that they
were to some degree armed, the muties were unable
to make their numbers count. Those surviving Sunchildren, including Sunchild himself, beat an early retreat, leaving the unarmed stickies to take the brunt
of the attack. But not before Sunchild had imparted a
chilling message.

The mutie leader had been considered a congenital
idiot, and perhaps he was: but not so much that he
couldn't sidle up to Alien in battle. Before the baron
had a chance to chill him, he hissed, "Big chill come
your way soon." And even as Alien leveled his
blaster, the mutie leader was gone.

Ryan was close enough to hear, and wondered what
the mutie meant by his statement. But that was for
later. Now there was chill or be chilled.

The battle was over as soon as it had begun.

"Leave them," Alien roared as a few of the sec
men turned to pursue the straggling stickies who were
able to make their escape. "There has been enough
slaughter. Let's collect ourselves and return home.
They won't come back in a hurry."

Ryan gave the baron a quizzical look. Would he

mention the mutie's threat to Harvey later, when they had privacy?

Even as the baron spoke, Mildred began the task of attending to the wounded. There were two sec men with blaster wounds, four who had knife wounds of varying degrees, one of who would need to be carried home, and twelve minor bite-and-scratch lesions. Blake was one of these, with two scratches on his face and a bite out of his left arm. Jak also had scratches on his face and on his neck, the red weals standing out ugly on his white skin.

"Hey, Jak, think those'll turn us into stickies?" the sec man joked.

"Chill me if fingers start to suck," the albino returned good-humouredly. He admired the way the sec man fought, and felt a rare trust to have the wizened warrior at his back.

Alien took one end of the improvised stretcher holding the seriously wounded sec man. "Come, let's return," he said simply.

Ryan, admiring the way the baron automatically took the load, grabbed the other end of the stretcher and followed Alien as he led the way back.

The one-eyed warrior pondered Sunchild's warning, and also the dark glances Harvey received from J.B. and Mildred. Things were perhaps coming to a crossroads.

Chapter Eleven

There were celebrations in Raw when Alien returned with his sec force. Celebrations that were obviously muted for the baron by the injury to one of his men. While the majority of the ville celebrated in the central hall with the help of their local brew and a band of musicians whose sobriety and ability to keep in tune was severely called into question by the end of the proceedings, the baron was at one point noticeable by his absence.

The reserve that the majority of the inhabitants of Raw had held for Ryan and his people evaporated on the strength of their performance during the firefight with the mutie raiding party. Blake in particular, his arm around Jak partly from comradeship and partly from the need to hold himself upright, was vociferous in retelling the events of the day.

There was no mention of the fact that Harvey had attempted to hold his men back from the attack, although J.B. did notice that Downey and Rankine, after an intense discussion, had thrown a few askance glances in the direction of the sec chief. It was something worth noting for later, something he would discuss with Ryan. That was, if he could find his friend and leader.

Ryan had slipped away from the celebration. He had noticed Alien exchange a few words with Jenna, who had nodded dismissively, before the baron had unobtrusively left the proceedings.

The one-eyed warrior was curious: why would a victorious baron wish to leave a celebration that was basically in his honor? Following him to find out would leave Ryan open to trouble if he was caught, and the baron had slipped away for some reason that was dangerous to himself and his companions. But if it wasn't, then Ryan was sure he could talk his way out of trouble. Ryan had more to his armory than his fighting skills.

The baron moved through the near deserted corridors of the subterranean ville, his ceremonial cloak of faded, wine-stained damask billowing behind him, his hair moving in rhythm with the heavy tread of his bulky frame. Only those citizens with vital tasks to perform weren't in the main hall, and the baron greeted them cordially as he passed. They returned his greeting, then quizzically viewed Ryan as he followed a few yards behind. He made no attempt to conceal himself, as that would only have been ridiculous given the geography of the ville.

After five minutes' striding through the maze that was Raw, the baron came to a halt in front of a unit that had a ragged curtain across its entrance. With a delicacy and care that surprised Ryan, Alien lifted the curtain and looked in. Ryan heard him whisper "Good time to see him?" and wait for a mumbled reply before stepping in.

As he did, he turned to the one-eyed warrior. "You may come, as well, if you wish, Ryan Cawdor."

Ryan, feeling like he did when Baron Titus of Front

Royal—his father—had caught him at mischief when a child, followed Alien into the sparse unit.

It was obviously a medical-care center, equipped as best as possible, and scrubbed clean, possibly by the woman who tended to the wounded sec man. He was unconscious, but seemed peaceful. Alien asked a few questions of the pale, haggard woman who tended him, listening intently to her answers before wishing her well and leaving, beckoning Ryan to follow.

Outside, Ryan felt an absurd need to explain himself.

"I wondered what you were doing, if there was anything wrong—"

"And besides which, it doesn't hurt any to keep an eye on a baron in a strange ville when he wanders off in the middle of celebration." He waved silence as Ryan attempted to speak. "No, save your words. I would do exactly the same in a strange ville. You have your people to worry about, just as I have. I like you, Ryan. Most barons—and that is what you are in your own way—are concerned only with their own power, not with using that which they have. I know my ways may seem strange after all you have seen, especially if the stories traders bring with them about other villes and other barons are true. But I feel that you will understand me."

The one-eyed man assented. "Mebbe I do. What you were taught you believe, and you try to live right by it. A man can do no more than try to live right by his code."

The baron smiled, almost to himself. "A rare thing, to find two such as us together. Not a boast, but a sad

reflection, I think." He looked back over his shoulder.
"That young lad hasn't been under Harvey's charge
for long, and it's doubly hard for his mother as she
is one of our medics. Her own son... It's right to
celebrate defending our way of life, though." He
clapped Ryan on the shoulder, almost to bring himself
out of his reverie by a forced goodwill. "Come, let
us return."

THE CELEBRATIONS continued for some time, with almost the entire ville drinking themselves into a stupor. For the companions, it was difficult to stay sober.
The ville's own brew was a sweet vegetable liquor,
with a syrupy texture, and was deceptive in its taste.
It was, as Jak noted, far more potent than most brews
they had encountered, and after a certain amount in-
duced a mild hallucinogenic euphoria due to fungal
spores that had crept in with the vegetable matter.

Despite their best efforts to stay sober, only Dean
managed to remain upright by the end of the celebration. He had a reason: the young Cawdor was suspicious not of the baron, but of his wife. Neither did he
trust Harvey. Whether this dislike was exclusive, or
whether it was because they were allied in some way
he didn't know, but one thing was for sure: he would
never get a better chance to explore the ville and find
out what—if anything—the baron's wife was plotting.

So when Krysty had settled a maternal eye on Dean
and warned him against the brew, he was only too
happy to play along with her for once, and swear off
the alcohol. He carried a small cup with him for most
of the evening, to ward off those who wanted in their
exuberance to thrust it on him. He tried a sip, but

found his abstinence helped by the fact that, to him, it tasted like he imagined sugared horse piss would taste. He feigned intoxication, and with almost everyone around him blissfully drunk, he was able to get away with it easily.

As the celebration died down, the drunken revelers either found their way back to their own living units or just collapsed on the floor, resting happily among the debris. One of those sprawled in this manner was Jak, unconscious and beyond being roused. Dean discovered this with rising dismay, as he had hoped that the albino would take him to the section of the ville where he had discovered the locked room. For some days, Dean had been brooding on this, and was sure it held the answer to whatever questions he was asking.

Now he would have to find it on his own. That was one problem. The other problem—perhaps two—consisted of Harvey and Jenna. Dean had kept a wary eye on both, and had noted that neither seemed to be drinking in any great amount. Both were now absent from the hall, and in the chaos he hadn't seen them leave, so was ignorant of their sobriety.

If they were both alert and going about their business, then that could prove a possible danger to him.

But Dean knew in his gut that he would never get a better chance to answer any questions he may have. So it was now or never.

He had been slumped against one wall for some time, feigning drunken stupor and sleep, using it as a shield from those who would try to get him drunk, and as a cover from which to observe his surroundings.

The hall was now quiet, the silence broken only by snoring and sleep-addled mutterings. Carefully, Dean rose to his feet and picked his way over the prone bodies until he was out of the hall and into the maze of tunnels, basements and units carved in the walls that constituted Raw. His playground for now: a playground for a most serious game.

Dean remembered Jak telling him that the room was located on an outer corridor, almost as far as the pipes would run, and that it was in the opposite direction to that in which they entered the ville.

It wasn't much, but it was a start.

Dean walked casually through the central sections of Raw, trying his best to create the impression of someone who was drunk and trying to find his way back to his unit. He had realized that there would be members of the community who had abstained from the celebration because of their duties, and he had no wish to attract their attention to him in any way other than that of being another reveler.

It worked. The few people who saw him as he wandered around the tunnels smiled indulgently and left him to his wandering, thinking him drunk. His staggering gait also enabled him to wander down some passages and then out again without attracting attention to his methods. He wished that Ryan or Krysty were with him, as he felt the need of some kind of backup. He had seen them leave the celebration, as he had seen Mildred and J.B. leave. He guessed that they were snatching a few moments of relaxed peace together, and had no wish to disturb them until—or unless—he found something to justify his suspicions. Even Doc would have been good as backup; but he had seen Doc unconscious on the floor in the same manner as Jak, and so knew there was little hope of reviving him until he had slept off the brew.

All the time he was thinking, he was searching, crossing off corridors in his mind, exploring nooks and crannies to see where they took him. He had plenty of time. A celebration like the previous night's would take a long while to sleep off, leaving him free to explore.

One direction had been closed to him by Jak's words. That left three directions out from the area around the central hall. Three directions, all of which had more than one corridor or passage that led off like spokes from a wheel.

But Dean knew what he was searching for: the metal door that Jak had told them about. That held the key, and that narrowed his search. Still so many corridors and passages, but at least he knew what he was searching for.

His patience and nerve were beginning to wear thin when he finally found it. He shivered as he walked down the deserted corridor, feeling the drop in temperature and also feeling that his search was nearly over.

The lamps were still lit, not having been doused because of the celebration, the lame lamplighter now lying drunk in the main hall. But although still alight, the oil was nearly used, and the lighting was dim, some of the lamps along the corridor guttering and casting a moving shadow across the wall. Dean found the corridor as eerie as Jak had done before, an atmosphere chilling the air more than the cooling pipes. The fact that, as he turned the final corner, he could see that there was no place to hide made the corridor even chillier for the young Cawdor.

Dean lost the drunken gait, his footfalls now kept as quiet as possible and his posture changing. He walked now on the balls of his feet, his balance thrown slightly forward, springing on each step. He quieted his breathing until he could almost hear the blood flowing in his veins.

The metal door ahead loomed large in his vision. Dean looked over his shoulder, and paused midstride. There was no sound behind him, and he could see nothing. He looked ahead at the patchwork metal door and took a deep breath.

Stepping up to it, Dean reached out a hand, finger-tips extended. His fingers touched the cold metal, pushing gently.

He didn't expect the door to yield, but to his surprise it swung open on well-oiled hinges, belying its looks.

The room inside was well lit. And empty. The door swung right back to the wall, confirming this.

It was all too easy. Dean stood on the threshold, wavering for one moment, and then he was in.

Dean advanced to the middle of the room, keeping alert for any sound or movement other than his own. It was only when he was certain that he was alone in the room that he allowed himself to relax enough to take in his surroundings.

The room was lit by a number of lamps suspended from a beam across the ceiling. They were in a line, laid out to cast their light directly down on a work-bench that occupied the center of the room. It was a scientist's bench, with retorts and tubes fashioned from junk. A closed book stood on one corner.

Looking around the room, Dean could see that there was little else inside apart from a table that had not only been scrubbed clean down to the wood grain, but also had leather restraints for ankles and wrists. Just seeing it made Dean shiver with a barely re-strained fear. His thoughts turned to the stories of predark whitecoats that Doc had told him.

There were two other doors, one leading off each side of the room. The far wall, opposite the door he had entered, was a blank wall of concrete.

Dean went to the door on the left. It was wood, with a bar lock that worked from his side. Listening up against it, he could hear faint sounds of breathing, sighs of sleep. Carefully, with infinite care lest he cause a sound, Dean removed the bar from its brack-ets, placed it against the wall, then opened the door.

The room was in darkness, broken by a beam of light that streaked across the floor from the open door. Dean stepped into the room and saw that there were five sets of bunk beds. Eight of the ten beds were occupied by small children. Without disturbing them, Dean could see that they all were blond, but not if they were male or female. One thing for sure, though: he was certain that if he could have looked, he would have seen that they all had blue eyes.

Unwilling to awaken them and cause a disturbance that would alert anyone to his presence, Dean crept out of the room, shutting the door carefully and qui-etly behind him before replacing the bar.

So now for the other door. Dean shook his head to clear it, to focus his mind as he crossed the workroom floor. Why was Jenna producing little blond children? For he was sure that the baron's wife was behind this. Come to that, how was she doing it? He paused by the workbench and examined some of the tubes standing on the pitted and scarred surface. He tentatively sniffed at the chemicals in the tubes, and hurriedly looked away, nose wrinkled and eyes smarting at the tart and acrid fumes.

Dyes of some kind. Dye the children's hair and perhaps injecting dye into their eyes?

He reached the other door. It had a bar lock similar to the opposing door, and as Dean removed the bar he could hear whimpering from within the room. Whimpering from more than one voice, mingled with the low hum of a hard-fuel-driven generator. What it was powering, he couldn't imagine. Neither did he want to imagine what was whimpering.

He would find out soon enough.

Laying the bar up against the wall, Dean carefully opened the door.

The room beyond was well lit by fluorescent tubes powered by the generator. Old tech equipment with digital displays and flashing lights stood against one wall, flanked by the generator. Cables and thinner wires ran from the equipment toward two beds that were against the opposite wall. The whimpering came from the beds.

The two beds stood side by side, old hospital beds with Perspex sides raised above mattress level, obviously rescued from the remains of the city above-ground. The Perspex was scored and scarred, which made it difficult for Dean to see what was lying on the beds, whimpering pitifully.

Apprehensive, and feeling the bile of anticipation rise in his throat, Dean advanced toward the beds.

When he was able to see over the Perspex, he wished he hadn't bothered.

How the creatures in the beds had been conceived and birthed he couldn't begin to imagine, but it certainly hadn't been a natural process. They were children, but only just. The heads were too large for the stunted and twisted bodies, with overly large foreheads to which clung wisps of hair. Both had small torsos, with shortened arms and only vestigial fingers. The legs were withered. They looked almost identical, like twins or clones. They were pincushions for a number of tubes that fed liquid into them, then extracted it. They were the results of an ongoing and not particularly successful experiment.

But they were still human beings, and their eyes showed constant pain.

The bile rose in Dean's throat, choking him. He tried not to make any noise as the creatures looked at him with fearful eyes, and yet begged for pity. He couldn't face them any longer.

Dean turned on his heel to leave, but was brought up short by the figure looming in the doorway. Silently, and with an infinite stealth, his pursuer had encroached on the room.

Harvey.

The sec chief stood easily, hand on hip, scratching his head. Neither hand was anywhere near the snub-nosed Colt Magnum Carry that was his chosen blaster. This was snug to his hip in its combat holster.

"Well, son, looks like you've really blown it this time. You should have been more careful, like your pa. If you ever stumble on something, you don't pry and you don't snoop. That way you might actually get to stay alive.''

Dean was aware of his Browning Hi-Power. He could feel its shape and weight. Could he outdraw the sec man? Certainly, his body weight was much more poised and alert, whereas Harvey seemed much too relaxed.

Uncannily, it was as though the sec man could read his thoughts. Without moving a muscle, except to lower the hand that had been scratching his head, Harvey said, ''Now, you see you could try and draw, mebbe risk beating me. But if you do, then you've awakened the whole ville, and have to answer why you've chilled the sec chief. And that wouldn't be easy, 'cause my Jenna, well, she can wrap that old fool Alien around her pinkie.''

Dean made no move, but neither did he relax. His adrenaline was racing, and time seemed to be moving at half speed as he frantically searched for a way out. His eyes searched past the sec chief to the room beyond. It seemed empty.

''You're right,'' Dean said simply. ''I'd have to be triple stupe to try and chill you. But on the other hand, you'd have to be more than that to chill me. You know there'd be trouble if I went missing.''

''You forget that you're on my territory, boy. Your father and his few rad-blasted scum against the whole of Raw? What kind of odds are those?''

''Odds I'll have to take,'' Dean breathed almost to himself, conserving his energy for his spring forward. He had estimated that one break, like starting a sprint in training at the Brody school, would propel him forward with enough force to catch the sec man in the midriff and push him back. Harvey would land, hopefully winded, on his back. Dean would roll forward from the thrust and be on his feet first, heading for the corridors. His only hope was to head back to his father and his companions. Harvey would then be in a difficult position. He may have to act covertly, which would hamper his ability to do them harm, especially if they were on triple red.

All these thoughts raced through the boy's head in a fraction of a second as he threw himself forward, lowering his head to catch the sec man off guard and in the solar plexus.

Which was exactly what he did. Harvey had instinctively read the movement of Dean's body, and was ready for the attack, but was a fraction of a second slower than the youth in reaction time. A vital fraction of a second as Dean's head caught him beneath the breastbone, driving the air from his lungs with a gulping gasp as the sec chief tried to replace the air almost immediately.

But Dean was already in a forward roll, his legs cutting through the air, using the prone Harvey as a cushion against his impact on the hard floor.

The young Cawdor sprang to his feet, almost stumbling as his ankle twisted on the uneven floor, but managing to stay erect with only a sharp knife of pain, too brief to stop him, to mark the stumble.

He had made two steps to the door, leaving a floundering sec chief twisting on the floor, cursing and trying to pull his Colt from where the holster had slipped on his belt, almost underneath him, when he was brought up short by a wave of paralyzing fear.

Dean had seen rabbits before they were chilled, frozen in a sudden burst of light. He had seen a mutie fox, so terrified at being cornered that its muscles were almost frozen in rigor before its chilling; but he had never experienced such a crippling fear—nor did he think it was possible for a human being.

But now he knew differently. Try as he might, he was unable to move a muscle voluntarily. They trembled and quivered in his legs as though they would, at any moment, dissolve to liquid. Although he could hear the cursing sec chief struggle to his feet, although he could hear him free his blaster, still Dean Cawdor was frozen, unable to move from his absurd position of being midrun.

And it wasn't just his being frozen; it was the fear itself. He had been scared before—terrified, even. His father always told him that fear could be a positive thing in a dangerous situation. It would help you clarify and make priorities when things were tough. But this was a different kind of fear. This was a blind, all-encompassing terror that made it impossible for Dean's mind to focus on one thing, flitting as it did from moment to moment between abject terror at dying, fear of torture, and even a ridiculous scaredness at wetting himself in his terror, feeling the urine flow down his leg.

"Well, I'll be fucked by a mutie leper!" Harvey exclaimed. "The little fucker can't even move—and he's pissed himself. I've got to hand it to you, babe...."

Dean was confused. Who was Harvey talking to? And then she entered the room. Although Dean couldn't conquer the fear, or think clearly through it, a part of his brain suddenly realized why he was so scared.

It was Jenna. The baron's mutie wife stepped through the outer door. She had obviously been waiting for Harvey to clean up the situation, but since he had failed she had decided to step in herself. Both Jak and Krysty had mentioned her obvious feelie ability, and now Dean was aware of how strong it could be when she chose to exercise the faculty.

Her sharp, pointed face was clouded with anger as she stood in front of the boy. The raven eyes glittered with nothing so much as childish petulance, and the dark curtains of hair that hung down over her shoulders only accentuated those eyes...the eyes that bore into him.

Dean's fear grew to the point where he wanted to gibber and moan with fright, even though some still rational par of his brain frantically tried to scream to him that it was all manipulation.

Jenna's face, which could, if not clouded by her twisted nature, have been beautiful, contorted with hate as she spat into Dean's face. Her acrid spittle stung his eyes, but he was unable to blink, his vision blurred by the liquid.

"Harv, you're a fuckwit," she said in a quavering voice. "You can't even get the better of a whelp like this. You know I hate using the taint in my soul unless I have to, so why make me have to?"

"Kid took me by surprise," Harvey muttered in return.

"Yeah, right," she said, sneering. "Nothing to do with you getting old and useless."

Harvey, now in front and facing Dean, tried to slip

an arm around Jenna's waist. "That's not what you say when—"

"No, not now," she screeched, shrugging him off violently. "You moron, you always were led totally by your dick."

Harvey's face hardened, but he said nothing. Dean figured that he would be the one to pay for the sec chief's humiliation, and knowing this didn't help the fear that was still flowing through him.

Jenna stepped back from them both and crossed her arms, looking askance at the young Cawdor.

"You're obviously a bright boy, like your father. And you'll grow to be as handsome as him... No, you won't, because you won't live that long. Shame. Mebbe I should take your father instead of old Harv here," she said mockingly.

Harvey was stone-faced, his attention fixed on Dean.

Jenna continued. "I suppose you feel disgusted by what you've seen here. And I'll grant that my experiments have not been that successful as yet. But progress takes time, and that fireblasted war came far too soon. You see, boy, one of the little projects the Illuminated Ones were working on was the creation of the perfect human being. It wasn't a widely known project, even within the group. Everyone has their secrets. But my father worked long and hard on it, trying to rebuild what his father had started, and what had been smashed when they left the redoubt and came into the open. Oh, yes, there were many little wars within the group, some of which even Alien knows nothing...despite what the fool thinks."

"You sure you should tell him this?" Harvey asked, still stone-faced, his eyes fixed on Dean.

Jenna shrugged. "He's going nowhere. Anyway, I want him to see that this has an aim, a point." Her eyes began to shine. "Some of the Illuminated Ones were against the idea of the perfect human being, but those with vision could see it was the only way forward. A way that became more of an imperative when skydark happened. How else are we ever going to rebuild? It's too late for me, cursed as I am by these mutie traits. But for others? Those children are the future. They may not be perfect yet, but they tell me much for the next time around. And when I have reclaimed that lost knowledge, then…"

She trailed off, lost in thought. Dean struggled to assert his will over his own body, hoping that her reverie would cause to weaken—if only for a moment—her grip on his mind.

He was right. It took an immense effort on his part, but he managed to move his limbs, could feel the strength start to flow back into his muscles. He made as if to move forward.

But he was too sluggish, still too much in thrall to Jenna. He was far too slow. Harvey stepped forward and punched Dean, using the time the boy's sluggish movements allowed him to draw back his arm and put all his weight behind the blow, knowing that Dean wouldn't be able to move his protesting body quickly enough to protect himself from the blow.

Dean saw it coming toward him, but was unable to get out of the way. The fist hit him like a jackhammer in the face. He felt the blow as if in slow motion, blood filling his mouth as one tooth loosened and others bit into the flesh of his cheek. The bone of his jaw groaned and grated in protest, perhaps at breaking point.

He was aware of the evil smile on Harvey's face as consciousness slipped away from him.

RYAN WAS AWARE of the jackhammer pounding in his brain as he slowly slipped back into consciousness. He slowly lifted his head, which felt as though it had little connection with the rest of his body. Looking around the sleeping unit, he saw that he and Krysty were alone.

The flame-haired beauty was wrapped around him, her body heavy with sleep. As the one-eyed man slipped from beneath her, he remembered with a smile the way they had made love, long and passionate, savoring the opportunity to take a few moments of peace and use it in that manner, knowing that they could—just for the moment—let down their guard on the outside world and be totally wrapped in each other.

But before that? The celebration was little more than a set of random images, each distorted by that fearsome brew and its incredible strength. As Ryan planted his feet on the ground and felt the impact travel up each calf, he wondered how the others felt as they awoke.

JAK HAD an aching head, but the will to dismiss it. Too long had he spent hunting and living in hostile territories to let a hangover get to him. He smiled as he spotted Doc, attempting to rise among a heap of bodies. Considering that the surrounding ville dwellers were used to the brew and mostly much younger than Doc, it was a measure of the old man's constitution and wiry strength that he was conscious before the majority of them.

The albino stepped over the bodies and assisted Doc to his feet.

"My thanks, Jak," Doc said, wincing at the apparent loudness of his own voice in his aching head, "I fear that I—in common with most—imbibed far too much last night."

"Not much celebrate in this place," Jak commented. "Why not enjoy?" he added.

"True, true...but there was something troubling me last night. Something I felt I had to speak to Ryan upon... But I cannot for the life of me remember. Where are the others?"

Jak shrugged. "Too busy to notice."

"A fair point." Doc grinned. "I have not been that drunk since New Year's in Vermont. For one wild, intoxicated moment I could almost have been back there...." His eyes misted over as he recalled his beloved Emily, and his children, Rachel and Jolyon, long since dead and buried even before skydark.

Jak took the old man's arm. "We find them," he said.

Doc looked confused for a moment. "What? Why, yes. It was just that I could almost see them, before that hard rain began to fall and— Wait!" He gripped Jak's arm so hard that the albino felt Doc's bony fingers bite into the muscle. "The hard rain—Sunchild. That's what I wanted to remember. Something I saw at Samtvogel. They have more than just blasters, and now that they have been routed, let us pray that he does not know how to use it, or that it isn't operative."

Jak frowned and took Doc's chin in his free hand so that he could focus his red eyes directly into Doc's.

"What worry you?"

Doc seemed to struggle for the words. "Hard rain...like the cursed whitecoats and their appalling methods of destruction. It must have come from the redoubt or a silo nearby. Thank whatever God is left that they didn't somehow detonate it then."

"Doc!" Jak barked, snapping the old man back to attention. "What it?"

Doc's voice was reduced to a whisper. "A nuke, my friend. They have, in the middle of their ville, a nuke. The very thing that created them. A splendid irony, is it not?"

WHEN DEAN REGAINED consciousness, he felt no pain from the blow that had rendered him unconscious. He felt no headache, nor any of the pain and nausea from concussion or waking from unconsciousness. In fact, he felt as though he were adrift on a sea of wool, muzzy but completely happy. He felt drugged.

He slowly realized that had to be the case, as he became aware of the fact that his wrists and ankles were secured and that he was lying on the table in the middle of the room.

Turning his head, he saw Jenna. There was no sign of the sec chief. Dean smiled stupidly at her, unable to do anything else.

Jenna returned his smile, but with a sinister edge. "As you may have guessed, young Cawdor, you've been sedated to keep you quiet and make you more malleable. You'll make an interesting experiment. I've never had a subject as young or as fit as you, nor one from outside this gene pool. I hope you're not hiding any mutie traits, or that the redheaded mutie bitch isn't your mother. Unfortunately, it's not easy to synthesize the drugs that were used on previous experiments, not with what I have available at the moment. But I do my best. I think you'll find the chemicals I'll be using on you will perhaps hurt more than they should, which is why I've put you under such a heavy dose. We'll begin tonight, after I've appeased my idiot husband for disappearing from his stupe celebration last night. Until then, rest well, my little one.''

She came over to him and kissed him gently on the lips before turning to go.

Dean smiled stupidly, although every fiber of his being screamed silently, unable to find release through the drugged haze.

He was still smiling when she locked the door, imprisoning him until his ordeal would begin.

Chapter Twelve

"Ryan, my dear boy. The teeth of the hell-monster are forever housed in slavering jaws that await nothing more than our perennial destruction. We are forever condemned by our past to not only repeat its mistakes but to enlarge upon them, increase them in volume to a deafening roar that cuts across the world—such as it now is—in a wave of increasing fear and loathing, even in Las Vegas, that will—"

"Doc!" Ryan roared, taking hold of the shaking, rambling man and holding him still, trying to penetrate his wild-eyed gaze with the steely glare of his good eye. It was no use. Doc's head was rolling wildly from side to side as the old man was gripped in a convulsive anxiety attack.

He had burst into the sleeping unit a scant few seconds before, disturbing the peace. Krysty had joined Ryan in the land of the waking, and like him was suffering from the results of the potent ville brew. It was unlike any white lightning or spirit they had encountered across the Deathlands, and for the first time in what passed at this moment for a memory, she had a hangover, her head thumping and the lights seeming too bright.

She and Ryan had conversed in muted, hushed tones, trying not to trigger each other's headaches. They both recalled similar segments of the previous night, and there was enough time for a moment of fond remembrance—a time that was in short enough supply.

Their muted reverie had been broken by the return of J.B. and Mildred. They had found an empty unit for themselves, wanting their own privacy as much as granting Ryan and Krysty theirs, but in contrast, both seemed to be suffering no ill effects from the spirit.

"Simple," Mildred said when Krysty asked her. "Just a lot of water and some juice. It may be mutie fruit, but it has something resembling vitamin C in it."

Krysty remembered back in Harmony, when Uncle Tyas McCann had taught them something similar. But it had taken Mildred's predark medical-trained and methodical mind to remember this, even in the midst of such a celebration.

"So do we go on or do we stay?" J.B. asked eventually, polishing the minisextant he carried with him.

Ryan was aware that the Armorer's producing the instrument as he posed the question was by way of a hint, and not a very subtle one. But then, J.B. was a straightforward man, not given to subtlety...unless it was in the line of a booby trap.

"I think we should go, move on. These aren't the Illuminated Ones. Yesterday's firefight would have been a lot easier if they had been. These people have little old tech remnants, and even though that doomie wife of Alien's gives me the creeps as much as all of you, I think Alien's on the level. He's a good man, doing his best to live by the code they set up here. There's no great stockpile, no Erewhon here."

J.B. nodded agreement. "Harvey's a coldheart who

doesn't like us around. I don't like the idea of wasting time and ammo on an unnecessary firefight. That's triple stupe, but that's what it'll come to if we stay."

Mildred agreed, and was about to tell Ryan and Krysty of Harvey's willingness to leave them to fight alone the day before, when she was interrupted by the sudden appearance of Doc, bursting in wild-eyed and anxious.

And now, after he had blurted out his halfstory, Mildred was helping him to one of the beds. He was breathing fast and heavy, sweat spangling his forehead and sticking strands of snow-white hair to his skull. His head turned wildly from side to side as he lay, the whites of his eyes all that showed as his eyes rolled in their sockets.

"Shit, the old fool's really got himself worked up about something," Mildred stated. "I need some kind of sedative to calm him. His heart will burst, the way his blood pressure's going."

Ryan crouched beside them. "No. He was trying to tell us something important. The last thing we need is him out of his head on something."

"Ryan, I'm not disagreeing with you," Mildred said through gritted teeth, "but unless we get him calmed down, we'll never find out what the old fool means."

The one-eyed warrior nodded. "I know where the medic is in this ville. I'll take you."

Mildred rose to her feet, turning to Krysty. "Keep an eye on him," she said with a trace of worry in her voice. "It'd be just like the crazy buzzard to buy the farm before telling us something important."

JAK KNEW exactly where he was headed. He had listened to Doc's story, and although finding it hard to fully understand the rambling tale, he could grasp enough through the old man's excitement to realize that it was vitally important that Ryan know of it. So he sent Doc back to the unit to tell his tale, while the albino took it upon himself to find Dean.

As with many things, Jak would have found it impossible to explain why he knew Dean wouldn't be with the others. But something was telling him that Dean had gotten himself into big-time trouble. He knew that his little exploration of a few days before had whetted the boy's appetite for the ville, and for nosing out his suspicions of Jenna and her activities. In a way, Jak wished he hadn't mentioned the metal door at the end of the isolated corridor.

Sure, the albino had gotten drunk the night before, completely insensible. But not before some alarm bell in his brain had registered the fact that he had seen Dean wandering on the periphery of the main hall. The youngster wasn't taking the opportunity to get drunk—in fact, there had been a clearness to his eyes and bearing, even at such a distance, as to suggest he was staying sober for a purpose.

And although Jak hadn't mentioned this to Doc, he had an idea what that purpose may be.

Jak's instincts had imprinted the route to that isolated corridor on his mind, and he had an almost perfect recall. The fact that he still had so much alcohol running through his system failed to slow him.

There were few people about; only those who were going about their daily tasks, those vital to the running of the ville. The other inhabitants were still shaking off the aftereffects of their celebrations. So Jak had few people to delay him, or to ask awkward questions.

But a few could be more than enough. On the way to the corridor he sought, Jak made a few detours—mostly to throw off the suspicion of any who may be observing him, and partly to scout any areas where Dean may have ended up if he had taken a wrong turn. The youngster was good, but not yet that good.

Jak had hoped to find Dean lost, as he worried about the time lag between Dean's disappearance and his search beginning. If the boy had found the door and had gotten beyond, then his not reappearing was a bad sign.

A bad sign that got worse as Jak neared the beginning of the corridor. It led off the last few desultory units, occupied by those who could no longer complete any useful tasks for Raw. They were given food and shelter still, but necessity and the harsh mode of life—even in such a fair and ordered society—meant they were exiled to areas where others didn't wish to live.

From the units, Jak could hear snoring and groaning as the celebrations took their toll on the old and infirm inhabitants. It would be useless to ask them if they had seen Dean. Even if it wouldn't arouse suspicion, it was doubtful whether many of them could remember their own names at this point.

But at least it left the way clear for Jak to move on unobserved…or so he hoped.

As the albino approached the curve of the corridor, a figure stepped from around the curve and into the poor light.

"Hey, Whitey—what y'all doing here, then? Get a little lost or something?"

Jak stopped, his pitted and scarred white face set like marble, giving nothing away.

Harvey stepped forward. His gait was casual, but there was a faint tenseness to his body language, a tightness to his movement that told Jak the sec chief was anxious beneath his seemingly calm demeanor.

"Y'all not talking to me? I didn't know you white muties got mute, as well as mutie."

Jak's anger rose like a thick bile from his stomach to his throat. His fingers twitched toward the concealed knives. With an effort of will, he stayed his hand.

Harvey walked slowly around Jak. The tall sec chief towered over the albino, but Jak knew that he was quick and strong enough to take the sec man if he pounced.

If... It would be stupe of Harvey to do this now, not with Jak so close to the metal door.

"Look for Dean. Young, not drunk before."

Harvey laughed. It was forced. "Well, I guess there always has to be a first time. And the kid has gone missing, eh? You won't find him here. I've just been patrolling this sector, and I haven't found him."

"That so?"

Harvey's tone gained a hard, threatening edge. "That's so, Whitey. So if I was you, I'd get back to the old man and tell him his whelp is still lost. Or you could look somewhere else."

"Mebbe do that," Jak said slowly. His eyes blazed as they fixed on the sec chief. Harvey looked away. He knew Jak had seen through him. But Jak didn't

have the full story, and the albino knew he would
have to be contented with that for now.

He turned, every muscle on triple red in case Harvey should try to attack. With every step he took from
the corridor, even as he passed the first of the dwellings, he could feel the sec chief's eyes burning into
his back.

Burning like the slugs Harvey would want to put
there from his Magnum Carry blaster.

As Jak passed the first of the dwellings, he knew
that their stay in Raw could become very bloody indeed.

DOC LAY SEDATED, whimpering softly while Mildred
tended to him. The nurse whose son had been injured
the day before left the unit, accepting with a sad grace
Ryan's best wishes for her son. The one-eyed warrior
could see her sorrow, and after hearing Doc's story
had the uneasy feeling that it would only be added to
in the short time to come.

While Ryan and Mildred were gone, Doc had
gasped out enough garbled detail, in with his ram-
blings and memories, for Krysty and J.B. to grasp
what he had seen in Samtvogel.

When Ryan and Mildred returned, while the nurse
and Mildred sedated Doc with an opiate taken from
a mutated strain of poppy that was grown aboveground, J.B. and Krysty had filled in the few details
they had gleaned.

Mildred left Doc and turned to her companions.
"You know, it's a shame they couldn't harness some
old tech from the redoubt down here. If they had
some kind of hydroponics plant, they could grow

those damned poppies instead of having to risk going aboveground to collect them. It's the strongest— What's wrong?'' she added, changing the subject rapidly when she caught sight of their grim faces.

Ryan explained as briefly as possible. Mildred whistled to herself. ''Shit, that really does upset the cart. If there's even the slightest chance that Sunchild knows how to activate that nuke, he may just be pissed enough to do it after yesterday.''

''Right,'' Ryan agreed. ''And there's too many good people down here to expose to that danger. And ourselves. Even if we left now, then there's no way we could get out of range quickly if he decides to act soon.''

''Only one thing for it, lover. You've got to tell Alien this, and we've got to go in and get it,'' Krysty said grimly.

J.B. pushed his wire-rimmed spectacles up on the bridge of his nose, a nervous gesture in times of stress. It was the only sign the ice-cold Armorer ever showed.

''Chill a whole ville? Wipe them out with whatever we can find in the armory here? Without knowing, that's a hell of a task.''

''We've been in worse than this,'' Ryan said simply. ''I'll go to Alien as soon as we've told Jak and Dean. Fireblast, where the rad-blasted hell are they? Always when you need him, Dean is off somewhere getting himself in shit!''

''Like his father?'' Krysty murmured.

Ryan looked at her. ''Guess so... Okay, I'll go and see the baron now. If Dean and Jak should bother to

let us know what the fuck they're doing, then tell
them—''

But the one-eyed warrior didn't get a chance to
voice his thoughts, as Jak burst into the unit.

''Ryan, trouble,'' he said shortly, gulping breath
from his journey. As soon as he was sure he was out
of Harvey's view, he'd run back to the unit.

Jak explained what had happened in his search,
ending with ''So need get Dean out.''

''Sec chief behind Jenna, that's gonna mean a
whole lot of trouble,'' J.B. muttered. ''Especially if
Alien's in on it all.''

Ryan shook his head. ''I don't think so. Don't ask
me why, but I just trust him, and it feels right. What
do you think?'' he directed at Krysty.

''I'm kind of with you on that, lover,'' she agreed
cautiously, ''but Jenna's got me worried. It depends
what kind of a hold she has on the baron.''

''True. I guess we'll just have to play this one by
ear,'' Ryan mused.

ALIEN WAS in his unit, although being the baron of
Raw, the term *unit* was perhaps inappropriate. It lay
at the rear of the main hall, with the entrance behind
the long table and the old drapes. Raw being the kind
of ville it was, he had no sec guard, and when Ryan
cautiously pulled back the drapes he found the baron
sprawled across his large bed, covered in the finest
linen and velvet that could be found in Raw. The
covers were thrown back, revealing the baron's torso,
running to middle-aged flab, but still heavily muscled
and crossed with scars that attested to his courage in

leading his people. His long beard rested on his chest, his long white hair untied and covering his face.

He was snoring and wheezing softly.

In stark contrast to the white of Alien, Jenna was a dark pool on his skin, her jet-black and flowing hair spreading in tendrils across him, her darker skin smooth and young against him. Ryan found his eyes drawn to her small breasts, her dark nipples erect where they brushed against her husband.

She was awake, her glittering raven eyes catching Ryan's azure blue orb, twinkling at him with a superior smile that made him suddenly look away.

In her triumph, she sent out a psychic wave that made Krysty feel nauseous and ill at ease.

"Well, excuse us..." Mildred spoke to allay the rising gorge within her. She didn't have Krysty's seeing power, but as when she had first seen Jenna, she felt the same wave, albeit in a milder form.

Jenna rose from the bed, making no attempt to cover herself and knowing that her petite and shapely frame was drawing the eyes of the three men present, feeling their gaze run down from her sharp face, to her erect nipples and down to the black nest of her pubis. Knowing that they would want her instinctively, and drawing on that for her own strength.

"Do you make a habit of insulting your hosts?" she asked with an artificial sweetness to her tone.

"There's no insult intended," Ryan said slowly, picking his words and trying to focus. He knew she was deliberately toying with him—with them all—and attempted to overcome that feeling. "We just need to speak to Alien. Urgently."

"But as you can see, he's asleep," Jenna returned.

Alien grunted, showing no signs of being awakened by the disturbance.

"Then mebbe you should wake him," Ryan said carefully, pitching it somewhere between a request and an order.

Jenna's raven eyes gleamed and glittered, flashing a mixture of hatred and lust at the one-eyed warrior. For a moment there was a stalemate. Then, just as suddenly as she had begun, Jenna averted her gaze and shook the slumbering baron.

"Wake up!" she snapped in a tone of voice that suggested she harbored nothing but contempt for him.

Alien awoke with a groan, mumbling and rising on one elbow to stare blearily at the sight before him. He was only half-awake, and unsure why there were people in his rooms. His brow furrowed as he recognized the intruders.

"What is the meaning of this, Ryan Cawdor?" he asked.

"We need to talk to you," Ryan replied, holding up both hands, "and there's no need to reach for your blaster."

Alien smiled and withdrew his hand from under the cushions and pillows that covered the far end of the bed. As he had been questioning the one-eyed man, he had slipped that hand—unobtrusively, he hoped—toward the cushions in search of the concealed blaster.

"How did you know I had one there?"

"Even the fairest baron in the most peaceful ville can't take chances against an enemy from within," Ryan replied simply. His eye flickered toward Jenna as he spoke, almost involuntarily. If she noticed, she gave no sign.

"Very well. Then tell me what it is you're wanting," Alien said, now fully awake and alert.

So Ryan began. Doc described what he had seen in Samtvogel, and when Jenna interjected with a query as to how the old man knew so much about predark tech, Doc bluffed his way out of it with a story about finding a stash of old vids in a ville during his travels. She didn't seem convinced, but Mildred hurried the proceedings along with a query to the baron as to whether they could attack Samtvogel with any degree of stealth.

Alien stroked his long beard, twisting it between his fingers in intense concentration. "I'd have to consult Harv to be really sure, but there isn't any safe way of hiding a large sec force along that route. It's too open. But those mutie fucks don't come out of their ville that often, so mebbe if we sent scouting parties ahead..."

"We have to get that nuke," Ryan said urgently. "Sunchild is pissed off, and if he has any idea how to use that thing..."

"I agree," Jenna interjected. "We should get that as soon as possible."

And as she said it, Krysty shuddered, her hair coiling about her neck. The titian-haired woman's seeing traits rose to the fore as Jenna sent out an unconscious wave of pure hate. She wanted that nuke for her own purposes. Krysty knew at that moment that recovering the missile from Samtvogel would be but the beginning of their problem.

While this raced through her mind, Ryan had swiftly moved the subject on to his missing son. It was a difficult matter to broach, as Ryan's people were all firmly of the opinion that Jenna had him secured someplace. But it was up to Ryan to raise the matter without arousing the dark mutie's suspicion.

The one-eyed warrior outlined the barest details of Dean's disappearance, and the baron was suitably sympathetic.

"We'll get Raw searched while we raise a raiding party," he stated. By now he had risen from the bed and was dressing, pulling on the freshly cleaned fatigues that marked him as the baron. Others in the ville had clothes that were patched and darned many times, repaired and faded. But as baron, Alien had the pick of any new stock from a passing trader.

When he finished, he picked up a cupped speaking tube and blew down it. Jak had noticed many small runs of similar tubes during his explorations of the winding underground ville, and had wondered what they were for. That question was now answered. They were a means of quick communication between links vital to Raw's sec.

A whistle from the far end of the speaking tube announced that the sec chief had answered. From where the companions stood, it was difficult to make out what he said, but there was no mistaking Alien's meaning from his loud bellowing. He ordered the sec chief to get his ass over right away, and before he had finished lacing his boots, the sec chief appeared in the doorway.

Jak wasn't the only one to notice that the sec chief's eyes dwelled lustfully on Jenna's naked form. There was a look in his eye that also suggested a familiarity with her form. For the albino, this added a few things together in his mind.

Alien barked out the situation to the sec chief, beginning with the missile and ending with Dean's disappearance. The sec chief's next words surprised everyone:

"Perhaps the muties got Cyclops Jr....."

"Dark night!" J.B. whispered to Mildred. "Has the triple stupe got a dose of rad poisoning?"

Ryan stared at the sec chief coldly. "You going to explain what that means?"

Harvey matched Ryan's stare. "Just exactly what I say. Chances of the boy going astray in Raw are next to nothing. Where the hell could he be? I reckon there was a revenge party out for more kids—mebbe some kind of sacrifice to appease their gods or something—and young Cawdor got caught."

Alien looked thoughtful. "You could be right there, Harv," he replied at length. "Sure as shit can't imagine where he could be in here." The baron looked at Ryan. His face was so open that the one-eyed warrior had no doubt he believed the sec chief completely. "Mebbe we should get that party under way and land two prizes."

"And if Dean isn't in Samtvogel?" Mildred pressed.

Alien shrugged. "Then we'll mount a search when we return. Trust me, Ryan Cawdor, there's little harm the boy can come to in Raw."

"I trust you," Ryan said slowly and pointedly. "I trust you completely. That's not the problem."

His eye met Jenna's gaze. She seemed to peer deep into him, and despite himself he felt a stirring in his loins.

It took some effort to look away.

THE RAIDING PARTY assembled in the main hall about two hours later by J.B.'s wrist chron. The Armorer had taken more of an interest in these proceedings than in the assembly of the interception force from the previous day. There were a number of problems that presented themselves to any sec chief who wanted a raiding party of sharpness and quality assembled at such a short notice.

To begin with, the Armorer doubted that the previous day's blasters had been stripped and cleaned. One of the first things he had learned during his time with Trader, before Ryan had even joined the infamous party on Trader's War Wag One, was that predark blasters needed regular cleaning and overhauling. When the large stockpiles had first been found, the weapons had been taken from their packing cases, and in some instances were immediately capable of being fired. But for many, the years of being stacked and inactive had led to the grease drying out, the bearings seizing, working parts becoming fixed and dangerous.

Every new blaster that had been acquired by Trader, whether secondhand or fresh from a stockpile, had been stripped, cleaned and greased before being reassembled and tested before being handed out for use in an everyday or combat situation.

And regular stripping and cleaning became even more important in some areas of the Deathlands. The nuke-raddled landscape and tainted air meant that in some areas the blasters were more susceptible to conditions. Blasters thought cleaned and greased were prone to corrosion and drying out, conditions that made combat dangerous. Many had bought the farm from a misfiring or exploding blaster. But not many of those had traveled with Trader.

So J.B. was interested to see how the armory at Raw would cope with this, given that the celebrations had begun almost as soon as they arrived back, and many in the newly constituted raiding party had been forcibly turned from their beds and even now were showing signs of still recovering from their drunkenness.

This was no idle curiosity. He knew that his own weapons were in the best condition. He knew that Ryan also kept his weapons that way. As for the others in their party, none would have survived as long as they had without that discipline being second nature. Neither would Ryan allow any to endanger the others by risking a misfire during a combat situation. They could back up one another all the way, but now they were also dependent on the inhabitants of Raw, a ville of which they knew nothing.

Therefore, J.B. resolved to keep an eye on the armory, to spot any weak points and if necessary to step in, to insure his friends' safety as much as that of the Raw dwellers.

When he arrived at the armory, he found that the small group of men and women who acted as Armorers were hard at work. There were five of them, two men and three women. The men were stacking small piles of plas-ex and grens to be distributed, while a selection of handblasters, semiautomatics, machine guns and rifles were neatly laid against the wall, the women working their way through the task of cleaning them with as much rapidity and accuracy as they could muster.

J.B. was pleased to see that everyone seemed to have checked their blasters in for maintenance. He recognized Downey's Sharps rifle, which stood out as it was the only Sharps in the armory. The two shot-guns belonging to the dreadlocked twins, Ant and Dee, stood to one side, their appalling condition caus-ing the Armorers to set them aside, perhaps for spe-cial treatment, perhaps because of a fear that their dirt and poor condition may spread to the other blasters. He recognized Blake's 9 mm Walther PPK by the nicks on the walnut stock. They formed a starlike pat-tern that was distinctive and obviously of meaning to the sec man.

On his previous visits, he had been treated distantly but politely, even though his vast knowledge had been recognized.

"Welcome, friend," one of the female Armorers greeted him, looking up briefly from the blaster she was greasing. She was small and rotund, with apple cheeks that should have marked her down as a cook rather than the mechanic she undoubtedly was. "Have you come to aid us in this preparation?"

"If you want," J.B. replied in a laconic tone. "You didn't seem too keen when I came around before."

"Nothing personal," she replied warmly, "just as we like to keep to our own tasks is all. But if you know your business, then we can use you now."

"Be glad to help."

She held up the stripped blaster she was holding. "Just as a matter of interest, what would this be?"

J.B. eyed the blaster before replying. It was a large weapon, of the type used for static positions rather than carrying in combat. Just from that, the Armorer was able to guess part of Harvey's tactic for the raid. But that was for another time. For now... J.B. grinned.

"That's light machine—RPK, drum fed. Supposed to go on a tripod, which I guess you've got stacked somewhere. Shit useless on the run, but okay if you mount it somewhere to provide cover. Course, it's supposed to do 660 rounds in a minute, but it never works that way 'cause the stupe bastards who designed it didn't figure on how hot the barrel would get. You do too much and the mother heats up the ammo in the drum and sets it off. Then you can't stop it firing, no matter what—and you got no control over it."

The fat woman whistled. "You sit your ass down here and start helping, son."

J.B.'s wry grin broke into a smile as he joined her. He felt confident that no matter what the state of the people in the raiding party, the blasters and grens wouldn't let them down.

IN A FEW SHORT HOURS, the party was ready to leave. The previous day's party of twenty sec men had assembled, minus the injured man who was still unconscious in the hospital unit. Alien headed the nineteen, bringing them to twenty. With Ryan's party, minus the missing Dean, they numbered twenty-six.

Added to this were thirty men and women from Raw, all taken from their regular tasks in order to augment the raiding party, and give strength in numbers to the attack on Samtvogel.

"Sure all know what doing?" Jak whispered to

Ryan as they assembled in the main hall for a briefing from the baron.

The one-eyed warrior replied softly. "If they match Alien for courage, even if not for fighting skill, then they'll be hard enough to chill. What we've got to think about is the strengths of Samtvogel."

While they exchanged these comments, Krysty was looking around the hall for Jenna. The baron's wife was nowhere to be seen, which wasn't what Krysty would have expected from her on the verge of such a battle. But then again, that completely summed up Jenna's attitude to her husband and to her people.

All the same, the flame-haired woman would have liked to have had Jenna where she could see her for as long as possible, for she was sure that the baron's wife was holding Dean captive, and she wanted Jenna to have as little time as possible with the boy until they were able to find him.

Mildred, too, was unhappy about unfinished business. Standing beside J.B., she murmured, "John, do you think it would be possible for one of us to stay behind and look for Dean?"

The Armorer tried to hide his surprise. "How the fireblasted hell would we work that?"

"I don't know, but if only Jenna and Harvey know what's happened to Dean, they couldn't say much about another one of us going missing without giving themselves away."

"I suppose so," the Armorer muttered in reply, polishing his spectacles before placing them back on the bridge of his tanned and scarred nose. "But with all these people around, you've left it a bit late to just slip away. We're going to have to roll with this."

Meanwhile, Alien was outlining the situation to his people, skimming over the potential destructiveness of the nuke in favor of the advantages of getting it away from the muties. He then had Harvey outline the plan of attack—two scouting parties would go in advance of the main group, in order to prevent any outriding parties from Samtvogel spying the main party and taking advance warning back to the ville. Once at the valley, they would surround and attack as soon as they could get in position, using the RPKs and grens to blow an advance path for the first warriors down the slopes and into the heart of the ville.

It all seemed straightforward enough, but relied heavily on surprise and not allowing the Sunchildren time to defend their ville. If Harvey had a contingency, then he was keeping it to himself for now...which, to Ryan's mind, was a bad idea. Any force could only be effective if it had a clear idea of what it was doing.

Then again, it did cross the one-eyed warrior's mind that this would be the perfect opportunity to "accidentally" get rid of Alien if Harvey and Jenna had any notions of ridding themselves of the baron.

Finally, Alien mentioned the disappearance of Dean, asking if anyone had seen the boy since the night before. From the muttered conversations, Ryan and his people gathered that few had any clear recollections at all of the previous night, let alone if they had seen a lad they barely knew.

It was unsatisfactory to leave the situation like that, but Ryan and his companions were forced to let the matter rest.

At least, for now...

Chapter Thirteen

It was daylight aboveground. The forest was lit with a radiant, twilight glow that was as bright as the day would ever be. The humidity was intense, and Doc could almost feel the drops of moisture in the air, causing him to wipe his face every few minutes. Moreover, as he breathed, the air seemed to scald his lungs, making him cough. He could almost see the droplets as a fine, drizzling rain around him.

Mildred had hung back to keep an eye on Doc, wary of how the trek would affect him, hitting such humidity so soon after so much alcohol, lack of rest and the psychological stress he had endured when remembering the nuke. Doc was incredibly strong, but had moments of contrasting fragility that meant he always walked a tightrope, balancing precariously. The last thing Mildred wanted was for Doc to fall off the rope at that moment.

They were in the center of the group that marched through the forest, using the well-worn paths. They had already passed the area where the previous day's firefight had taken place, picking their way over the corpses that were still strewed across the path. The Sunchildren hadn't returned to claim their dead, and the corpses were already bloated and rotting in the heat, swollen with gases that emerged as moans when the dead meat was touched by a passing foot, making the ordinary ville dwellers jump with fright and the hardened sec men laugh. It helped to relieve the tension for the sec men, who in their view had a whole heap of inexperienced chill fodder to nursemaid, as well as attend to their own task.

The sickly sweet smell of death blended with the scents of the flowers, following them for some way down the path. Krysty had noticed how the creepers across the forest floor had already started to entwine around the corpses, preparing to bury them beneath, turning them to a mulch that would fertilize the earth. How long, she wondered with a shudder, before the vines got greedy and started to ensnare the unwary and alive as they passed?

The party was large, and even moving in almost total silence made a considerable sound in the quiet forest. The creeping vines squealed in echoes as the footfalls of the war party crashed down time and again. The undergrowth on both sides of the narrow path was pushed back with a rustle as people passed, then sprang back for the next member of the war party passing to push it back once more, creating a continuous wave of sound.

That made Ryan uneasy. He looked back over his shoulder and caught J.B.'s eye. The Armorer made a small inclination of his head, a minute gesture that communicated his displeasure with the circumstances of their progress. The sounds of the creepers and of the moving undergrowth could mask any sounds made by an ambush party.

Ryan had mentioned that to Alien as they began their journey, but the baron had deferred the matter entirely to his sec chief. Harvey had listened to

Ryan's concerns, then dismissed them out of hand. "Those fuckers'll be back in their shitpit still licking their wounds and asking their dumb god what the fuck to do, Cyclops. Trust me—I've been here all my life, and you ain't been here for shit."

There had been an implied threat and put-down in the words that Ryan noted but chose to ignore for now. At one time, his hot blood and temper would have pushed him into a fight with the sec man. But now there was too much at stake for a battle with an uneasy ally. Save that score for later.

So Ryan and his people concurred with Harvey, and joined the vast war party as it tramped through the forest. All the same, Ryan didn't have to tell any of them to be on triple red, just in case Sunchild wasn't as dumb as Harvey supposed. There was no way Ryan could call Sunchild using more stickies than his own people for the retaliatory raid a stupe move. Sunchild may well be an insane mutie, but that wasn't quite the same as being dumb.

The trees and shrubs closed in on them, seeming somehow to loom overhead with a hidden threat as the war party made its way through the forest. The flowers, with their heavy scent, swayed in the ripples of the massed movement, their heads bobbing as though to strike. The moving forest canopy overhead created a disorienting strobing of what little light could penetrate if you looked up too long; yet to look down you could see the creepers moving beneath your feet, bending and twisting under the heavy tramp of rough-shod feet.

The humidity seemed to wrap them in a blanket of

damp mist, clinging to the pores of their skin and preventing them from sweating.

"There's too many of us in too small a space," Ryan said softly to Krysty, who was walking at his side. She had left her heavy coat back at the ville, knowing that it would be more of a hindrance than an aid. Her jumpsuit clung to her body, molded to her shape by the damp air and the sweat of exertion. Her titian hair was plastered to her head, the limp tendrils swirling against the skin of her throat and neck.

"Makes the forest heat worse," she agreed. "Trouble is, I can't say I'll be glad when we're out of here, 'cause it just goes from one set of problems to another."

Ryan nodded. "I'm not sure we should do this during the day. It'd be much cooler in the night, and offer us more cover."

"Night by the time we get there—mebbe that's what Harvey's figuring on," Krysty mused. "Mebbe he feels we'll all have cooled down by the time we get there. Except that we'll all be exhausted."

"Trouble with that coldheart is that every time he says something, you get the idea that there's a whole lot more he won't say," Ryan mused quietly, keeping his phrasing a touch cryptic in case he should be overheard too much.

Krysty silently agreed, a feeling of nausea sweeping across her when she considered Harvey and Jenna. What kind of a power base were they attempting to build, and would the sec chief use this attack as a means of getting rid of his baron?

They continued in silence for some time. Gradually, the path grew wider, the shrubbery and undergrowth less dense. The ruins of the buildings that constituted this section of old Seattle became more and more visible. They were also more whole than the fragments that remained deeper into the forest.

The path widened into an old road, with the fragments of a sidewalk still barely visible through the creepers. Storefronts and apartment buildings became apparent, and once again the city took on the aspect of what, in the predark world, Mildred had heard of the remains of Angkor Wat, the Vietnamese city in the jungle. Vietnam had been a buzzword for the generation before her, and was now just a memory, but for Mildred as she looked around, she figured she had an idea of what the ruined city had to have looked like to U.S. Army units who had stumbled on it in the middle of war.

Except that Angkor Wat had taken thousands of years to evolve to the ghostly jungle city, whereas the nukes and rad mutation had achieved this in a fraction of the time.

In the silence of the march, J.B. had time to think. The difference between this section of old Seattle and the area where he and Ryan had met up with Trader and Abe again—it seemed like forever, though it couldn't have been that long—was immense. The way in which rad-ravaged nature set up areas of complete contrast was frightening. The way there had been dense forest on one side of the redoubt and virtual desert on the other when they had arrived…

The train of thought brought the Armorer back to the Illuminated Ones. He didn't entirely share Ryan's views on the remnants of the old secret society. Although the bizarrely clothed sec force they had encountered on the old blacktop had arrived in a working wag that sounded well tuned, and they had the laser blasters that worked okay, still it seemed to J.B. that they had been far too keen to firefight and ask questions later. They seemed to have the tech, while Alien's ancestors had kept the ideals. So even if there was a stockpile of old tech they were sitting on, even if their Erewhon was the promised land away from the struggle and shit of everyday Deathlands living, there was no guarantee they would want to share it. And if there were more of them, with those laser blasters, then it would be a very uneven firefight to get pulled into.

He knew Ryan better than almost anyone. He trusted him, both as a man and for his tactical judgment. But even so, the Armorer's more suspicious and cautious nature could see them getting themselves caught beyond a rock and a hard place.

His train of thought was lost as the war party, straggling slightly but still fairly compact, turned a corner and reached an old intersection he recognized too well.

On the left was the old apartment building where they had stood on an upper floor and observed the Sunchildren. Ahead of them stretched the road out of the old ville. The two-lane blacktop was about an hour's march away, and on the other side of it the ville of Samtvogel.

Say an hour and a half at their current pace. J.B. breathed in the hot air. It was less humid now and would soon become dry. The heat would also be direct as there would be no deflecting vegetation.

It was going to be tough. They would be exposed, and although there was no chance of their being ambushed, it did mean that they would have to stand and fight if a rival party advanced. There would be no cover.

Which was why an advance scouting party had been sent ahead.

J.B. wondered how they were faring. Obviously, there was no trouble as they hadn't doubled back with a warning. But they had been in the heat a whole lot longer.

"EASY ON THE WATER, Whitey. We need it a lot more than you."

"Why?"

"'Cause there's a whole lot more of us."

Ant creased up with laughter, Dee cackling and shaking his head, dreadlocks flying in the arid air.

"Man, you are one stupe mother," he gasped between the laughter. "Any fool knows that us brothers got the skin for this rad-heat weather. Shit, we already got tans. That was Mama's gift to us."

"Will you two shut the fuck up?" Blake yelled. "We're supposed to be an advance scouting party, and here we are making enough fuckin' noise to drown out a gaudy house."

"So who's yelling, man?" Ant asked in a mocking soft tone.

Blake narrowed his eyes. "They should have left you guys back at Raw. You're still jolted out of your fuckin' skulls."

Dee smiled, his eyes sparkling with the chemical high. "True, my friend, true. But that's kind of good in a way, you know? It means we won't give a fuck if some mutie son of a bitch takes our legs away. Just keep fighting.''

Jak sealed the canteen of water and returned it to the pouch that was slung around his waist. Despite the heat, he had kept on his camou jacket, protecting his white skin as much as possible from the searing sun. One of the problems of his albino heritage was that he burned easily, and in the cancerous sun of a postnuke atmosphere, he had to be careful. Sunstroke was a minor thing, but it could get you chilled if you weren't one hundred percent focused during a fire-fight. For the twins, it wasn't a problem. Their dark skins were better adapted than Jak's to the sun, the extra pigment giving them that fraction more protection. As for Blake, his wizened and weathered brown skin was a testament to the number of patrols he had undertaken in the sun.

The advance scouting party was four strong. Harvey had picked Ant and Dee because they survived better in the sun, and because they were junkheads who were still high on jolt. The powerful narcotic had a tendency to affect people in different ways, perhaps because of the different and minute mutations that had followed the period of skydark. In the case of the dreadlocked twins, it acted as a stimulant to their senses, and dulled their perception of danger. They were ready to fight.

Blake was one of Harvey's senior men. He had survived longer than anyone except the sec chief himself, and had spent a long time in the desert regions. He was the obvious party leader.

It was Blake who had insisted that Jak come with

them. His admiration for Jak's fighting skills, and the bond that had formed, told the experienced sec man that Jak's instincts, along with his own experience, would act as a perfect foil for the twins' jolt-enduced recklessness. The albino, trusting the sec man's judgment, had agreed.

The scouting party had set out with forty-five minutes head start on the rest of the war party. That was enough time for them to get a good lead, but not so long that they would be out of reach should they discover anything.

The journey out through the forest had been uneventful. The twins were high, and chattered incessantly, yielding little to Blake's pleas for them to keep the noise down. He and Jak said little, trying to block out the prattle of the twins and try to discern any sounds from the undergrowth that may speak of a mutie raid. It wasn't an immediate worry, but there was a chance that Sunchild had rallied his people immediately on his return, and was planning yet another, larger retaliatory raid. There was also the chance of a random mutie party in search of sacrifices. If they chanced on the advance scout party and the noise the twins were making acted as enough cover, then the scouts wouldn't even make it out of the forest.

But things were quiet, and the twins only ceased to talk incessantly when the scouting party had traversed beyond the edge of old Seattle, entering the fringes of the desert area.

"Typical of you stupes," Blake remarked, "to stop fuckin' yammering when it don't matter no more."

"It's the heat, man," Ant replied.

"Kind of dries your throat too much to talk," Dee finished.

So, apart from a few outbursts actuated by things like Jak taking water, the party continued in silence. They trudged wearily across the arid desert, the few scraps of scrub tree and mutated, twisted cactus providing not even the briefest respite from the sun, burning orange and purple in the chem-stained sky.

After the twins' last outburst, they continued in silence for some time. Jak kept his eyes, aching from the bright light, cast down apart from the occasional sweep around and a very occasional glance up to judge the position of the sun.

It was sinking lower in the sky, although the heat at this point was still harsh, beating down hard.

"Soon be dark," he husked through a phlegm-blocked and dried throat.

"Not soon enough for me," Blake replied. "Too exposed out here in the day."

"What you moaning about, man?" Dee questioned him. "We don't have to fight them. We see a party coming, we just turn tail and head back with the information, covering our asses on the way. Shit, they can't ambush us here, can they?" he added, opening his arms expansively to the empty wastes of the desert.

Blake shook his head. "Nearer we are to them, the tireder we are and the fresher they are. Get that through your jolt-fucked skull and think about it."

Jak silently agreed with the older sec man. They were beaten down by the sun and weary from the journey. It was possible that an outrunning mutie party could catch them up and force a stand before they reached the main war party.

On the other hand, so far there had been no sign of any activity. With luck, the Sunchildren were still licking their wounds from the previous day's firefight.

It was only when he looked up and saw the pall of smoke seemingly rising from the earth that Jak realized how well protected the valley of the Sunchildren was. On their previous, dark-shrouded excursion, he hadn't realized that the sudden dip of the valley, almost a hollow crater, made the ville invisible on three of its four sides.

They were approaching obliquely, Blake leading them out in a southwesterly direction so that they couldn't be seen from the gentle incline that formed one side of the valley and serviced the only road into the ville.

The twins had fallen silent as they drew nearer, their attention becoming more focused on their task. It was eerily silent, despite the nearby presence of the ville. The bowl of the valley acted as a sound barrier, and kept the sound contained within its natural walls.

Blake indicated for the twins to spread out to his left, and for Jak to move across to the right.

"I just want us to have a look-see what they might be doing down there. Don't do anything to attract their attention, for fuck's sake. We just want them to go about their business, see what they're about, then get the hell back to the main party."

"Why can't we just give them a little taste, dude?" Ant asked, running his hand lovingly along the barrel of his newly cleaned shotgun.

Blake shot him a warning glance. "I know you

boys got a reason to hate the muties, but there's still just four of us. We can't keep them all down there until the others arrive. Besides, Harv wants us to scout out trouble and report back…and he's the boss, right?'' The twins didn't answer immediately, so Blake rapped again. ''Right?''

''Guess so,'' Dee murmured. His brother nodded.

''Okay, so let's do it,'' Blake said softly.

Jak moved away from the other three, leaving them in the rapidly darkening light to move around the rim of the valley. Despite the fact that it would have been almost impossible for him to be seen, he still kept low to the ground, moving in a light-footed crouching run that raised little dust from the dry earth around.

Dropping to the ground so that he was on all fours, then lowering himself so that he was on his belly, Jak advanced to the lip of the valley. The dust itched on his exposed skin, granules of the dry earth insinuating themselves under his clothes and irritating him. He blinked the dry dust from his eyes, which were itching and raw. The tears ran down his cheeks where his eyes watered. Not content with this, the dust caught in his throat and clogged his already dry mouth.

But it was worth it. Anything that cut down the chances of being spotted was worth the effort and discomfort he may have to endure. He could only trust that the twins were doing the same. He knew Blake would be, recognizing another born survivor in the wizened sec man.

Jak carefully picked his way over the wire fencing that ran around the top of the valley. He ignored the stench of the rotting bird corpses that were speared on the wire at regular intervals as a deterrent. He had no fear of dead things, only a caution against cutting himself on the wire and letting any infections from the dead creatures enter his bloodstream.

He took his time, negotiating the wire carefully. There was no one in sight, and no need to hurry. Once over, he picked up speed once more.

As he neared the lip of the valley, the sound increased. Most of it consisted of the everyday sounds of living, amplified and distorted by being trapped within the confines of the valley's bowl. Sound overlapped on sound so that it was difficult for Jak to pick out individual noises. He was, however, aware that in the mainstream of the noise were the sounds of some chanting.

It was only when he was in a position to look over the lip and down into the valley that the source of the chanting became identifiable.

The vast majority of the Sunchildren in Samtvogel were going about their business in a manner that changed little, whether norm or mutie: children ran and played, women cooked and made clothes from the rags, men fashioned weapons from what was at hand or made tools. But in the center of the ville, something a little out of the ordinary was taking place.

The main arena, where Jak and the others had recovered the chilled children, was mostly empty. Only mostly. A small group of Sunchildren—all male— were gathered in their bright robes, their assortment of salvaged and homemade knives visible on their makeshift belts. They were chanting along to cues from their leader.

Even at such a distance, Jak could see that the mutie leader now only had the use of one arm, the limb that had been grazed by a blaster shot now limp and possibly gangrenous, covered by a primitive dressing. If it was infected, then Samtvogel would soon lose its leader, which may mean that he figured he had nothing to lose on one last throw of the dice.

This notion was amplified by the fact that the mutie leader was standing in front of the painted and decorated predark nuke, gesturing to it while he led the chanting, as though offering it a prayer.

There was nothing in his action to indicate that he knew how to arm and trigger the nuke, or even that its old tech was still operable. But it wasn't a certainty, and they couldn't depend on anything except certainties.

Jak withdrew his head and crawled back from the edge before raising himself from the dust so that he was on all fours rather than flat to the earth. He snorted the dust from his nose and throat, hawking a lump of blackened phlegm onto the ground with a noise that sounded louder for the quietness around.

He headed back to the wire, and over it. Once more he avoided contact with the insect-crawling bird corpses. Jak would much rather have fought a dozen stickies than an infection. Once over the wire, he looked back to the valley.

They were beginning to light fires and lamps down in Samtvogel, the smoke of the cooking fires being joined by these, and the light reflecting up a little way, prevented from spreading out by the enclosed valley. It seemed to form a small dome of light over the valley, a dim beacon in the encroaching dusk.

A light they would have to extinguish.

Jak heard a low whistle coming from Blake's direction, followed by two, more distant, replies. For his own part, Jak whistled low, cracked by the dryness of his mouth and throat. He turned and headed back to where he had left the others, maintaining his crouching run even though it was almost certain that they were alone along the top of the valley and were safe from observation.

Ant and Dee were already with Blake when Jak arrived back. The four men quickly exchanged what they had seen. It all added up to the same thing: Sunchild had something in mind, but there was no immediate attack and there was no increased guard.

"Okay," Blake decided, "we head back to the main party, tell them what we've seen."

"They'll be exhausted after coming through in this heat," Ant began.

"Mebbe Harv'll let them rest before the attack, cool down in the night."

Blake laughed shortly. "Hell no, boys. You know Harv better than that. He'll just want to go in hell for leather. Hit 'em hard and hit 'em fast. Just in case."

Jak kept silent, but wondered why Harvey would want to risk additional losses by sending in people who were tired and not one hundred percent after such a long journey. He suspected it may have something to do with the fact that Alien would, as the fair baron he was, put himself in the front line of the action. The older man would be weary, and Jak knew that he wasn't a good fighter. More than that, the baron had a woman back in Raw who was in some way connected to the sec chief, and to whatever was going on behind that metal door.

And just mebbe it had something to do with that and with whatever had happened to Dean. Because Jak was as certain as could be that the boy wasn't in Samtvogel.

All this went through his mind as they began the journey back toward the two-lane blacktop. They had spent almost half an hour on their survey, which meant that the war party should only be about fifteen minutes away. If the light had been better, then they could possibly have seen the party advancing. But as it was, the sun had now set, and the cold air closed around Jak like a vise, colder somehow after the intense heat of the day.

As they marched back, it was as much the thought of Dean being trapped still in Raw as the fall in temperature that made the albino shiver.

THERE WAS a blackness.

A blackness like the thickest blanket placed over him, a blackness that enveloped his face, cutting off air, as well as light, wrapping itself around his head until it blocked out sound. Blocked out everything, so that the only impressions he had of anything around him were the faintest of impressions, muffled in the blackness.

But gradually it improved. Gradually, things began to filter back. Slowly at first, but then with an increasing speed until the sound became too loud, every last breath from his own body like the rasping of a saw on metal, every step in the room like the pounding of a hammer on a wall. The light became stronger than staring directly into the sun, creeping through his closed eyelids until he screwed his eyes tight, so tight that he felt he would pop his eyeballs back into his forebrain.

And the taste. Like raw earth and salt as his own sweat and dust from the air around coated his tongue, matting on his taste buds.

The air suddenly came back to him, acrid with sweat and fear, great drafts of air, the slightest breeze like a hurricane in his nostrils, the previous struggle for air now replaced with the fear that he would drown in the onrush of oxygen.

All the time he tried to move his arms and legs. But they were constrained still. At first he couldn't tell, as his body felt detached from his consciousness, and then as his body and senses became overly sensitized it felt as though every muscle and tendon were borne down by their own weight, pained by its own sensitivity.

Somewhere deep within him, he clung to the knowledge that he was still alive, and that he wasn't mad. He knew that this had to be part of the drug testing he had been told about, and that these sensations would soon pass. The balance would soon be restored.

That part of him that wondered if she really knew what she was doing, and if he would make it back still sane or still alive, he quelled with a ruthlessness he could only find from the knowledge that giving in to it would mean certain insanity.

So he clung, and rode the wave.

However long it may take. That is, assuming he had any real idea of what time was anymore.

WHEN HE FELT it was safe to open his eyes, she was looking into them.

"Ah, so you're still with me, young Cawdor. For a while there, I thought you might be lost...alive, yes, but reduced to something less than a vegetable."

Jenna smiled. Her sharp features were softened by her broad mouth. She had even, good teeth, and although her lips were thin they were red enough in contrast to her dark complexion to warm her features. Even her hard, glittering black eyes seemed for a moment to become warmer.

"I don't want you to become that," she continued. "I have other ideas for you." Her voice took on a husky edge, clogged with desire.

Dean felt his body respond to the change in her voice, rising to the occasion. It was when he felt her hand fondling him that he realized he had to be naked. At some point in his drug-induced journey, he had been briefly unshackled and stripped.

Jenna laughed softly, feeling the change in him. "So you're pissed at missing a chance of escape, eh?" She gently manipulated him back to his former state.

"What... Why?" Dean croaked, unable to voice the questions that raced through his head, his parched voice failing to respond with the requisite speed.

"You'll find out in time," she replied softly. "The good thing is I don't need to change your eyes, already blue like your father, like the perfect ones. Pity about the hair. Mebbe the genetic modifications I've been trying will help. Old gene tech is a bit unreliable still, even though I've been trying to pull all the old notes, research and equipment together. Still, you've responded well so far.''

Dean couldn't keep the fear out of his eyes. What had she been doing to him?

Jenna sensed his unease. ''Just a few modifications, sweetie. They won't kill you. Mebbe make you more productive. I'm going to need a good stud, and you're old enough to produce. I know you are, because I've already milked and tested you. You're not firing blanks, boy.''

Dean looked away, feeling his cheeks run hot. Her hand was still stroking him, keeping him erect, and he felt strangely ashamed at the way Jenna had used him while he was unconscious.

The woman kissed him gently on the cheek. ''Don't feel upset, sweetie. That raddled and seedless old fool I'm married to can't give me the child I want. Besides, it'd be impure. So would Harvey's, despite the enjoyment I get from him. But he's a moron. You and your father, though...I can see the both of you giving me the progeny I need. With you or your father to give me the new barons, and my experiments to perfect and clone the others...life'll be peachy again.''

Chapter Fourteen

"Dark night! But it's cold and I'm tired," the Armorer chattered through frozen teeth.

"Why, John, that's almost a joke," Mildred commented mildly, looking up at the stars that still shone in the clear sky. Funny how it always surprised her they were still there. Just because the whole damned world had changed, why should they?

She was cold, as well. Like Krysty, she had left her jacket back in Raw, unwilling to face the humidity of the forest and the heat of the day with the thick protective covering. Problem was, the night had come down too quickly, and they still had distance to cover.

"What is Harvey's little game here, John?" she continued. "Wouldn't we have been better setting out at night?"

The taciturn J.B. nodded. "Mebbe it suits his purpose better. Certainly not for the good of all."

"Which should be his job..." Mildred looked ahead of her. The moon was only a crescent, casting little light on the arid and flat plain. The fact that they hadn't been visited by the scouting party suggested the way ahead was clear. But how far did they have to go now before reaching Samtvogel.

The same question was crossing Ryan's mind as he marched beside Alien. The baron was breathing hard with the pace of the march, and the one-eyed warrior

was concerned that the man would be too exhausted
to fight well when they reached Samtvogel. Like J.B.,
Ryan wondered if this was part of some hidden
agenda from the sec chief, a way of disposing of a
popular baron without raising any suspicion.

"Hey, Harvey," Ryan called, keeping his voice
low but loud enough to carry, "how far now?"

"About a mile and a half, mebbe two miles, Cyclops. Why, you getting' tired there, boy?"

"No, but mebbe others are."

The sec chief looked back over his shoulder. The
light was poor, but Ryan was sure that Harvey's gaze
was on the baron rather than on himself.

"No time to rest," the sec chief said simply. "We
just gotta press on."

Krysty felt her hair tighten about her as the whispered words reached her ears. She was cold, shivering
and tired, but still her mutie sense was sharp enough
to pick up on Harvey's intent. At the same time, she
felt a sudden lift within her.

"Jak," she whispered.

"The scouting party is near," Doc called, walking
close to Krysty and catching the lilt in her voice.

Within a few minutes, black shapes appeared
against the darkness of the night. Two large, two
small: the scouts.

The war party halted under the stars, gathering
around the scouting party while Blake relayed the information gathered. There were no guards or patrols,
but it seemed that Sunchild himself and a few trusted
Sunchildren were preparing for something.

"Did they look like they were ready for an immediate attack?" Ryan asked, aware of the stare Har-

vey gave him, aware that by speaking before the sec chief he was speaking out of turn.

Jak shook his head, the pure white of his flowing hair seeming almost incandescent, like a flare in the darkness.

"No. If Sunchild know to trigger nuke, it gone by now."

Doc interjected. "May I?" he asked politely. Then without waiting for an answer said, "Did Sunchild have any kind of computer tech visible? Or perhaps he had the cone of the nuke open. Some of them have the tech within, so that they could be set off in the silos in the event of an invasion. Or it could be a remote control, handheld. But then he may have to—"

"You know a fuck of a lot about this shit," Harvey growled, interrupting Doc.

"I have had, um, some experience, you may say," Doc said softly, avoiding eye contact with the sec chief.

He returned his attention to Jak. "Was there anything like that?"

The albino shook his head. "Look like muties praying to it like god."

Doc nodded, ignoring some of the nervous laughs from the war party. "This is good. I would say that we are in no immediate danger. Perhaps," he added, eyeing the baron speculatively, as well as a few of the older members of the war party, "we could rest awhile."

Harvey shook his head. "Hit hard, hit fast and don't let the fuckers even get the slightest clue as to what's happening to them. We rest, they could send out their own scouting party."

"That's unlikely," J.B. murmured. "And if they do, then we just chill them. No one'll notice until it's too late."

There was a murmur of agreement among the weary war party, stilled by a gesture from Harvey.

"Who the fuck is the sec boss here?" he hissed at the Armorer. "We do what I say...right, Alien?"

The baron looked uneasy. "Well, I feel like the rest would do me good. But in these situations, I put you in sole charge, and it would be wrong of me to override this just for my own convenience."

"Okay," Harvey snapped, casting an eye over the assembled party. "Then we carry on."

ANOTHER FIFTEEN MINUTES of marching brought them close to Samtvogel. With Blake in the lead, they took the same oblique course as before, leading off and away from the sloping side of the valley and toward the obscurity of the steep inclines. The glow of the ville's lighting cast a wan illumination over the immediate area.

As they stood outside the corpse-covered wire, two of the three women in charge of the armory came forward. They were each carrying one of the drumfed RPK machine blasters. J.B. could see the mounting tripods, folded, in backpacks. The fat woman who had questioned the Armorer about the blaster to test his knowledge spared a second to wink at him before speaking to Harvey.

"If you want us to set these up on this side and that—" she gestured to the far side of the valley

"—then you need to give us help. We'll each need someone to help set and mount these bastards, and to first get us over that wire. Awkward with this," she finished, tapping the heavy blaster.

Harvey agreed and detailed Ant and Dee to assist. The heavy sec men were agreeable, and adjusted their wrist chrons so that they would be able to synchronize the beginning of the attack.

"That's how long we've got now, people," Harvey noted as the four people went forth to set up their posts. "Time to get our shit together. We know we can whip their asses—we just need to get it right."

The sec chief divided his forces, detailing parties to fan out and cover all along the bowed ridge of the valley, ending with two parties to take either side of the only road out.

"The plan is simple. We go in when the covering fire has started. That'll be over our heads, and will cease when we get into Samtvogel itself. We want the nuke, and we want Sunchild. We also want to find Cyclops Jr. dead or alive. We take him back no matter what—agreed?"

The last was directed at Ryan. Harvey was eyeing him carefully as he spoke the word, searching for the slightest sign of reaction. Ryan remained stony-faced, controlling the emotions that ran through him, knowing that the sec chief was looking for the slightest sign of weakness. Ryan was sure that Dean wasn't in the valley, but he was still his son, and the thought of him chilled like the children they had recovered previously made him shudder inside.

But not outwardly. Harvey turned away, dissatisfied by the lack of reaction. He continued. "When we've secured that objective, we trash the place. Completely. For once and for all we rid ourselves of the mutie scum—no offense, Whitey—and drive them out. If possible, we chill them all. Every last shitter.''

"Are you certain about that?" Alien asked, his voice strong and firm in the night. "We have never, in Raw, acted in such a manner—"

"Baron, you want them to escalate, get more and more trouble? If so, then fine. But you put me in charge of sec, and I say we ice the fuckers once and for all.''

The baron demurred. "Very well.''

Ryan felt J.B.'s hand on his arm and his breath in his ear.

"What's the idea, Ryan? The longer we stay around, the more of us stand to buy the farm...or is that the idea?"

"Mebbe. And mebbe not just Alien. Triple red, J.B. That coldheart may just decide to chill us at the same time.''

The one-eyed warrior felt, rather than saw, the assent from the Armorer as he melted into the crowd to spread the word to Mildred, Jak and Doc. Krysty had been close enough to hear.

"Okay, let's get to it," Harvey commanded.

The flame-haired woman lightly kissed Ryan on the cheek. It was a cover for her to whisper, "Be careful. Dean's not here, and we've got to get back to find him.''

THE RPKs WERE set up on each side, the drum-mounted ammo in place. On their respective side, Ant and Dee both secured the tripods, and left the two

Armorers seated, with the blasters at the requisite angle. The two dreadlocked sec men then both moved away as one after the final check, readying their shotguns and checking their wrist chrons.

Around them, stretching in a thin line around the lip of the valley, the war party readied their own weapons.

On opposite sides of the valley, the dreadlocked sec men checked their wrist chrons. As one, they turned to the Armorers seated behind the RPKs.

"Now!"

The firing began in short, controlled bursts, the twin machine blasters rending the air with tracer fire and peals of noise, louder for the quiet that had preceded it. As J.B. had pointed out when questioned earlier on the blasters, they were capable of 660 rounds per minute, but to fire at such a pace would heat up the barrel to such a degree that it would ignite the ammo left in the drum and set the blaster on a rapid and uncontrollable fire.

So each Armorer kept her firing to short bursts, rattling off fifty or sixty rounds before pausing and counting to ten. Then another fifty or sixty. The barrels of the RPKs were soon red-hot, but not the white-hot that would ignite the drum. The pauses were enough to keep the barrel just beneath that crucial temperature.

The tripods were raised at an angle that would keep the fire going over the heads of the war party as it descended the steep slopes that formed three sides of the valley of Samtvogel. The majority of the ammo would land toward the center of the ville, where the majority of the men were clustered. The outlying areas were where the women and the children were sequestered in their tents and shacks. Some of the shells cannoned into the faded and peeling stucco of the ranch houses, chipping off plaster that raised choking dust in the smoky light.

As he scrambled down the side of the valley, Ryan could see that the muties gathered in the center of the ville were thrown into confusion by the sudden attack. Some of them gathered around Sunchild in an attempt to shield him, but the mutie leader roared and directed them away. Some of them disappeared into one of the ranch houses, and Ryan guessed that was where they kept their small armory. They had already proved themselves next to useless in a firefight, but nonetheless it could prove a problem in close quarters, where a stray blast could go anywhere.

As he reached the bottom of the incline, he was pulled up short by the figure of a mutie looming up at him out of the semidarkness. There were fewer fires at the edges of the ville, and longer and deeper pools of shadow. This was the danger zone, as the invaders were still descending and could be caught easily as they reached the valley floor.

The one-eyed warrior was ready for this. Although the SIG-Sauer was in his hand, he couldn't rely on finding much time and space to reload, so was unwilling to waste ammo. As his combat boots thudded on the dirt floor, his hand snaked down his thigh and withdrew the panga.

The mutie was screaming wordlessly, a high note of fear mixed in with the savagery. As the misshapen creature approached, Ryan could see that it was a woman, the pendulous and wrinkled breasts riding free of the stained and patched dyed robes that she wore. She had only half a face, the majority of her lower jaw and one side of her cheek being a mass of scar tissue and weals. She was virtually bald, and her toothless mouth was open in the scream, strings of drool running between her lips.

Her eyes were lit by hate, fear and a light of pure insanity. She was brandishing a large, scythe-shaped blade that had a small wooden handle. The blade, even in the poor light, seemed to be stained and pitted with something that was probably blood.

Ryan had no intention of letting his own blood be added to that which had dried on the blade. He held the panga in front of him, across his body, waiting for the optimum moment.

The mutie approached him in an open stance. She was shuffling rather than running, which slowed her enough for him to relax into the move rather than hurry it, for she was holding the blade above her head, ready to bring it down in a sweep.

This left the right-hand side of her body completely exposed to attack, the line down her arm and ribs undefended from any blow that may be struck.

Ryan stepped forward, ducking under the blow as her arm fell uselessly past his shoulder, the scything blade hacking at empty air. At the same time, he brought his own blade across and up, so that he sliced beneath the ribs, carving open the soft flesh and spilling the mutie's intestines into the dirt with a slooshing sound and a rise of steam as the warm flesh and blood hit the cold night air. The blade continued its upward thrust, carving into vital organs before being withdrawn as Ryan stepped back.

The mutie woman stood for a moment, a bewildered light in her eyes. Then the light died, and she tumbled forward onto the ground at Ryan's feet.

JAKE, THE HUGE, bearlike sec man, roared loudly and had a blood lust in his eyes. Like the berserkers of Viking legend, he had almost tranced himself into a state where he had no feelings or emotions, no sense of morality or justice, nor even any sense of his own being beyond being a killing machine.

Which was exactly what Harvey wanted from him. The sec chief had seen Jake in this state before, and had spent no little part of the journey persuading the sec man that he should adopt this persona for the raid. The bearlike, grizzled fighter had taken little persuading, and had spent the few minutes at the top of the valley, waiting for the signal of covering fire, to put himself into that state where he saw only fresh meat for the chilling.

And now he was in full cry, a deep-throated roar escaping him, barely registering the sweeping knives and rough-hewed blades of the muties as they attempted to stop him. He had discarded his Heckler & Koch blaster in favor of two long samurai-type swords, the strangely shaped blades arcing through the air before him in a complex pattern, sweeping and crossing in a way that prevented the mutie Sunchildren from getting too close. There were a few random stabs that penetrated his defenses, and the jagged edges of blades had cut and marked him, streams of blood ribboning down his chest and back. He seemed not to register them, except that it spurred him to greater savagery.

The flashing blades cut through soft mutie flesh, hacked at jagged bone, with barely a pause.

"DARK NIGHT! Could have sent that big bastard in on his own," J.B. muttered.

"Be fair. You don't want him to have all the fun, do you?" Downey replied, snapping off another round from the Sharps, scoring cleanly through the forehead of a passing mutie. The mutie staggered on for a few steps, not seeming to realize she was dead, before crumpling into a heap.

"Fun?" the Armorer grunted, rattling off another short blast from the Uzi into a group of muties emerging from one of the ranch houses. He and Downey had both gravitated toward covering the ranch houses, the two of them assuming that any blasters the Sunchildren had would best be stopped as soon as they came out of what passed for an armory, rather than let loose as a random factor into the firefight—except that it was much more of a night chill than a firefight.

J.B. had descended the eastern slope of the valley almost on his butt, sliding down through a cloud of dust and feeling the rough earth tearing at his fatigues. It didn't matter if he ripped some skin on the way down. If he was going to use the M-4000 to maximum effect, then it was necessary to arrive as quickly as possible.

Hitting bottom at a run, the Armorer had headed for his self-appointed task: the ranch-house armory. There was still confusion as he sprinted through a crowd of mutie Sunchildren, using the Tekna knife to carve a path. The blade was razor sharp, the muties keen to avoid it. He was relying on the element of surprise and the fact that others were following to cover his back on the outer fringes.

But now he was coming into the main area of light, lamps and fires making the central arena of Samtvogel seem almost in daylight. There was a clutch of muties around the ranch house, blocking his way.

Without breaking stride, J.B. sheathed the knife, and brought up the M-4000, which he had been cradling in his left arm, so that he grasped it with both hands. He stopped for a moment, planting both feet firmly to take the recoil, and fired the charge of barbed metal fléchettes into the packed group of Sunchildren, who were too bewildered by this sudden apparition to move.

The white-hot metal, shot at enormous velocity and spreading over a wide area as it left the confines of the barrel, bought death and pain to the group, which disintegrated suddenly into a mass of writhing, blood-stained flesh. Some of the muties at the front of the group took the full brunt, their faces and torsos ripped to shreds by the load. Their already chilled remains were flung backward into the group, the force pushing other muties down and saving their lives—at least temporarily. They thus avoided the main load of death, but were still wounded by the storm of fléchettes that had spread low and wide.

The Armorer had wasted not a second in slinging the M-4000 and bringing the Uzi into play, his short bursts directed at mopping up those sections of the heaving mass that still seemed to be alive and dangerous.

Passing the now chilled pile of mutie flesh, the Armorer established a safe position by a sheet-metal shack, firing a quick blast through the opening to clear the inside of any possible danger. Covering his back, he began to pick off any muties that passed his view, with his attention primarily focused on the ranch-house windows and doorway, from which the wood and glass had long since disappeared.

"Only me," a breathless cry had announced as J.B. had whirled to greet the sounds coming up behind him. "Had the same idea, eh?" the sardonic Downey announced, settling himself in beside J.B. and sweeping the long, iron-gray hair from his sweat-spangled face. Somewhere along the line, his habitual ponytail had come loose, and the strands of hair across his vision were both irritating and dangerous.

J.B. could smell the powder and heat from the discharged Sharps, and knew that the sec man had been busy at his task, and that he, too, had the foresight to target the ranch house.

"Better to chill them as they emerge, not let the bastards get those blasters all over the show." The sec man grinned in answer to J.B.'s unasked question.

And now they were picking off passing muties and had a group holed up in the ranch house, loosing blaster shots that whined high and wide past the sec men.

There were also shots from inside the ranch house itself.

"Think we could leave them to chill themselves like that?" Downey questioned. "Guess I'm getting cramp around here."

"Could risk a gren," J.B. answered. Squinting through his spectacles, the Armorer took a hand from his Uzi to push his fedora back on his head and scratch idly at his forehead. "Doesn't seem to be too many of ours around this point, and the house looks strong enough to contain the blast. Problem is, what if they've got a stock of grens in there themselves?"

"Good call," Downey replied thoughtfully, realizing why the Armorer hadn't risked a gren before. He looked around. There was no localized fighting. The ville was small, but large enough for there to be none of the war party within a radius of about fifty yards. "Wouldn't they have blown themselves up by now, if they had any?" he asked.

J.B. pursed his lips and blew. "Odds are," he said simply, reaching into one of the pockets stuffed with ammo and grens that littered his jacket. He produced a gren, pulled the pin and rose to a standing position. A seemingly lazy swing of the arm, along with a perfect eye for distance, saw the gren arc in the air and land through one of the windows.

"Down," J.B. commanded, pushing Downey to the rear of the shack.

The explosion was muffled, only the open doorway and windows allowing the force to escape. The structure of the building seemed to blow out, almost to the point of crumbling, before returning to normal. The sound of the ammo supplies firing off filled the immediate area, and then died.

The building was darkened and still, all the more obvious in the light and confusion surrounding.

"Guess that's seen to that," Downey remarked. "Let's go and get that mother nuke, my friend."

J.B. grunted his assent, and they left the shelter of the tin shack to enter the fray.

KRYSTY FOUND herself alongside Rankine and Bodie. The rangy sec man was striding through the mayhem with ease, firing off shots from his .303 Lee Enfield and then swinging the stock to club Sunchildren out of his path.

"Impressive dude, eh?" Bodie panted in Krysty's ear, the exertion showing on his fat face. He was using his blaster sparingly, a Tekna knife like the Armorer's clasped in his other pudgy hand. "Me, I'm not really much of a fighter. Always get nerves, you know? Talk too fuckin' much, like I am now. Nerves, y'see?"

Krysty raised her blaster and took off the top half of an advancing stickie's head with one shot. There were still a few of the stickies that had been in Sunchild's attack party at the ville, and they were now robed like the other Sunchildren—although instantly identifiable from their tiny eyes, needle-sharp teeth and splayed sucker fingers, as well as their almost bizarre lack of hair.

Bodie whistled. "Nice shootin', babe."

The titian-haired woman turned to him. "Don't call me 'babe.'" Then added, "Look out!"

Distracted by his nervousness and the finely muscled female fighting machine at his side, Bodie hadn't noticed a robed Sunchild come flying at him from his unprotected left-hand side. He was turned toward Krysty, and although her cry had made him turn, it wasn't quick enough. The mutie was on him in a flying leap, bellowing wordlessly as he clawed at the sec man, attacking even while still in midair.

The two hit the hard-packed earth with a thud that drove the air from both their bodies. Krysty couldn't blast the mutie as he and Bodie were too entwined, so she grabbed a handful of robe and flesh from near the mutie's neck and heaved upward.

The muscles in her arms stood out, and the cords on her neck grew taut. Her flaming hair whirled wildly with a life of its own as the mutie flew back in the air.

While he was still above the ground, she had leveled her Smith & Wesson blaster, putting a slug into his soft chest.

"Wow!" Bodie exclaimed. "That was something else!"

Krysty shook her head in amazement. "Just be careful unless you want to be chilled. I won't be beside you all the time," she added, chucking his chin as though he were a child.

Before Bodie had a chance to say much else, Krysty had disappeared into the fray, leaving him to watch his own back.

DOC HAD BEEN one of the last to hit the floor of the valley, picking his way down carefully so that he wouldn't fall and either chill himself or be a burden for any well-meaning Raw dweller who was close.

He needn't have worried. When he reached bottom, Mildred was waiting for him, using her ZKR to pick off approaching muties.

"By the Three Kennedys! Could it be that you are awaiting mine own humble presence?" Doc muttered as he righted himself.

"Well, I figured a crazy old buzzard like you may need some nursemaiding," Mildred said.

"Less than graciously put, my good woman, but nonetheless I appreciate the sentiment."

"Then stop talking and let's get moving," Mildred said quickly. "I figure it would be best for all concerned if you and me got to that nuke first, seeing as we're the only ones present who may have some idea of the tech."

"If Harvey is that close to Jenna, then he'll know of the technology involved," Doc replied. Then, as Mildred spared him a glance, he added, "Although I agree that such a thought only reinforces your point."

They began to move into the main body of Samtvogel. By the time that Doc had descended, the battle had moved inward, the advancing force pushing back the surprised Sunchildren until they were almost entirely contained to the central clearing, around their sacrificial altar—and, more importantly, the totem-decorated nuke.

Progress for Doc and Mildred was easy…almost too easy, so much so that an attack from the rear was so unexpected as to almost catch them off guard.

Almost, but not quite. They advanced through the slaughterhouse that was the outer reaches of Samtvogel, stepping over the chilled corpses and the dying, none of whom were conscious or fit enough to put up any kind of fight. Doc cradled the LeMat and had the swordstick unsheathed, but to preserve ammo Mildred picked off the few muties that came within range with her ZKR. There were other pockets of attack who, like themselves, had arrived after the first wave of attack. The main body of fighting was in front, as it was up to the stragglers like themselves to mop up resistance.

It was only because the sounds of strife were in front, and had the echo of distance, that Doc could differentiate the sound of movement from behind them. He whirled with a speed that belied the care with which he had advanced.

Behind himself and Mildred was a group of five muties, three men and two women. Two of the men were wounded, one dragging a heavily bleeding leg, the other with an arm hanging limp and useless. But all five had the fire of battle in their eyes, and were brandishing blades of varying sizes. They were only a few yards away, and advancing rapidly.

Mildred began to turn, but Doc snapped at her, "Eyes front, Doctor. Leave this to me. I would like to feel useful to some degree."

As he spoke, Doc raised the LeMat, and his last words were almost lost in the explosion of the percussion pistol.

The round caught the mutie with the injured arm full in the face. His head disappeared behind a spray of blood, flesh and bone. The woman to his left— perhaps his mate—screamed as she saw him disintegrate in front of her. It was a scream cut short by Doc's next shot, which caught her throat, ripping out her larynx and almost severing her spinal column. The rest of the shots were evenly spread over the group, cutting them down and either mortally wounding or instantly chilling them.

"Onward, onward, Doctor," Doc commanded.

"Yes, sir," Mildred murmured.

JAK HAD BECOME a fighting machine once more. Like Jake, he was primed, honed and let loose on an enemy. But unlike the giant sec man, Jak still kept his entire wits about him. There was a coldness within the albino, as icy as the whiteness of his hair and skin, that enabled him to stay detached in the middle of battle.

The mutie Sunchildren around were no match for the fighting skills of the albino. Eschewing the .357 Magnum Colt Python in a close-fighting situation, he used the leaf-bladed knives to slash his way through the collected tribe, with only one objective in view. Harvey had wanted the ville trashed and scattered, but Alien wanted information, and had made a request of the albino he had noted as such a strong fighter.

"Over to the left, Jak," Blake shouted from a few feet away. He still gripped the 9 mm Walther PPK he favored, but had let off few rounds, preferring to use the long, double-edged bayonet that was in his other fist, the honed blade almost as long as the small sec man's forearm.

Jak moved gracefully and seamlessly away from his compatriot, and to the right of the nuke.

Three passing moves with the knives disposed of dull-witted guards, too slow to even move before their lifeblood pumped from severed arteries.

Sunchild raised a rusting sword and bellowed in rage and frustration at his crumbling empire. He brought the blade down toward Jak's head, but the albino skipped around the blow, allowing the momentum to carry Sunchild forward…enough for Jak to chop at the exposed back of his neck, rendering him unconscious.

"Need alive...for now," the albino muttered as the mutie leader hit the ground.

HARVEY WAS in trouble, and it was all the fault of his own arrogance.

The sec chief had led the charge down the sides of the valley, arriving on the earth-packed floor only shortly after Ryan had chilled his first Sunchild. Like the one-eyed warrior, he had cut a swath through the surprised muties by using his Colt Magnum Carry blaster sparingly, and mostly chilling his opponents with the knife he always carried with him. The old Emerson CQC-7 was a highly prized tactical folding knife, and the razor-sharp blade was maintained by the sec man in the same chisel-sharpened state as when he first acquired it from the armory. Some-how—and the facts were vague enough to be wor-rying to Raw's baron if ever he heard them—the knife had found its way from a passing trader to the armory via the sec chief himself, with no questions asked or answers wanted.

Harvey had wanted the knife, and he had taken steps to acquire it. As with everything, his attention was focused. As it was now focused on attaining the nuke.

But that focus could be one-dimensional, and as the sec chief cut through the swarm of muties, he didn't notice that one of the Sunchildren he had cut wasn't quite chilled.

Ryan was in the vicinity, having fought his way through toward the nuke. Looking across, he saw the injured Sunchild drag herself up from the earth, her robes splattered with blood. A slash from the Emerson had cut her throat, and she had collapsed from the shock. But only veins had been cut, not an artery, and although she would eventually bleed to death, she was mustering all the strength she could for one last assault on the sec chief.

Ryan was in hand-to-hand combat as he saw this, and guessing what was to happen, doubled his efforts to dispose of the mutie he was battling. Shifting his balance, he knocked out the grip the mutie had on him by thrusting his arms up and out. While the Sunchild was off balance, Ryan's own powerful forearms crossed, catching the mutie's head in the middle of the cross. A flexion of the powerful muscles and a twist of his body weight insured that the mutie's soft-boned neck broke.

He was dead before he hit the dirt, and Ryan had already turned his attention to Harvey's predicament.

Ryan covered the few yards in a matter of seconds, but he was still not quick enough. His SIG-Sauer was holstered, and by the time it was unsheathed a clean shot would have been impossible, with the Sunchild and the sec chief too entwined.

Harvey, for his part, was taken completely by surprise. The Sunchild threw herself about his neck, attempting to drag him backward. His attention focused entirely on what was to the front of him, it was only the wiry man's strength that stopped him tumbling back under the sudden force from behind.

Harvey could feel the warm blood trickling from her, her fetid breath in his ear and on his neck, the panting and grunting of her breath as she tried to pull him down with all the strength she had left in her body.

The sec chief fought against it, pulling himself forward and attempting to throw her over his shoulder. But her weight was centered too far down her body, and the whole force was dragging too much for him to get any momentum on his own movements. Even more urgent was the fact that her arms were locked around his throat, and he couldn't breathe properly, gasping for breath. He hacked at her flesh with the Emerson, but in her dying condition she seemed impervious to pain, and not even the razor-sharp blade cutting through the flesh of her fingers could force her to relent.

Ryan could see the difficulty the sec chief was having, and unwound the scarf from his own throat. The long scarf was weighted at each end by carefully concealed and secured weights, which made the scarf a useful and unobtrusive weapon.

Useful like now. With a flick of his powerful wrist, judging the distance exactly with his practiced eye, Ryan kept hold of one end of the scarf and sent the other shooting toward the mutie. The tip of the scarf, weighted as it was, gained momentum in flight and cracked against the temple of the woman's head. A large bruise, weeping a thin trickle of blood, grew up almost as soon as the weight hit home, and she grunted heavily, her consciousness dimmed by the blow.

Harvey heard the crack, felt her heavy breath as she grunted, then felt her grip ease as her weight increased and became dead. She slipped away from him and down to the earth, still bleeding from her throat wound, and now with no consciousness to impair her way to death.

"Thanks, Cyclops," Harvey said hoarsely, rubbing his sore throat.

Ryan retrieved the scarf and wrapped it around his neck once more. He fixed the sec chief with a glare. "Don't thank me. Just remember you owe me," he said shortly, before plunging on into the fray.

Mebbe—just mebbe—that favor would count for something....

THE BATTLE WAS finally over. It had been short and bloody, and the vast majority of the casualties belonged to the Samtvogel dwellers.

"When I was still a fairly young man," Doc remarked to Krysty as they watched the Raw war party moving among the chilled Sunchildren to gather blasters or to chill any muties who might still be alive and therefore a threat, "when I was still in that time before the whitecoat horrors, they would take the Native American and treat him like this."

"Uncle Tyas McCann used to tell us of those days," the flame-haired woman replied. "He used to say that the law of dog-eat-dog was all that ruled. And the inherent stupeness of it was that he'd never seen a dog eat a dog unless they were put into a ring to fight for men."

Doc smiled. "An interesting point, my dear. And appropriate, I think. Yes, in some ways. Fear can do strange things. Is this the way a man like Alien seems to rule the rest of the time?" he questioned, sweeping the area with the end of his walking stick. "Was it necessary to lay waste to their lives? Certainly, they had coexisted long enough."

"Sure, but that was before the nuke."

"Before the whitecoat horrors," Doc said softly. "They will always return to haunt us, I believe."

"And your point is?" Krysty asked. "Sometimes we have to do things we don't want, or don't like, just to survive. You know that as well as anyone."

"But at what cost to ourselves?" Doc looked her in the eye. His own gaze was clearer and steadier than she had seen it for several days. "Consider that man," he said slowly and with measure, indicating Alien. "A life spent living a certain way, questioned and perhaps destroyed in a night. Consider the people. This was…easier?"

Krysty looked at Raw's baron. He stood in the center of the ville while his people scavenged, and a party of sec and some of the stronger ville dwellers—the blacksmith and the armorers among them—rigged the nuke with ropes and makeshift platforms to effect a way of carrying it back to Raw.

Alien was bowed, more like the vanquished than the victor. This was in contrast to Harvey, who was directing operations as though he, himself, had assumed the baronial role.

Krysty's musings were stopped as Mildred came up to them.

"No sign of Dean," she muttered shortly, keeping one eye on the party securing the nuke. "I've looked all over, and so has John. Haven't seen Ryan or Jak yet, but I'll bet you a whole heap of self-heats that I know what their answers will be if you ask them."

Krysty nodded. "He never left Raw. That's something I guess we'll have to deal with when we get back. And quick, 'cause I think the power base may be shifting in the ville before long." She gestured in

Alien's direction with a slight inclination of the head. Mildred took in the situation at a glance.

The conversation was repeated almost word for word when Ryan, and then Jak, returned from scouting the remains of Samtvogel. But Jak had something more to add.

"Only Sunchild alive." He looked over to where the mutie baron was trussed, like a wild animal, tied to a stake driven into the ground while the nuke was secured. "Because Alien say."

"What about any survivors?" Mildred asked.

"Didn't you see them chilling any who hadn't already bought the farm?" J.B. asked softly.

"I meant those who may have got out of the valley during the fighting."

"None," Jak said simply. He indicated the road out. "Sec chill anyone reach there."

"Harvey's certainly made sure of this one," Ryan said grimly.

The one-eyed warrior led the way over to where the sec chief was preparing the nuke for the return journey. He seemed to be assuming sole charge of the nuke, while the baron—who should have been directing or overseeing operations—was standing to one side, seemingly lost in thought.

"Anything we can do to help?" Ryan asked.

Harvey cast an eye over the companions. "Not here," he said with an undertone in his voice. "Mebbe you could help fire the place."

"Fire?" Mildred asked.

"Damn, but I thought you blacks were smart," Harvey replied, ignoring both Mildred's angry look and the fleetingly hostile glances from Ant and Dee, who were busy with the nuke, but not so busy as not to hear. It didn't escape Jak's notice that Blake also cast a glance in the sec chief's direction.

Perhaps there was an ally there when the crunch came down.

Harvey continued. "Look, this place ain't got no one left alive. It's just some charnel house shitpit for the buzzards. Who knows what disease could spring up here unless we clean it up. Cleanse the area, y'know?"

"Alien's orders?" Ryan asked.

"Sure," Harvey replied. He called over to the baron. "Fire the place, Alien?" The baron replied with a noncommittal wave of his hand.

Harvey grinned. "Sure as shit good enough for me, Cyclops. So you want to do this?"

The sec chief's insolent and superior gaze met the rock-steady steely blue eye. Ryan's gaze was stronger, harder. The sec chief looked away. "Find Cyclops Jr.?" he added as a final shot.

"No, but I think you knew that," Ryan replied. "I know he'll turn up. But not here."

Ryan turned to his friends. "We might as well get this over and done with."

None of them were happy with the circumstances surrounding the firing of Samtvogel, but the catch was that the sec chief had a valid point. Samtvogel could become a hotbed of disease with so many rotting chilled corpses within the valley, and this disease could then be borne to the forest by the birdlife. So it was essential that the valley be cleansed with fire.

Ryan and his companions joined the members of the Raw war party who were engaged in preparing the firing. There were already numerous small fires blazing around the valley floor, and these would be the source of the bigger blaze. The lamps were being extinguished, and their oil collected. Some of the war party had discovered the storehouse where the supplies of fuel were kept, in an old outhouse to one side of one of the ranch houses, and this was added to that collected from the lamps.

Now came the part that seemed the most vile: the chilled mutie Sunchildren had to be doused with the oil, to enable them to burn. The areas in between were also drenched with trails of oil, stopping short of the fires. For the whole thing to go up before the war party had left the valley would be disastrous, and it was a fine line between leaving a gap that would prevent immediate firing, a gap that would be too large for the fire to jump when the real firing began.

But finally it was done. The war party assembled in the center of the ville.

"Okay, plan is this," Harvey called over the crowd. "The boys here haul the nuke out first, followed by Cyclops and his people, who get the pleasure of carrying that bastard—" with which he spit at the bound Sunchild, still tied to the stake "—and then the rest of us follow. Firing party take torches, start the burning at the back, then run like fuck to join us."

There was a ripple of laughter at this touch of humor, and the crowd parted to allow the sec men pulling the makeshift platform with the nuke on it. Using scrap from the camp, they had rigged up a trolley and pulleys that enabled the missile to be rolled with a relative smoothness, and once they had breasted the gentle incline of the track it became a simple task to haul it.

Ryan and J.B. followed, supporting the stake with the mutie baron so that it sat easily on their shoulders. They would take the first haul, followed by Jak and Doc, then Mildred and Krysty. They were none too happy at being volunteered for the task by Harvey, but had elected between them to say nothing and see how matters developed—especially in view of the manner in which the sec chief had assumed control of the situation, and the baron had said nothing.

The main body of the war party followed, with the firing party at the rear. Composed of the fastest and most nimble members of the war party, they lit torches from the fires that still burned, then skipped among the corpses and oil trails in a macabre dance, firing the oil trails and corpses at the rear of the valley and the outer edges, then outrunning the spreading fire as it consumed the ville.

The blaze was quick to take, and even in the dawning daylight the valley became an inferno of intense heat and light, the smell of charring flesh gagging and catching at the back of the throat as it drifted on the morning breeze.

Looking back, Doc saw the fire take hold in the enclosed oven of the valley, flaring brighter than the rising sun, with an intense heat that flared more brightly. He wasn't the only one. As he turned, left behind by the war party, he saw that Alien was also watching the fires.

There was an aura about the baron that suggested his power had been broken that night. An aura that snapped Doc out of his reverie and reminded him that, despite the holocaust behind them, their own fight was still far from over.

Chapter Fifteen

"Why don't you speak, you poltroon? Don't you see that this continuing pretense is only going to lead to more pain?"

"You old fool. I don't know who's crazier, you or that mutie bastard," Harvey muttered. "He's a half-crazed mutie fucker, so why should he be able to make any sense?"

Doc smiled, his oddly perfect white teeth reflecting the lamplight that hung over the bound and secured mutie leader, casting a pool of light in the center of the room that left the edges in shadow. He leaned toward the sec chief to emphasize his point.

"That, sir, truly does beg the question of why, if you believe that, you persist in torturing the poor soul."

"Poor soul? This fucker is a poor soul?" Harvey's disbelieving voice rose into a screech. "After all he's done, you can say that?"

Doc shrugged. "There is, sir, no feasible logic to your argument. Would torture bring back the dead and damned? No, sir, it would not. All t'would do is make you feel better for a short while. And that, sir, is not the purpose of this charade."

Harvey seethed. "Big words, you lanky fuck. But that's all. I say I should just ice the son of a bitch right now."

Jak stepped forward from the shadow. "Not what Alien want. Not what say. Anyway, Doc use big words but sometimes make sense. Why think talk sense anyway?" the albino added, looking to Doc.

Along with Harvey, Jak and Doc in the interrogation room were Ryan, Blake and Downey from the sec force. The purpose of the interrogation, as Alien had directed his sec chief, was to find out what had happened to Dean, and also to ascertain how much the mutie leader knew about the nuke that was now being safely stored in an outlying tunnel. The trip back had been swift, the makeshift transport for the nuke being more than adequate for the task. The men pulling the nuke had headed away from the ville entrance they had used to exit the underground lair, and had instead headed for the disguised entrance that led on from the subbasement of an underground garage in a ruined office building. The sec forces had camouflaged the debris that led into the garage so well that J.B. had assumed they were headed into a wall of foliage as he followed close behind with the staked Sunchild, sharing the load with Ryan.

Once inside, Alien had directed his sec chief to the interrogation, and had accompanied his men to where he planned to store the nuke. He had asked the Armorer to accompany them, and J.B. had taken that as a compliment to his abilities that he was being asked to help mothball a nuke. His rad counter had earlier verified that no radiation was leaking from the missile.

The rest of the force had dispersed to their units to recover, Mildred and Krysty accompanying the wounded to the small sick bay. There were few casualties, but more than the ville's small medical team would usually deal with, and they were grateful for the assistance.

And now Sunchild sat in the middle of the room, bleeding from a number of minor cuts and lesions about the face and upper body, heavily bruised from the repeated punches and slaps of the sec chief. Harvey had made a show of holding back, but it was obvious from the condition of Sunchild's earlier blaster wound, and the gangrenous smell emanating from the area around the pus-dribbling wound, that the mutie baron's stamina had been severely depleted, and it wouldn't take much to chill him once and for all.

Not once had he made any sounds that could be taken as words, but there was something about Doc's conviction that the mutie could speak, and perhaps tell them something, that made the one-eyed warrior stiffen in the shadows.

"Yeah, Doc, why do you think that?" he asked softly, echoing Jak's question.

"Our friend here is holding out on us, I fear," Doc said, bending toward the mutie baron so that his face was almost level with that of the bound man. The smell from the mutie's gangrenous wound made him gag, but he paused, waiting until Sunchild made eye contact. "You see, I feel sure that he is following every word we say. The body language of the man suggests that he is braced against the big chill, but that he has his pride, and will take his secrets to the grave with him. To protect part of himself, keep it close. By not giving in, he feels that ultimately he will win. Don't you?"

"Shit, bastard and fuck. Can you believe this complete bullshit?" Harvey raved, turning imploringly to Blake and Downey. "What the fuck kind of jolt is this old shithead on?"

The two sec men exchanged puzzled glances. If their chief was right, and Doc was wrong, then why the hell were they there anyway? And if the old man was right, then why was Harvey getting so worked up?

Ryan stepped forward into the light. He fixed Sunchild with his icy blue eye. "Do you know anything about my son?" he asked quietly.

Sunchild returned the stare. Doc stepped back so that there was nothing between the one-eyed warrior and the mutie baron except the charged and empty air. Despite the wounds, the blood and the ugliness of his mutated features, the mutie leader assumed a sudden dignity that took all but Doc and Ryan by surprise.

"I know nothing of your son, One-eye. Are you the one of legend? The one who searches for the north?"

"I may be," Ryan replied in a hushed voice. "What do you know of me?"

"Men we have sacrificed to the gods have spoken of you before dying. Yes, we know your tongue. My fathers and myself long ago learned that we would need it to communicate and learn from those who would join the gods. You and your people are legend to some. I tell you this—if I had your son, he would have been chilled and consumed as a sacrifice, and a noble one...one of much power. I would have welcomed that, and it would have been a fine chill for

him, to meet the gods as a chosen one. But we have
not done this.''

"I believe you," Ryan said quietly.

Time seemed to stand still, and there was no one
else in the room besides the two of them. All else
faded in the eerie calm of Sunchild's voice. Ryan had
only heard him bellowing the strange dialect and
chant of his people. To hear him speak a normal
tongue, and so quietly, was bizarre. He spoke it as
though it were a foreign language, haltingly but with
a measured precision to every word.

"You have taken our totem. The means of destruction, the coming of the purifying fire.''

"Yeah. The last thing we wanted was another
nukecaust around these parts," Ryan replied. "If the
positions were reversed..." Despite himself, he found
that he held a degree of respect for the mutie baron,
who seemed to carry with him the dignity of an in-
herited line.

"Our view would be different. Naturally, as you
do not believe. For many generations, we have coexisted here, allowing your heresy in this ville. But
things are worsening. I can feel her power growing.''

Doc stepped forward. "Her?"

"Mutie fucker's talking shit again," Harvey interrupted.

"Shut up, Harv," Blake hissed. "Let him have his
say.''

The sec chief shot the wizened deputy a glance of
pure venom but said nothing.

Sunchild continued. "The woman who would control. You think I have not been aware of her heresies?
The sacrifices that have been corrupted by her hand?

She is mutie like us. I can feel her near, feel the hate. Think what you like of us, One-eye, and you, old man,'' Sunchild said, turning to Doc. ''We are as noble as you, but we have different views. You are not bad, just wrong. But she is bad. Her blood was tainted in the underworld, and that continues. She has white-coat fever, and will seek the final solution—''

The shot that rang out in the air was deafening in the enclosed space of the locked room. Ryan's ears rang, and the smell of cordite filled his nostrils. The slug from Harvey's Colt Magnum Carry blaster was a .357, powerful despite the snubbed barrel. At such short range—and the sec chief was only a few yards from the mutie leader's head—the power and destruction of the shot was awesome. Sunchild's head seemed to explode like an overripe melon, his skull splintered by the explosive power that erupted as the bullet entered through his left eye and pulped his brain, the displacement at such velocity carrying an incredible motive power. The exit wound was so large as to take the back of his skull from off of his vertebrae, the gray tissue of his brain and the red of his blood forming a fine mist that sprayed out across the room, splattering Downey, Blake and Jak, who were behind and on either side of the seated mutie.

One second it seemed to Ryan and Doc that Sunchild was looking at them, his eyes strangely clear and lucid, his mouth formed into a word, about to speak. The next his head was nothing more than a blur of bone, flesh and gore, spreading out like a geyser.

''Fireblast! What the hell was that for, you triple-stupe son of a pox-ridden gaudy?'' Ryan yelled, rounding on the sec chief.

"Don't push it, Cyclops," Harvey answered in a calm voice betrayed by only the slightest tremble. "Damned fool was spreadin' shit, demoralizing my men. Can't have that. Right, boys?" He looked to Downey and Blake, who were wiping themselves off as best as possible.

Like Ryan, Doc and Jak, they were only too well aware that Harvey was the man with the unholstered blaster. Nonetheless, they didn't sound too convinced.

"Sure," Blake said hesitantly.

"Whatever you say, Harv," Downey added, his face betraying a confusion at his chief's action. There was a moment's awkward silence before Doc spoke.

"Well, my dear sir. I shall be most interested to hear you repeat that explanation to your baron..."

JENNA HAD BEEN standing, railing at Dean, when she went into convulsions.

He craned his head as much as possible, straining against his bonds, and could see that she was frothing at the mouth, moaning softly with the whites of her eyes showing.

Straining his muscles as much as possible, Dean was torn between hoping she was somehow dying, and hoping that she would recover. The latter because he would be trapped, with only Harvey knowing where he was. He didn't want to be left here defenseless with the sec chief, as Harvey had no reason—unlike Jenna—to keep him alive.

He pulled at every restraint and one at his wrist loosened.

As he worked to free his hand, Dean had to be careful. Jenna may come around at any moment, and he may have to cover his actions. There was a good chance that she wouldn't spot his deception unless she checked carefully, as the loosened restraint was on the opposite side of the bench to that on which she had fallen. Unfortunately for Dean, this just made it harder for him to loosen the leather restraint and also crane his head in the opposite direction and take in Jenna's condition.

The tendons on his neck stood out, the sinews strained and popped, but the youngster kept his head toward the prone woman, watching for the barest movement that would suggest a return to consciousness. All the time, he worked his wrist, until the leather was loose enough for him to slip his wrist right out. Carefully, and with an infinite caution, he brought his free hand over to work at the restraint on the other wrist.

Jenna moaned softly, the timbre of her voice changing as she slipped back into the everyday world.

Dean's heart raced, rising to his mouth. He thought he might vomit, such was the rush of adrenalined surprise at her voice. Yet, acting on an instinct already honed in dangerous situations, he moved with an ease and grace that surprised himself. His arm moved back across his body to its former position, his hand slipping back into the restraint and assuming a pose of being tightly bound. His head snapped back on his neck so that he was looking up at the ceiling. To all intents and purposes, he seemed to have moved not a muscle since Jenna had had her fit.

She pulled herself from the floor, still groggy from

passing out. Shaking her head and muttering, she stumbled across the room to the workbench. She picked up the hypo loaded with chemicals, then turned and looked at Dean with a narrowed gaze.

"No, I don't think so," she said slowly.

Dean turned his head so that he met her gaze. He could feel her mind snaking out to his, probing him. He was alarmed, hoping that she wouldn't be able to see in him that he had partially freed himself.

But she was looking for other things. "No, we didn't finish our little discussion, did we? No matter. But what happened to me? Yes…"

Dean said nothing, trying to blank his mind completely.

"Don't try and be clever, little boy," she snapped. "I only want to fill in some blanks. I remember standing beside you, then there was a sense of overwhelming danger, and this force that… Oh shit," she added in a whisper. "This can't be happening. That fuckwit idiot." She walked over to Dean, her mind still occupied. He hoped it would stay that way, and that she wouldn't check his bonds too closely.

Leaning over, she put her face close to his. "You'll keep, little one. Next time I'll finish you off properly, yeah?" And he felt her hand on him, squeezing so hard that it made him wince in pleasure and pain.

"Yeah, and your father, too," she said with a lustful gleam in her eye. "But first I've got trouble to settle. So you stay here and think about me. And remember this—if you give me an heir, then you live. If not, well…"

She let the answer hang in the air as she turned to leave him.

Dean closed his eyes, breathing heavily, heart thumping. He heard her leave the room, securing the door. The metal was thick enough that he couldn't hear her footsteps down the corridor, so he counted to twenty to himself instead, then slipped his freed hand from the loosened restraint.

Now he had some time—although he couldn't be sure how long—to free himself, find his clothes and try to get the hell out. He began to move, frustratingly aware of how his muscles had ached and cramped from being held in the same position for so long. But he had to ignore the cramps and move before Jenna returned.

BLAKE CLOSED the rough wooden door on the scene of Sunchild's slaughter. He secured the simple lock on the outside of the door that was designed to keep captives inside. Not that the chilled mutie baron was going anywhere. It was just habit.

"Well, Harv, you've got some explaining to do to Alien," Downey said simply, looking at his sec chief.

"Why?" the sec chief replied. He looked on edge, and there was the faintest hint of a facial tic as he spoke.

"Shit, Harv, he didn't want Sunchild chilled. He just wanted him interrogated," Blake exploded in exasperation. "I just dunno what was going on there, but if it's something we don't know about—"

"Why would it be that?" Harvey snapped. "Why the fuck would you say that?" He grabbed the smaller sec man by the front of his shirt and slammed him up against the wall.

Jak was the first to react. He snaked between them,

his arm flashing as he chopped up, breaking the grip. In one fluid movement, he followed through and pushed Harvey back against the far wall, where Ryan's tightly muscled arms secured the sec chief.

"Thanks, Jak," Blake muttered, shaking himself down and trying to keep calm. "Feel like this whole fuckin' place has gone crazy all of a sudden."

"Mebbe crazy all time. You notice now," the albino replied.

"You could have a point there, Whitey," Downey said slowly. "Listen, Harv. You just go and calm down some. I'll go and report to Alien, okay? It was an accident, agreed?"

Jak and Ryan exchanged looks. Should they go along with this? Doc merely assented. "It is your ville, dear boy, and your place to make decisions."

HARVEY STORMED away from the group, and they let him go. For Blake and Downey, it was important to smooth things over with Alien before they found out what the hell was wrong with their sec chief. For Ryan, Jak and Doc, it was important to link up with J.B., then with Mildred and Krysty. If any immediate action was to be taken to find Dean, then they should all know exactly what was going on while they were in the same ville, in order to avoid endangering one another.

It crossed Ryan's mind that he should follow Harvey. He felt sure that the sec chief could lead him to his son. But now wasn't the right time.

So Harvey was alone as he stalked the passages and tunnels of Raw. His mind raced. Time was suddenly running short on him, and he had to find Jenna.

She was planning to depose her husband, and although she hadn't planned to make her move yet, Harvey was sure that this would have to change.

He approached the corridor at the end of which stood the metal door. It was as he turned the corner that he found Jenna locking Dean in the lab.

"Listen, we've got trouble," he began in a low, tense voice, too worried to bother with preliminaries.

"You think I don't know that?" she replied as she turned to face him. "I've just had an immense psychic wave throw me off balance. What have you done, Harv?"

The sec chief looked puzzled. "I've just chilled Sunchild before he could say anything about you. How the fuck he knew, and how you know—"

"My bastard mutie taint," she muttered savagely, halting him. "Feelie like him. I always knew that bad blood would bring trouble on me."

"Well, it's gonna fall like a hard rain now. We need to do something."

"Then the time has come," she said decisively. "Did you get the nuke?"

"Yeah. Alien's got it stored away, doin' that while I dealt with that mutie scum."

"Then we need it. If we have that, then we have the power. Order your men to seize it and await further orders from me."

"Whoa there, babe," Harvey said hurriedly. "I don't know if they'll all go for it. Yeah, they're loyal to me, but only because we're under Alien. I can guarantee a few, but others..." he shrugged, thinking of the attitude he had seen in Blake and Downey.

"Then we need reinforcements. Ryan Cawdor and

his people. They're good fighters, and he's a strong leader.''

Harvey narrowed his eyes. ''Yeah? Just you remember who's gonna be at your right hand, woman.''

''Oh, I know that very well.'' She smiled. ''But we need help to get there, sweetie. Now all you've got to do is get Ryan Cawdor—alone—to me, and let me do the rest.''

She pulled Harvey to her and kissed him. It never failed, and once more the sec chief was a pliable tool for her games. However, her thoughts as they kissed were far from him, far from any desire other than power.

RYAN HAD GATHERED his troops in the unit they had been allocated. Jak had sped through the twisting tunnels of the ville to find J.B. and take him away from the party that had secured the nuke in its new port of storage. Alien had been in conference with Jake about mounting a sentry on the storeroom, and then Downey and Blake had arrived to report to their baron, so it had been easy for Jak to whisper in the Armorer's ear, and for J.B. to melt away from the crowd.

Doc had gathered Mildred and Krysty from the medical unit, a task made easier by the fact that the majority of wounded had now been dealt with. He alluded to Ryan's urgency in a way that had confused them, but convinced them that something was wrong.

And now they were together. Ryan outlined the situation he, Jak and Doc had witnessed. When he finished, Mildred shook her head slowly.

''We've got big trouble now. How the hell are we

going to find Dean and still keep our backs covered for when the shit hits it?''

"The only thing to do is play it as it rolls,'' Ryan replied. "We can't plan anything at this stage, as we don't know how Alien will play things. It also depends on Harvey's next move.''

"Funny say that,'' Jak murmured from his position by the curtain that kept them private from the tunnel outside. He was keeping watch, and had caught the sound of a familiar footstep echoing through the tunnel.

Harvey entered the unit without any invitation or apology. "Cyclops, Alien wants to see you right now. His chamber. Come on.''

"Do not say please,'' Doc muttered as Ryan left with the sec chief, leaving his friends with a warning glance.

"Dark night, I think you'd better trail them, Jak,'' J.B. said to the albino, who seemed to understand immediately.

Mildred, however, wasn't as clear. "What's the matter, John?'' she asked the Armorer.

"Well, Millie, it's like this. Alien's gone to his chambers and been briefed by Harvey damned quick for someone who was overseeing the nuke just a little while back.''

Krysty was checking her blaster, making sure it was fully loaded. Her hair was coiled tightly. "The shit's already hit,'' she said, almost to herself.

DEAN ACHED in every muscle, but he savored every last drop of the pain, because it was the pain that came from freedom.

As soon as Jenna had left the room, he had freed his hand and started to work on the restraint securing his other arm. It had been simple to untie, and he had massaged life back into the dead limb. It tingled and ached, and the bites and scratches began to sting.

But the problem came when Dean tried to sit up and untie his ankles. His abs were strong, and a sit-up of that kind would normally have presented no problem. However, in order to secure him, his legs and arms had been stretched, and the muscles along his ribs and across his stomach had been tensed to an abnormal degree, then held rigid.

For the first two attempts, Dean found he was unable to raise himself, the only answer his musculature could give him being a sharp and repeated attack of cramps, like fire across his stomach and chest.

He sank back, breathing heavily and trying to quell the panic that rose within him. He had no idea how much time he may have, and to be floundering right now was something that filled him with fear.

No. Fighting it back, Dean tried for the third time, rising slowly and supporting himself with his elbows and forearms on the table. Pain shot through his arms, but it was more than compensated for by the decreased pain in his torso. As he freed his ankles and massaged pained life back into them, the sharp pains in his body reduced to a dull throb.

Then he tried to stand. Learning from his previous experience, he took his time, supporting as much weight as possible through his arms as he placed his feet on the floor, feeling the pins and needles in the soles of his feet, and gradually increased the weight his legs bore.

Eventually, he was standing. In pain, but unsupported.

He took only a few seconds to relish this freedom, and to adjust to being mobile again. He could afford no more. He had to move as quickly as possible. His clothes were still in a heap in the corner of the room, where they had been discarded before he was trussed. He dressed as quickly as possible, wincing at the pain of the scratches and bites, the agony of cloth touching skin still sensitive after the severe cramp engendered by his restraint. When he put on his boots, his feet felt as if they were encased in lead that tightened around his ankles, forcing the blood out.

Dean ignored it as best as he could, knowing that he couldn't afford the indulgence. He had to move as fast as possible.

He tried the door, but knew even as he did that it was pointless. It locked from the outside, and he had heard Jenna secure it. It was still fast.

Dean leaned with his back against the door and surveyed the lab. He knew the layout, and knew that it was used for experiments where fumes could be a problem in an enclosed space. So there had to be an air vent of some sort in the lab. It was no point just hammering on the door. The lab was secluded, and the only people likely to hear were Jenna or Harvey as they approached.

So the air vent was his best bet.

Stiffly, Dean moved around the walls of the room in which he had been kept restrained. It was the best place to start, as it was where the majority of experiments took place. Besides, he didn't want to face the results of Jenna's experiments unless he really had to.

Floor to ceiling he scanned the walls, moving anything that could hide a vent. The wall by the door was clear, and it was pointless to look at the wall housing the doorway into where she kept her hideous mutated children, as this was only a dividing wall.

That left the wall opposite the door to the tunnel, and the wall against which the restraining bench and operating table stood. He began with the far wall.

Nothing. So the vent had to be somewhere along the wall where he had been restrained. Dean set to searching with a renewed purpose, ignoring the small voice in his head that asked if the vent was too small to get through.

A metal cupboard and filing cabinet stood at the angle of the two walls. A drab olive green, they looked as though they were military salvage, possibly from the redoubt. They were standing free of the wall, very deliberately pulled away from the concrete.

Dean knelt, ignoring his protesting thigh muscles, and pressed his face to the gap. There was a faint draft of cold air.

Dean stood slowly, his energy renewed and increased by the knowledge that he may have found his escape route. This gave him the strength to fight against his protesting body as he struggled with the cabinet and cupboard. They were full and heavy to move, screeching on the concrete floor with every inch gained. The boy's muscles, sore and strained, filled with lactic acid at every exertion, betraying the urgent effort he put into his work. He gritted his teeth and redoubled his efforts, sweat pouring into his eyes, his heart racing with every screech in case it attracted Jenna or Harvey if they should be approaching.

He stood back, panting. They were far enough away for him to get behind them. He dropped to his knees and crawled into the space between the metal and the concrete. The light was dimmed by shadow and enclosure, but he could see that a metal grille covered the opening of the air vent. Groping blindly, he couldn't believe his luck when he found that the screws had rusted in their plugs, and it took only a little maneuvering for him to pry the grille loose.

Snaking around, tearing his already sore flesh on the corner of the opening, feeling the metal of the cabinet scrape on his already bruised ribs, Dean was head and shoulders into the vent.

It crossed his mind that he had no idea if the vent would narrow suddenly or take a steep upward curve that would be impossible to follow. Perhaps he would be so tightly enclosed that his already protesting body would cramp and spasm, refusing to move.

He put such notions out of his head. Instead, he focused on a single-minded determination to get away.

He had no other choice.

RYAN WALKED across the main hall with echoing footsteps. He wondered what Harvey had waiting for him. The sec chief had excused himself and hadn't accompanied the one-eyed warrior. J.B. and Jak had both wanted to accompany Ryan, but he had refused, instead ordering that his friends hurry to the baron's chambers after a ten-minute gap. Ryan figured he could keep it together that long, if necessary, until reinforcements showed.

It was deathly quiet in the main hall. The inhabitants of Raw were still too busy putting their own affairs in order after their return from the battle to think about celebrating another victory. That would come later.

It did seem ominous to Ryan that he could hear nothing from the baron's chamber. Not a sound, almost as though whoever was behind the heavy drapes was consciously keeping silent.

Every nerve ending in his body sang with the tension. The empty socket of his left eye ached beneath its patch, the scar tingling, a reaction he always had when trouble was imminent, and it was the time of tension before action.

Ryan reached for the drapes and pulled them back.

"Alien?" he said in a level tone. "You wanted me?"

"That fool may well do, but I want you even more," came a sibilant female tone from the shadows.

The dimmed lamp increased in brightness, illuminating the chamber.

"Well, well, I am surprised," Ryan murmured.

Chapter Sixteen

"You must have guessed," Jenna purred, her voice still carrying a harsh edge. She knelt upright on the fur-covered bed. She was naked, and licked the tip of a finger before running the nail down her body, between her breasts and down to her pubis.

"You must have guessed it was me who wanted to see you...and why," she added, fixing Ryan with her raven-black and infinitely deep eyes.

Despite himself, Ryan could feel her mind start to encroach on him, tendrils wisping around the edges of his consciousness.

"No, I came to see Alien. Mebbe find out something about Dean," he said, trying to block his mind and stop her seeing that he was lying. He had suspected a setup of some kind. But why Jenna? He had a notion, but what exactly was it that she wanted?

The small and exquisitely shaped woman licked her lips and smiled, taking a step toward him.

"You're not very good at hiding your thoughts, sweetie. More of a man of action, I would have said. You know damned well why I want you, and that's why I've got your son. He has potential, but I think you would be better."

She was now standing in front of the one-eyed man, who felt as though his limbs had become blobs of mercury, unable to move and infinitely heavy. She trailed the fingers of one hand delicately over his face, running a nail edge down his puckered scar with a tenderness that belied all he knew of her.

"You must have gathered that I have my own plans. You and your people could be a part of that. You and your son can be my concubines and you my right hand. And that old man seems to know much of the predark ways. He could be very useful, very interesting."

She now stood on tiptoe so that her face was against Ryan's. He could feel her mind snaking and coiling around his own, trying to bend his will to hers. Was this how she snared Harvey? Ryan wanted her, could feel the stirrings of lust despite his revulsion at all he knew or surmised about her. And she had Dean—she had admitted this. What had she done with his son?

Ryan used this spark to fight back against her. She brushed her lips against his, and he could smell the musky sexual odor of her body. It filled his lungs and seemed to spread around his body in the same way that her mind spread around his consciousness.

She began to kiss him, her tongue probing and licking, nibbling at his mouth. He felt her hands start to rove across his body, fingers searching for openings in his clothing. She was using every sensual trick she knew to break down his defenses.

To a casual onlooker, it wouldn't have seemed so, but Ryan was fighting one of the most important battles of his life. He knew that if he gave in to her, then he would be enslaved and his friends doomed. He had been here before. Countess Katya Beausoleil, the sadistic baron who had wanted to keep him as her personal stud, and who had perished when they plunged into a raging river. Her enchantments had been subtler, and he had resisted those.

Ryan pulled his head away from hers, a jerky, hesitant movement slowed by the lack of control he now seemed to have over his own body.

"No. You won't—"

He didn't get a chance to finish. While he had been struggling mentally, he had been unable to hear the approach from behind....

"SOMETIMES I WISH I'd stayed at Brody's," Dean muttered as he bit into his lip. His mouth ran salty with his own blood, but the distraction of the pain was working. Muscles that screamed for freedom of movement or rest were once again blanked out enough to allow him to carry on.

The air duct had run for what seemed like miles, but in all probability was only a few hundred feet, in a straight line before turning sharply to the left. The concrete inside the duct was rough and unfinished, snaring Dean's clothes and scratching at the area of exposed skin on his shins between his boots and the hem of his pants. Under his shirt, his back became raw and bruised from rubbing on the concrete ceiling of the narrow duct.

The sharp corner was a problem, and for all the sinuousness that he could muster, he still wasn't sure that he could twist his protesting body and get the push from his legs that would take him around and onto the next stretch.

There was no light at all now. The last vestiges

from the lab, bleeding into the duct, were now just a memory.

The cold draft of air had become stronger, colder as he entered the straight section, moving on. His elbows were rubbed free of skin, but he focused on the pain, using it to drive him on. He refused to think about the possibility of the duct narrowing. There was no way he could crawl backward, and the terror of being trapped was actually too great for him to even contemplate.

The air was freezing now, and his body shuddered with involuntary shivers, making progress even harder. But through the intense cold, Dean realized that he had reached a junction in the air ducts. The cold seemed to bear down on him from above, and his shoulders were like blocks of ice...blocks of ice that were no longer being rubbed raw by concrete.

It was too dark to see, but he could only surmise that he had reached a point where a larger central duct had been sunk as a shaft from the surface, which meant that there was more than this one duct. Logically, then, there had to be other exits.

It was something of which he couldn't have been sure before now, but knowing that there was another way out cheered him, and gave purpose to his determination. Testing the distance around him by extending his arms, he found that the central shaft was wide. Experimentally, he raised his head and shoulders, slowly lest he crack his skull.

There was no ceiling here. With great care not to cramp his protesting muscles, Dean found that he was able to stand in this part of the shaft, and stretch his aching and confined limbs.

He tilted his head and looked up. There was no sign of light, no indication of where the shaft eventually surfaced.

After pausing for a few moments to savor the lack of confinement, and to breathe deeply of the cold air, Dean began to grope blindly around the parameters of the shaft. It seemed to him that it was like the axle of a wheel, with the duct leading from the lab being one of the spokes that connected centrally to this point. Being sure to note where he began—not wanting to accidentally return the way he had come—he turned in a circle, feeling for the openings to the ducts.

There were eight in all, seven for him to make his choice. Picking one diametric to the duct from the lab, he dropped to his knees again.

"Just got to keep going now," he whispered to himself, striking out across the floor of the shaft and into the duct.

"WELL, CYCLOPS, this is a nice little surprise."

Ryan would have started at the sound of Harvey's voice behind him, but he found that he was still unable to move freely.

Jenna, on the other hand, had no such trouble. Squealing with faked fright, she jumped back from the one-eyed man, grabbing a fur from the bed and using it to cover herself. Her eyes took on an accusatory cast, and Ryan felt the heaviness lift from his mind, independence return to his limbs.

He turned, and saw that Harvey was standing in the opening to the chamber, the drapes held back.

Alien stood beside him.

"I think you may have some explaining to do, friend Cawdor," the baron said softly.

Ryan shook his head. "No explaining. You think what you will."

The one-eyed man knew that whatever he said, he wouldn't be believed. If he tried to explain about Jenna's power, about Dean, about her proposition, none of it would be believed. The baron was completely in her thrall.

"This is no way to treat your hosts, Cyclops," Harvey said with relish. "I reckon it's just plain bad manners. Shall I chill the fucker now, Alien, or do you want to do it yourself?"

The baron held up a hand. "Not now, Harv. This will require a ville meet. Send the word out soon as possible, I want everyone in the main hall. Then we'll decide what to do."

"What to do?" Jenna screamed, holding the fur to her. She was acting the part of the outraged baron's wife well, Ryan had to admit. "What do you mean? This one-eyed bastard is no use to man nor to beast."

"We will decide that later," Alien snapped with a harshness to his voice that Ryan hadn't heard during their stay in Raw.

The baron turned his attention to Ryan. "As for you, Ryan Cawdor, you and your people will attend, by force if necessary."

"That won't be necessary."

Alien nodded. "Good. You perplex me, Ryan Cawdor. But we shall see. Yes, we shall see. Now get from my sight."

Ryan made no reply and walked out of the cham-

ber, passing the baron and the sec chief without looking at them. He didn't look back at Jenna, either.

Now they were faced with a possible firefight to
get out alive, and there was still no sign of Dean.

THERE WAS ANOTHER tight corner in the concrete
duct. This tunnel hadn't seemed as long as those leading from the lab, but Dean had no idea whether this
was really the case or whether it was a matter of psy-
chology. In a sense, it was unimportant. All that mattered was reaching an exit.

And perhaps this was it. As he squeezed himself
around the corner of the duct, a faint light permeated
the gloom. The duct was on a slight incline, which
made it harder for him to crawl. His elbows felt as
though they were worn to the bone, no longer hurting
because the nerve endings had rubbed away. But the
growing light gave him the impetus to go faster. The
way out was almost in sight, and he couldn't fail now.

It seemed to take forever, the grille at the end of
the duct growing larger, tantalizingly always out of
reach. Each shuffling movement took an eternity.

Sound started to leak into the shaft: a buzzing of
idle conversation, the clattering of movement. Wherever Dean had landed, it was a heavily populated
area. He was relieved. If it was populated, then it had
to be central, so it would be easy for him to find his
way back to the rest of the party. And if it was central
and heavily populated, then it would be hard for Jenna
or Harvey to recapture him without giving away their
secrets to some degree.

This knowledge spurred him on, and Dean quick-
ened his pace, getting closer and closer to the grille.

When he reached it, he could see why he had traversed an incline. The grille was situated high up in the wall of the tunnel, above the level of the heating and water pipes and the brackets for the lamps. He could see the tops of people's heads as they went about their business. He was in the central area where trade and commerce took place. Although there were a few people about, there were fewer than he would have expected from previous exploration, and through the hum of conversation he caught something about a raid on Samtvogel.

It was all the more important he find his father and his friends—if they were still alive.

Dean tried to loosen the grille, cursing to himself as his constricted arms found it hard to get the necessary purchase to push the grille out of the wall. But slowly it began to give, with a grating screech.

Two men passing by looked up at the grille.

"Shit, it's the one-eyed man's boy," one of them said. "Quick, Ham, get me something to stand on."

His companion grabbed a stool that sat by an unattended stall and gave it to the muscular, thickset man. "Hang on, son, hang on," he said as he placed the stool beneath the grille and climbed up, pulling at the grille to assist Dean's restricted pushing.

The grille gave way, and the thickset man tossed it to the floor, taking hold of the boy as he slithered from the duct, blinking in the light.

"Ham, take the boy," the thickset man ordered his companion, and Ham—who was swarthy and squat—seized Dean with a strength of grip that gave lie to his fat frame, lowering the youth to the ground as Dean fell, upside down, from the opening of the duct.

Dean sat on the floor of the tunnel, a small crowd gathering around him. The thickset man seized the boy by the hand, pumping it and announcing himself as Donal. "Where have you been, son? Where have you been?" he kept repeating.

Dean found himself without the opportunity to answer, the man's concerned questioning cutting across his attempts to speak. So the youngster used the man's arm—hand still pumping—to pull himself to his feet.

"Yeah, yeah, please," Dean said quickly, trying to speak between the concerned questioning, which was now beginning to come from the small crowd as Dean still found himself unable to answer. "Look, thanks, but I really can't..." He shrugged, not able to finish the sentence. Detaching his hand, he backed away from his rescuer, through the crowd. "I can't stop, really, thanks...."

Dean turned, looking around to orient himself. He now knew which way he had to go in order to reach the unit where his father and friends had been billeted. He started to run, despite the protests of his aching limbs.

"Well, what do you make of that?" Donal asked no one in particular. "Is that what you call friendly?"

The fat man Ham shrugged. "Outlanders," he said simply, as though that were all the answer needed.

RYAN OUTLINED the situation to his party.

J.B. blew out his cheeks and pushed his fedora back on his head. "Well, I guess you're not chilled yet, so that's a start." He sighed.

"Yeah, John, I find that really reassuring," Mildred said with heavy sarcasm.

"He's right," Ryan replied. "We're here together, and we know what we're walking into later. If it's some kind of mock trial and then a chilling, at least we can make a fight of it."

"Or find Dean, get out first," Jak added.

"Always ask the impossible and expect the unexpected." Doc smiled. "We do not even know where he is."

But even as he said this, they all noticed Jak—on sentry duty—suddenly stiffen. The albino turned to them, a rare smile cracking his scarred white face. "Always expect unexpected," he said simply.

With which he disappeared around the curtain, returning a few moments later supporting an exhausted Dean, who had run despite the aches and strains of his muscles, and had collapsed into Jak's support gladly when the albino rushed to greet him.

Krysty aided Jak in seating the youth on the edge of the bed. Mildred immediately stripped him to the waist to stem the bleeding from some of the deeper scratches on his back, which had soaked the back of his shirt in blood.

"God in heaven, boy, what have you done to yourself?" she whispered.

"Listen," Dean said breathlessly, his head suddenly swimming with exhaustion now that he had reached relative safety and was no longer moving solely on adrenaline. He had to concentrate on every word, forcing them out. "Listen, you were right, Mildred. Jenna, she has old tech, and these muties that she's made. She wants—"

"The master race," Doc interjected. "As ever with these people. History never learns. It just keeps making the same mistakes on an endless loop."

"Yeah, right, Doc, but saying it doesn't help now," Mildred snapped. "Let Dean finish. We don't have much time."

Dean gasped out what had happened to him.

"You think that both her and Harvey will use the meet to get us chilled and mebbe try and get Alien out of the way, as well? Say he's weak for letting us in?" Krysty posed.

Ryan frowned. "Alien's a good man, and popular. That'd be hard for them, unless they've got the whole of the sec force with them, and I doubt that from what I've seen."

"Yeah, second that," Jak added.

"So we need a game plan," J.B. said, cutting to the heart of the matter. "We've got to get our asses out of here, and keep our backs covered as we go."

Ryan nodded, but was cut short from adding anything by the voice of Blake behind him.

"Time for the meet. Harv sent us 'cause he don't trust you," the small sec man said apologetically. He and Downey, blasters in hand, stood at the entrance to the unit, both looking embarrassed by their appointed task.

As the drapes opened, Dean had reacted quickly, sliding off the bed so that he was sheltered from view. Downey and Blake wouldn't be expecting to find him, so would not search the unit if he wasn't with the party that left; he had to hope that they hadn't heard him or glanced at him when they entered. Doc, nearest to the youngster, pulled a blanket from the bed,

catching the bottom hem with the toe of his boot and
dragging it down so that Dean was covered.

No one else noticed.

"It is a pity we did not get that chance to look for
young Dean, and that the lad seems destined to stay
lost," Doc said with a perfectly straight face.

The inference was clear, and no one spoke of Dean
as they assembled in silence, then followed the sec
men from the unit and on the journey to the main
hall. There was nothing to be said that wouldn't give
clues as to any possible course of action. It would be
every man for himself, staying triple-red alert. It
wouldn't be the first time they had been in such a
situation.

The one thing that did puzzle them individually
was that the sec men had made no attempt to take
their weapons. Still armed, it would have been easy
for them to overpower Blake and Downey and try to
effect their escape. The problem with that being that
if sec men had been sent, it wouldn't be beyond Harvey to set up sec parties to ambush them if they attempted it. At least dealing with Alien they had some
chance of reasoning with him.

BACK IN THE SLEEPING unit, Dean waited until the
footsteps had receded into the distance before emerging from behind the bed. While he was there, he unholstered his Browning Hi-Power and checked that it
was fully loaded. He was thankful for Jenna and Harvey's confidence in the restraints on the operating table. They deemed it unnecessary to remove the blaster
from the carelessly discarded pile of clothing.

He slipped the blaster back to its place of concealment, fingers lingering on it to feel the position of the butt and grip, mentally mapping it for when it was necessary.

Dean then crossed the floor and drew back the drape. They had disappeared around a bend in the tunnel, but he knew the route to the main hall, so it wasn't necessary to keep them in sight.

He followed at a pace he calculated—from their speed on leaving—would keep him equidistant from them until he reached the main hall himself. What he would do when he got there, he wasn't sure. He would have to assess the situation as he found it.

Dean kept his head down and tried to blend in with his surroundings. He was aware from the reception he had received when Ham and Donal had helped him from the ventilation duct that his disappearance had been well noted, and that there had been a search for him. Obviously, word of his escape hadn't yet reached the ears of the sec men who had come to escort his companions. He hoped that it hadn't had time to spread, and that he could remain fairly anonymous.

The ville seemed to be almost empty as he made his way to the main hall. This was good for Dean, as it allowed him to pass unnoticed. However, he did find the fact that his father and companions would be facing the whole of Raw a cause for concern.

As he neared the hall itself, there was a swell of sound as the muttered conversations of the whole ville gathered in one room hit him. The sound was too overlapping and confusing for Dean to make out anything in particular, but from snatches that could be discerned, he gleaned that not even the ville dwellers themselves knew what this was about.

Whether that was a hopeful sign, he didn't even want to consider. He reached the entrance to the hall, which was unguarded on the outside. Beyond the opening, he could see the mass of people. His father and friends, Blake and Downey, and even the baron himself were lost to view, somewhere in the center of the vast room, surrounded by the residents of Raw.

Two sec men stood on the inside of the entrance, their backs to him. Like everyone else, they seemed more interested in what was about to transpire than in keeping watch.

Good. Dean approached the entrance, light-footed so as not to give them cause to turn around. His entrance was aided by a sudden call to silence from Harvey. Everyone, even the sec guards, suddenly craned forward, their attention so focused on what was happening in front of them that they ignored the young man pushing into their midst, unwilling to take their eyes from the spectacle in front of them.

"I WISH EVERYONE wasn't staring so hard," J.B. whispered to Mildred as they stood in a group, flanked by Blake and Downey, in the center of the hall. The inhabitants of Raw had formed a circle around them, and were studying them with interest, appearing to have little idea as to what was occurring.

"Why, John, don't tell me you're shy," Mildred replied, her acid sense of humor surfacing as an indication of her own concern.

Jak turned to Blake. "Why?" he asked simply.

The small sec man looked uncomfortable. "Not my

choice, Jak. Harv is still boss, and he says word comes from Alien. They didn't tell me or Downey what it was about. But mebbe you know?'' It was half plea, half accusation.

"Mebbe believe if I tell, but mebbe not most,'' Jak replied.

"Thing is,'' Downey commented, "it can't be that bad, 'cause Harv never said we should disarm you. In fact he was sure that we shouldn't.''

"A most interesting stratagem,'' Doc mused, hearing this.

"Meaning?'' Krysty queried.

"Work it out regarding our earlier conversation.'' Doc smiled cryptically. "It is not, perhaps, for the general consumption.''

Krysty's hair curled tight to her neck. She had a good idea what Doc meant, and knew that it caught them even more between that rock and that hard place than ever. Harvey wanted to set them up and chill them in a firefight, giving himself ample time and opportunity to dispose of the baron in a seemingly accidental manner.

The one thing they had in their favor was Dean. It seemed more than likely that Harvey didn't know he was loose, or if he did, was unaware that he had returned to the group. And the youngster was somewhere in Raw.

Mebbe, she thought as she scanned the puzzled and not yet hostile faces of the Raw dwellers, mebbe even somewhere in this hall.

Her train of thought was interrupted by the shrill yell of Harvey's voice as he pushed through to the entry of the hall, followed by Alien and Jenna.

"Hey, move over there, we gonna begin. So quiet up!" the sec chief yelled. Behind him, the baron was grim faced. Jenna found it hard to hide a sly smile, and Krysty recoiled at the psychic wave that hit her when their eyes locked.

It was show time.

DEAN HAD BEEN MOVING through the crowd, keeping his head down so that he wouldn't be recognized, but had been brought up short by the sound of Harvey's voice.

Looking up, he saw the sec chief, the baron and Jenna enter the circle left in the center of the hall. He saw the expression on the woman's face and felt his stomach flip.

Trouble was coming. And now.

Harvey addressed the crowd. "Okay, people, you're probably wonderin' why you're here, and what this is about. Well, these people—" he spat the word as though it were poisonous "—have betrayed us. Alien wants to talk to y'all about it."

The sec chief stood back, looking pleased with himself, as the baron stepped forward.

"My friends, I have come to seek a consensus from you. As you are aware, Ryan Cawdor and his fellow travelers have aided us considerably in our recent and most vital struggles against Samtvogel. Indeed, without them our task would have been much harder. And yet I have discovered that behind our backs, Ryan Cawdor has been plotting to overthrow me and to assume control of Raw."

A ripple of surprise and shock spread through the crowd. Even among the companions, there was surprise at the charge itself. Dean kept his shock down and used the ripple as a means to move forward a little more, nearer to the center.

"Shortly after our return to Raw today," the baron continued, "I returned to my chambers to find Ryan Cawdor alone with my wife. She was naked and distressed—"

Another ripple of shock, this time not shared by the companions. Dean, for his part, found the idea of Jenna distressed by her nakedness sickly amusing, considering what the woman had told him about her plans for his father and himself.

Alien held up his hands for silence, and continued, "When I had dismissed Ryan Cawdor and had calmed my wife, I discovered that Ryan had told her he wanted to rule Raw, and use the people to help him achieve his aims. Also that he wanted her as his woman, as he was tired of the one he has now."

Krysty felt sick at the accusation coming from the mutie woman, but also amused at how far wide of the mark she knew it to be. She felt the raven eyes of the queen searing into her, but refused to meet them.

Tiring of that game, Jenna stepped forward and interrupted her husband. "When I told him that I wasn't interested, the bastard tried to take me by force. It was only my husband arriving that saved me from that animal," she cried, her voice trembling with an anger and fear that was convincing—unless you knew the truth.

The muttering in the crowd started again, but with an uglier undertone. Jenna had never been popular, but Alien was loved and respected by his people, and she was his wife.

The baron held up his hands. "I've called you here to announce that they will be expelled. I want no chilling, as the rest of the party are not to blame. They will be escorted from the ville. If, however, they do so much as come near us again, then they will be chilled. That is my ruling."

There was a buzz among the crowd as they debated between those who agreed with the baron, and those who favored a chilling. Dean put aside his own surprise, and moved to the front of the crowd, making ready to break into the circle.

In the middle, it was hard to tell who was the more surprised, Ryan and his companions, or Jenna and Harvey.

"J.B., better be triple red just in case," Ryan whispered, leaning close to the Armorer. He was careful not to approach his weapons and spark a reaction.

J.B. nodded agreement and swept his gaze over the others. While shocked, they had all taken in the judgment and were prepared to believe the baron. No one had reached for a blaster. Not even Dean. The Armorer blinked, momentarily surprised at the stealth with which the youngster had infiltrated the center of the circle.

J.B. wasn't the only one to notice Dean. Harvey reached for his Colt Magnum Carry blaster as soon as he spotted Dean, but was stayed by the hand of the baron, who said something that J.B. was unable to make out in the surrounding noise. The Armorer also noticed that Jenna had turned pale.

Alien held up his hand once more for silence, and

made to speak as the hubbub subsided. But before he could actually speak, Dean began.

"Listen to me! Alien is being lied to—Jenna and Harvey have a lab hidden at the end of one of the tunnels, and they're making muties down there. It was them who took me, and I wasn't able to escape until now."

Alien listened to the youngster with a puzzled frown. Noticing this, Jenna grabbed her husband's arm.

"Don't listen to that shit! Get them out of here," she screamed with an almost hysterical edge to her voice.

But when her husband looked at her, there was a coldness in his eyes that made her shrink.

"No," he said quietly. His voice was almost a whisper, but over the shocked silence of the gathered ville dwellers, it carried like the loudest shout. "No, let the child show me. If he lies, then it will be shown for that. If I do not allow him that chance, how can my people ever trust again that I am fair and honest?"

"Don't do it," Harvey said, his voice trembling with a mixture of fear and anger. "It may be a trick of some kind."

"Well, if it is, Harv, then mebbe we'll chill anyone in sight," Downey said slowly.

"Right. 'Cause we'll go along, just to keep things safe…all of us. With the boy and his father, and the rest, in front. Just to be sure," Blake added. He looked at Jak before adding, "You learn who to trust when your life is on the line, and let's just say I've been having a few doubts about you lately, Harv."

There was nothing that the sec chief or the mutie

woman could do at that moment to change things, and as the crowd parted to allow Blake and Downey to usher Dean out of the hall, followed by his father and companions, Harvey held Jenna back from her husband as he followed.

"Shit's about to hit," he said softly. "Follow, I'll try to round up those who'll follow me straightaway. We've got to move now."

Jenna nodded her agreement, then followed Alien, who was looking back to see what had happened to her.

In the swell of the crowd, Harvey managed to slip away in order to locate those he knew would be loyal to him first and foremost. The moment of truth was approaching.

DEAN LED THEM through the tunnels and corridors of the ville, heading unerringly for the outer reaches and the tunnel that terminated in the metal door. He felt better for having Jak by his side, as the albino also knew where the lab lay.

"I hope for your sake this isn't true," Alien said to Jenna in a quiet voice. "Because if it is..."

"Of course the child lies," she hissed back at him, venom dripping from her tone. "You trust him against me?"

"You forget I have the legend and history of Raw and the Illuminated Ones passed down to me from my forefathers," the baron replied. "I know something of your forefathers, and the taint that may have traveled down."

"You've never said anything of this before," she said quietly.

"I had hoped...but perhaps not," Alien replied with an infinite sadness in his voice.

They had now reached the tunnel that terminated in the metal door. Dean halted before it. The lock was still in place. He turned and looked back at Alien and Jenna.

"This is it. She has the key," he said simply.

Alien turned to his wife. "Well?"

"I don't have a fucking key," she spit. "I know nothing about this place."

There was such conviction in her tone that, for a moment, Dean found he was even doubting himself.

"Well, we've got to get in somehow," Blake said, stepping forward and examining the lock. "Think I could shoot it off?"

J.B. leaned forward to get a better look, being careful not to move quickly or arouse any suspicion about his actions. "I'd say you need some plas-ex for that," he commented. "I've got some, so if you'll let me..."

Blake nodded. "I'm pretty sure I've got nothing to fear from you," he murmured, "but just for show, make it slow."

The Armorer grinned and reached slowly into one of his capacious pockets before producing a small container of plas-ex.

"Now I think we'd better get back around the corner before we go any further," he said.

Blake nodded and ushered Alien and Jenna back around the bend in the tunnel, followed by the companions, with Downey bringing up the rear. J.B. stayed by the door, attaching a small amount of the plas-ex to the lock and fitting a fuse before running back to join them.

"Down," he shouted, clutching his ears and opening his mouth as the plas-ex blew, taking the protective measure as the explosion was in such a relatively confined space.

The lock had indeed blown, and the door was hanging open, the thick steel buckled by the force of the blast.

"Hot pipe, you made sure there." Dean whistled as he led the way toward the lab.

The baron turned toward Jenna, who was noticeably hanging back. "Well?" he asked. "Why not come with us, if you have nothing to be afraid of?"

He felt a creeping sickness in his head, and closed his eyes against the pain. When he opened them again, scant moments later, he could see the back of his wife as she ran from him. Setting his jaw, already knowing what he would find, the baron turned and strode toward the lab.

As soon as he entered, he could smell the decay and corruption, as though they were tangible.

"It's true...." he whispered to himself.

"THIS IS SICK. I remember the reports about Mengele, and how they always said it couldn't happen again. My daddy always said they were wrong. Jesus Christ, Dad, you were right."

Mildred fought back the tears as she stood over the cots where the hideously mutated results of Jenna's experiments lay. The eyes of the speechless mutie children looked up at her in fear and despair. They had known nothing but hate and pain, but knew that she was a stranger, and may end that pain.

Alien joined her. "There's no hope for these poor souls," he said softly. "We must—"

"I know," Mildred interrupted. "But I can't."

"Then I must. And as her husband I must take responsibility for not knowing."

Alien held out his hand, and Mildred knew what he wanted. She handed him her ZKR.

The baron took the blaster, checked the breech, then put the barrel to the head of the first mutie child.

"Please forgive me," he whispered before pulling the trigger. The noise was intense in the small room.

Alien repeated this with all the children, tears coursing down his face.

When he had finished, Mildred took his arm, and they reentered the main lab. The others were standing there, not knowing what to say to the shattered baron.

Alien looked around at the legacy of his wife.

"Destroy it," he said quietly, giving Mildred back her ZKR. "Destroy it all. Then we find her, and put her on trial."

"I don't think it'll come to that," Ryan said gently. "If she's gone, and so is Harvey, then you're going to have to fight for your ville. 'Cause we're the only ones who have seen this for sure, and there's no telling who'll side with who if the truth isn't yet known."

The baron nodded. "So be it. If it comes to a firefight, then we must be ready. So smash it all, as quickly as possible."

"How?" Downey asked. "You want us to blow it up, mebbe set fire to it? We need to get rid of those chilled experiments, that's for sure. Can't risk disease on top of this."

"Too dangerous down here for grens or firing," J.B. commented. "The best thing would be to shoot up the equipment, and plas-ex that room to bring the ceiling down in there and bury those poor bastards."

"Let it be so," Alien said quietly, striding from the room.

He was joined by everyone except J.B. and Ryan. While the Armorer sprayed the comp and medical equipment with his Uzi, Ryan laid the charnel house of the side room with plas-ex, which he fused and timed.

"Okay, people, let's get the hell away," he said urgently as he and the Armorer exited the lab. They ushered the others down the tunnel and around the corner as the plas-ex detonated in the lab, bringing down the walls and ceiling of the side room, burying the corpses of the experiments.

"Some of those children were from the ville," Alien said quietly. "She and Harvey must have been taking children and experimenting on them."

"How come we never knew?" Blake asked, bemused. "I mean, it ain't that big a place, right?"

"I believe I may be able to offer a possible solution," Doc commented. "The Sunchildren have always taken children that strayed to the outside. What better cover for Jenna and Harvey to abduct children? Then, when they had finished with them, they turned them loose on the outside, where they did, actually, become victims of Samtvogel."

Blake shook his head in disbelief. "I thought I knew that bastard."

"Throughout history, man has had an almost boundless capacity for deception and savagery. There are some things, friend Blake, that never change.'' Doc pursed his lips, an expression of infinite regret crossing his brow.

"That may be," Ryan said, bringing matters back to a practical level. "What we've got to worry about now is what sort of a reception we're heading back to. Stay triple red, friends."

As if in answer, the sounds of a pitched battle began to reach their ears.

Chapter Seventeen

It had taken Harvey only a few moments to melt into the crowd. Despite the doubts voiced, the sec chief had his followers, as did the baron's wife. There were those who had often wondered if the ville would prosper more under a firmer hand. Alien was, in their view, too nice to be a baron. He lacked the ruthless and sadistic streak that kept people in line. People like themselves. And so they had harbored, some openly and some in secret, the view that the steely sec chief and Jenna would make a better team. There was something about Jenna. No one but Harvey knew the extent of her experiments and her evil, but she had an aura that some could sense, and this made them respect and fear her.

And fear was what they wanted. What drove them and led them.

So it was that there were hands to cover them as they both tried to hide themselves in the uproar that followed the exit of Alien, Ryan, the sec men and the companions. Was this just a trick to buy them time, to chill the baron and take control? Or was it true that Jenna and Harvey had contrived to keep such experiments secret?

After the raid on Samtvogel, and coming on top of what had seemed like the sudden and shocking end of years of relatively peaceful consolidation, the confusion among the inhabitants of Raw was immense. In the main hall, people argued and started to get heated, pushing and hitting out. Tempers flared and the temperature was raised.

"Boss, this way, and quick!"

Harvey, grabbing behind him for Jenna's hand and trying to keep her close, heard the voice loud and urgent to his left. Looking up and across, he could see Bodie pushing through the packed mass of humanity, using the butt of his snub-nosed blaster as a club to hammer down on the necks and skulls of those who would block his path. Considering the frayed atmosphere and the confusion, Harvey was more than glad that only his sec force carried, by habit as much as enforcement, blasters on a day-to-day basis. At least no one was going to take a shot at him.

"Let's get the fuck out," he yelled at Bodie. "Regroup, get the boys together."

"They ain't all gonna come with you, boss," Bodie replied.

"Don't matter. That stupe Alien is out of here right now, with Cyclops and his goons. That gives us time to rally those good ol' boys who'll stay the course."

"Okay, boss." Bodie grinned, savage and humorless. "Follow me."

The fat sec man chopped them a path out into the ville. Most of the people inside were too busy fighting one another to try to get out, and those that did found themselves hemmed in by the sec men at the sole entrance. The two men carried longblasters, which they held across their bodies, using the whip-thin barrels as weapons, not wasting ammo as they hit anyone trying to get out.

Anyone, that was, except Bodie, Harvey and Jenna.

"Stay here while I round up our forces," Harvey ordered crisply. "Any sec who go against you, they ain't with us, so chill the fuckers."

The sec men exchanged vaguely puzzled glances.

"Our own?" one of them queried.

Harvey fixed him with a glare. "Son, if they ain't with us, then they're the enemy. Understood?"

Not waiting for an answer, he turned on his heel and rapidly sped toward the armory. The first step would be to secure all weapons for his force alone.

ANT AND DEE STOOD in the center of the fray, possibly the only two people calm in the center of the storm.

The dreadlocked twins still carried their battered shotguns, cleaner than at any time in the past but showing the scars of use and misuse. Ant raised his, looking at it with a shadow of regret crossing his face.

"Looks like we're gonna need these again, bro, and sooner than I would have liked."

His twin returned the look, gazing at his own weapon with sadness. "Sure looks so. You reckon that one-eyed dude and his sprog are right, or should we go with Harv?"

Ant gave his twin a look of disbelief mixed with disgust. "You kiddin'? Harv hates anything and anyone except himself and mebbe that weird bitch. Think we've got any chance of a good life with him as big boss?"

Dee laughed, a hollow, bitter sound. "Yeah, like fuck."

Ant shrugged. "Then let's get to it, dude."

And with a cry that sounded as one, both twins let out a bloodcurdling shriek, turning in opposite directions, waving their blasters and cutting themselves a swath through the crowd until they reached the exit, where they came up against the twin longblasters blocking their path.

"Where you going, boys?" asked one sec man.

"Who you with?" asked the other, so rapidly the two almost sounded as one.

"What do you think?" Ant asked in an exasperated tone. It was, however, a neutral question. It elicited exactly the kind of response they both wanted.

"I knew you'd be good ol' boys for a pair of blacks and side with us," one sec man said, grinning.

"Yeah, make the new order work," the other added.

Ant and Dee exchanged the briefest of glances before moving as one with a speed like a striking rattler. Their powerful arms pumped, using the stocks of their respective blasters as baseball bats, coming from the level of their elbows in an upward arc that caught each sec man under his chin, jawbones shattering on impact as both sec men crumpled into unconscious heaps, neither having time to respond to the attack.

"Never did like those dudes, bro," Ant said sadly.

"Yeah, even the best of places get insects," his twin replied. "Figure we should find Cawdor and the baron. Reckon Blake and Downey'll be with us, if no one else."

"Yeah, they're good people. But where the fuck were they going?"

Dee grinned. "Shit, you got the one flaw in my plan, dude!"

WITH THE SEC GUARD now rendered ineffective, the fighting in the main hall spilled out into the tunnels and passages of the ville. Men and women who had peacefully coexisted in the enclosed ville all their lives now found that they hardly knew their neighbor at all. Those sec men who were still loyal to Alien tried in vain to calm the crowd and prevent the violence and conflict, but they were outnumbered both by the crowd and those sec men who wanted to stick with Harvey.

It wasn't long before the crowd had separated into two distinct forces, and lines of demarcation were drawn up in the ville as each side took whatever cover it could, using whatever came to hand as weapons to augment the few sec blasters.

It was clear that whoever controlled the armory would win the war. Something Harvey was already attending to…

"HEY, HARV. What the hell are you doing, you rad-blasted gaudy spawn!"

The chief armorer had elected to miss the meeting in the main hall, figuring that her presence wouldn't make much difference. Besides, someone had to clean and stockpile the blasters, grens and plas-ex after the raid on Samtvogel. It would be a lengthy task, and she figured that the sooner she got to it the better. Besides, she'd taken a liking to J.B. Dix, and had the feeling that his people would be hitting trouble. It made her feel uneasy, and she felt happier with complex but inanimate pieces of metal than she did with complex but animate human beings.

She had been in the middle of stripping one of the

RPKs when Harvey, Jenna and Bodie burst in on her. It was hard to know who was the more surprised. Harvey had truly believed that everyone was in the main hall, and that he would find the armory empty. The chief armorer had no idea what to make of the sec chief, one of his trusted lieutenants, and the baron's wife bursting in on her, wild-eyed and looking for all the world as though they were about to commit mass murder.

Which, of course, was their very intention.

Harvey stopped dead, staring at her, and then without another word took the Uzi from its wall mounting, grabbed spare ammo from the carefully labeled and stored boxes and tossed it to Jenna.

When he ignored her, she repeated her question. But this time, suspicions aroused that something was very much amiss and that she'd have no choice but to get involved, she left the RPK and reached slowly and stealthily for her own personal blaster, the Springfield Loaded 1911 that she kept secured in the waistband of her old camou pants. They were faded and patched, but she kept them because of the special loop she had sewn into the back. Stitched time and again until it held the Springfield perfectly balanced, it made her pants almost a second skin, and she didn't feel comfortable unless she could feel the Cocobolo grip's texture nesting against the base of her spine.

Her finger snaked around the lightweight match trigger while the palm of her hand flattened against the high hand grip. The flat mainspring housing meant that the blaster nestled into her plump body just about as unobtrusively as it was possible to get, and she was careful to move with a slow and easy motion, so it would appear just as though she were scratching an itch.

Harvey looked at her. "Donna, don't do this," he said slowly and evenly.

"Do what, Harv? And don't fuck with my blasters. They ain't cleaned yet, not all of them."

Harvey smiled despite himself. He had always thought her dedication to the hardware was a little weird, and mebbe she was only pissed at him for messing with it.

In which case he wouldn't have to chill her.

"Listen to me, Donna," he said softly. "The time has come to decide which side you're on."

Her finger was still on the trigger, the grip still nestled into her palm, but she stayed any movement.

"Side, Harv? What sides do you mean? We're one people, right?"

"No, Donna, it ain't that simple anymore. That damned Cyclops, he's got Alien all confused and wantin' to go against how we've always been. If we don't stand up for what we believe, then we're sure as shit gonna be under the one-eyed bastard's thumb. We won't be us anymore. Is that what you want? Or do you want to fight with us?"

The chief armorer narrowed her eyes, trying hard to assimilate all that Harvey had said. Was that what the meeting had been about? But if so, then why would Ryan Cawdor's people want to take control and change things? She thought about their aid in the battle against Samtvogel, and more importantly she thought of J.B. Dix. Mebbe it was just the way the man seemed to be like her with weapons, but she figured that he was good people. It didn't figure....

Donna delayed just that little too long for Jenna's liking. The dark mutie snapped the safety on her blaster, the click sounding loud against the faint background noise that was beginning to permeate the tunnels. Her raven eyes glittered hatred.

"She doesn't believe you, Harvey, and we can't afford to waste time."

She raised the Uzi as though to fire.

It all happened in the same second. Suddenly, intuitively aware of the situation as her instincts broke through her confused thinking, aware only of the Uzi pointed at her, Donna drew the Springfield, snapping off a shot as her hand whipped around her body.

"No!" Harvey yelled, both at the chief armorer and at Jenna. He flung out an arm, snatching the Uzi from Jenna's grasp before she had a chance to pressure the trigger, and simultaneously pushing her from the path of the slug, which bit into the wall of the armory, raising a small cloud of dust.

The crack of the Springfield was echoed a fraction of a second later by the roar of the sec chief's Colt Magnum Carry, as the snub-nosed blaster spit its .357 load at the seated woman. Drawn as he moved, and aimed low, the slug ripped into Donna's chest cavity and upper abdomen, spreading fatal damage as the slug tore cartilage and splintered bone, ripping bands of muscle and splattering layers of fat, scoring through major organs and causing massive internal hemorrhaging.

In the fraction of a second of life she had left to her, Donna was acutely aware of great pain and a rapidly spreading numbness. Her vision dimmed on the sight of Harvey and the baron's wife about to argue.

She figured that even if she was chilled, arguing like that they wouldn't be far behind her.

The merest flicker of a smile formed her death mask.

Meanwhile, Jenna shot a venomous glance at her erstwhile lover and partner. "What the fuck did you do that for?"

Harvey held his temper. "In the first place, I didn't want you chilled. And in the second, if you let that fucker loose even on controlled bursts in here, you're likely to hit some grens and blow us to hell."

Her temper cooling rapidly as she fought to stay on top of the situation, Jenna was able to see Harvey's point.

"Okay, Harvey. So what's your great tactical plan?" she said with as much sarcasm as she could muster.

"We've got control of the armory. We get the hardware to this who are with us and keep the rest down, chill 'em if necessary. Then we find Cyclops and Alien and blow them to fuck."

Jenna smiled a slow, evil smile. "That's good, but we need the real whiphand, sweet."

Harvey gave her a puzzled frown. "What's that?"

"You'll see." She called to Bodie. "In here, boy. When we've gone, you get these to our folk, you hear?" she continued as he entered the armory from his sentry post outside. He had ignored the blasterfire, trusting the sec chief to keep things under control.

"Yes, ma'am," the fat sec man replied. "We'll soon have things under control for you."

Harvey was still puzzled. "What's the idea? Where are we going?"

Jenna's evil smile took on an icy edge. "Sweetie, if you want total control of them, you have the total weapon. We need fear to still the opposition, keep them down and under us. Every strong society needs its menials. They stay menial by fear. So why don't you show me where Alien stored that little ol' bomb he got from Sunchild?"

"COMING THIS WAY. Back!" Jak whispered as they came to a crossroads in the tunnels. Ryan had sent the albino on slightly ahead of himself, changing his usual practice to lead the way. It seemed to the one-eyed warrior that Jak's ability to detect direction would be better employed leading until they had some idea of the situation in the center of the ville. In such a maze of passages and tunnels, Jak's ability to pinpoint sounds was a vital weapon.

They had heard the pitched battle commence, and the occasional blasterfire told them that the armory hadn't yet been raided to a full extent. As they were all armed, apart from the baron, this gave them an edge. Ryan handed the baron his SIG-Sauer as a defensive weapon, feeling that Alien would cope better with the handblaster than with the Steyr.

They had advanced this far without a pause, and with hardly a word between them. J.B. kept point as was usual, Downey close to him. Blake was beside Ryan, following hard on Jak's lead. Strung out between them in the narrow tunnel were Krysty, Dean, Alien, Mildred and toward the rear Doc.

At Jak's command, they flattened against the tunnel

wall, closing ranks so that they were ready to flank across the narrow space should an enemy round the corner.

But it was no enemy. Voices, indistinct, became clearer as they neared: the breathless voices of the twins.

"Shit, bro, I hope we find them soon."

"Ain't nowhere else to fuckin' go, dude. They've got to be around here somewhere."

"Sure as shit hope so, 'cause I think my lungs are gonna fuckin' burst!"

The twins laughed despite themselves, coughing hard but still keeping the pace.

Ryan and Blake exchanged glances as the footsteps neared. The wizened sec man nodded, agreeing without the question even being voiced.

"Hey, boys," he called, "who you lookin' for?"

The footsteps pulled up short. Ant called, "Shit, Blake, man, where the fuck you been? We've been all over here looking for ya. You got Ryan and his crew with you?"

"Mebbe," the sec man replied cautiously. "What you boys wantin'?"

"You, dude. You gotta get back, man, 'cause all hell's broken loose. Harv and that bitch have got some sort of takeover goin' down, and we need all the help we can get."

Ryan and Blake exchanged glances once more.

"Trust them?" the one-eyed warrior asked.

"With my life. Crazy fuckers, but too crazy to lie if they even wanted to," he replied.

"Good enough for me," Ryan said.

"We're coming out, boys," he called to the twins.

Ryan and Blake stepped out simultaneously into the junction between the corridors, blasters ready as a precaution.

"Whoa, dude, easy!" Ant exclaimed as he and his twin held their shotguns away from their bodies. "I know what one of those fuckers can do, so 'scuse me being nervous," he added, gesturing with his free hand at J.B.'s M-4000, which Ryan had borrowed.

The one-eyed warrior allowed himself a small grin as he lowered the M-4000. "Okay, so fill us in," he said as the rest of his party, including the baron, stepped out into the junction.

The twins explained the situation, keeping it as concise as they could without contradicting each other too often. When they had finished, Ryan turned to the baron.

"Seems to me that most of your sec force want to take their chances with Harvey."

Alien shook his head sadly. "Whatever happens, I can't go on now."

"Worry later. Get Harvey chilled first," Jak snapped pithily, not allowing Alien to slip into self-pity.

"What's the state of play with the armory?" J.B. asked. "Right now, only sec and us have blasters. But if everyone on Harvey's side gets them..." He trailed off, feeling it unnecessary to go on.

Ant shook his head. "I guess he's headed straight for it, but the problem the dude's got is that our side is between the armory and his side, ya know?"

"Then he'll need another tool to bargain with," Ryan stated flatly.

"By the Three Kennedys," Doc whispered, "he wouldn't."

Mildred caught Doc's inference. "He might not, but I bet she would."

Alien looked at them blankly. He was a broken man, and unable to focus on events.

Ryan, on the other hand, had clicked into combat mode, and his mind was racing.

He turned to Blake. "You take Downey and Alien and head for the center. Take Jak and Dean with you. They're good fighters, and you may need them."

The sec man nodded, glad that he would have Jak by his side. "And you?" he asked.

"We're going after Harvey and Jenna. Reckon they've gone for the nuke. You with us, boys?" he asked the twins.

"Bet your ass," Ant replied.

"Yeah, and whip that sorry mother Harv's ass," his twin added.

With a brief farewell, the two forces parted company, both headed for what they knew to be the final showdown.

Chapter Eighteen

The area where the nuke was being stored was deserted. Alien had felt it unnecessary to mount a guard while he had the ville meeting, and Harvey had been only too pleased to go along with that, wanting all his people concentrated.

One thing he hadn't foreseen was the willingness with which Jenna would turn to the nuke as a bargaining tool.

There was an almost eerie quiet about this part of the ville. Away from the pitched battle, and on the other side of the tunnel and passage complex to where her lab was located, Jenna was certain that they would be left in peace until she had worked out how to arm the bomb.

"Are you sure about this?" Harvey asked her as she opened a panel on the garishly painted side of the nuke, near the nose cone.

"In what way?" she replied calmly, partly as a result of her preoccupation and partly because she felt the power within her grasp, and the self-confidence that engendered. "What's the problem, sweetie? Until I've actually examined this, I don't know for sure if it's even armed."

"But what if it is?"

She looked at him with an expression of complete

calm that froze his blood. "Then if it is, I set it going."

"Another nukecaust?" Harvey queried, unable to keep the quaver from his voice.

Jenna laughed, harsh and cold. "Of course not, you cretin. I set it going, and then turn it off on the failsafe when my idiot husband and the one-eyed fool have acquiesced to us. For fuck's sake, you don't think I'd be doing this if I couldn't stop it?"

"Yeah? How can I be so sure you even know how to get it going properly?"

"You know I can. You know I have the learning. After all, if you really thought I couldn't set it running, you wouldn't be shitting yourself right now, would you?"

Harvey didn't answer. She was right.

Jenna turned her attention away from her lover and fully to the nuke. The old comp circuits were still in operation, and using codes she had learned from books and papers taken by her forefathers from the redoubt, she punched in a series of commands that told her that the nuke was armed and ready. She set the timer and punched in a sec code so that only she could turn it off. It was a sec code set by the original programmer of the missile from the redoubt, and was a name the like of which she didn't recognize, but had memorized earlier.

"There." She smiled, standing back from the gaily colored instrument of destruction. "That's done."

"Good," Harvey breathed. "Can we get the fuck out of here now?"

"Of course we can. We've got another little battle to win. I wonder how your people are doing right now?" she asked, shrugging the Uzi off her shoulder and flicking the safety catch, switching the firing mechanism to short bursts.

"Only one way to find out. Let's get the hell back," Harvey muttered, leading them away from the nuke and back toward the center of the ville.

IN THE CENTER, the battle had reached stalemate. Those sec men and ville dwellers who had sided with Alien were blocking the route to the armory. Although they outnumbered the opposition, they had fewer sec men on their side, and so had fewer blasters, which evened things up.

The battle had died down to a war of attrition, with both sides adopting a siege mentality. The occasional shot was fired, the occasional seized object thrown over the hastily erected barricades. But there was a general tense silence.

Into which arrived Blake, Downey, Jak and Dean, with Alien close behind them.

Rankine was one of the few sec men who had aligned himself with the baron, and he had assumed command for want of anyone else. However, he was at a loss how to break the deadlock, and the relief on his face was evident when Blake and Jak picked their way through the line to arrive at the front of the barricade.

"Thank fuck you're here," he said gladly.

"Where are the rest of you?" he added, speaking to Jak.

"After Harvey. Never mind. Get this finished," the albino said shortly. "Alien not happy."

"Yeah, his heart ain't in it," Blake chipped in, speaking softly. The other ville dwellers on the barricade had spotted their baron, and the atmosphere had noticeably lifted at the sight of the big man. "Listen, we need to act before it becomes obvious and has a bad effect. What's the score?"

Rankine filled them in on the details, and Blake listened carefully. "Okay," he began when Rankine finished, "the first thing is to get people armed. Have you raided the armory yet? No, obviously not," he said, spotting the furrowed brow on his fellow sec man. "Get some people back there. Meanwhile, I think we need to do some scouting. How much hardware do we have right now?"

Rankine made a quick head count. "We got eight sec here, so eight blasters—nine including me."

Dean had made his way forward with Downey. Blake turned to him.

"Whaddaya say, kid? Covering fire from the marksman here and a few of the boys while you, me and Jak make a little scouting foray?"

Dean took a look over the barricade. The lines had been drawn in the main stretch of the tunnel at the center of the ville, with a distance of two hundred yards between the two barricades. Not a lot of room to play with, but with plenty of cover in the shape of empty units and overturned barrows.

"More than scouting. I reckon we could make a bridgehead out there. Think so, Jak?"

The albino nodded. "Enough cover if you give enough cover to make it," he said to Rankine and Downey. "Get blaster from armory triple quick and we got them. Get grens mebbe."

Downey shook his head. "Risky down here. Better if we can avoid it."

Jak nodded. "Make sure you sharpshooter."

Blake called two sec men over and ordered them

to accompany a party of ville dwellers to the armory and return with blasters. While they assembled the small party and headed off, he directed two more to join Rankine and Downey in laying down covering fire. Meanwhile, Jak and Dean made note of the best cover, both for themselves and for Blake.

The wizened sec man turned to them, his face set in stone. "Okay, ready from my end. You?"

Jak nodded. "We head there and there—" he indicated two positions of cover "—and you there," he added, pointing to the easiest spot.

Blake smiled appreciatively. "You trying to tell me something?" he said simply before turning to the four marksmen. "Okay, guys, now or never..."

The four marksmen assumed positions along the barricade and started to lay down a barrage of covering fire.

"Hot pipe, this better work," Dean shouted, as much to himself as to Jak and Blake, as the three clambered over the barricade and began their zigzagging run for cover.

IT WAS a long haul across the ville from where Ant and Dee had met Ryan's party to where the nuke was stored, and the one-eyed warrior pushed the pace at which they crossed the distance. All the time, he was aware that Doc was the weak link, but he wanted the old man on hand when they reached the nuke. If it had been set running, then Doc's knowledge of pre-dark tech, as sketchy and clouded as it was, may prove useful. Mildred knew more about comps per se, but she hadn't had the firsthand experience of the Totality Concept that Doc had. That might make all the difference.

They had to circumvent the tunnels and passages, avoiding the strife-torn center, and that made their task all the more difficult. Ryan cursed with almost every step he took, the twins keeping pace with him. Krysty followed close behind. Mildred and J.B. hung back a little more, assisting Doc to keep pace.

"Go on ahead," he puffed, moving as fast as he could. "I swear by all that is holy that I shall not be far behind. Besides, you may have to chill a path to the nuke that will take time."

Ryan assented with a gesture, and in company with the twins and Krysty, he increased his pace, allowing Mildred and J.B. to stay with Doc. The old man was right. He could assume that only Jenna and Harvey were with the missile, but they may have others with them. If so, it may take valuable time to dig them out before trying to shut off the nuke.

"Down here, shortcut," Dee puffed, swerving down a smaller tunnel.

"But be careful at the end," his twin added. "It brings us out on a sharp turn. Take it easy."

It was advice that Dee would have done well to heed. At the moment he reached the end of the small tunnel, and stumbled around the blind corner, he came straight out on Harvey and Jenna, who were making their way back toward the barricades in the center. Like the twins, Harvey had decided to utilize the shortcut.

The dreadlocked giant stumbled as he cornered, and crashed to one knee, momentarily losing his grip on his shotgun. It was a vital fraction of a second before he looked up…directly into the barrel of Harvey's Colt Magnum Carry.

It was difficult to know who was more surprised by the encounter, the dreadlocked twin or the sec chief, both stopped dead in their tracks. For one absurd moment they were frozen. Then Jenna's shrill voice rent the air.

"Chill the fucker!"

Harvey didn't think. The voice made him jolt, his finger tightening and squeezing on the trigger as the twin began to raise the shotgun.

The explosion from the snub-nosed blaster was deafening in the enclosed space, and the impact at such close range blew Dee backward into the mouth of the smaller passageway, where his already dead body cannoned into his brother.

"No!" It was an anguished yell from Ant as he saw what had happened. Without pause he pushed past the inert form and out into the larger passage.

Jenna, leaving Harvey to deal with things, had already brushed past him and was heading in the opposite direction without a backward glance. Harvey, stunned, looked after her. Things had happened just that bit too fast for him to react. He was still looking as Ant emerged.

Stupidly, Harvey turned his head back in time to see the twin bear down on him, spattered with the blood of his brother. His shotgun was raised. Harvey's own blaster was at a lowered angle, and in the fraction of a second it took him to bring it up, the dreadlocked sec man was on him, his shotgun rammed up against Harvey's throat.

"You chilled my brother, you fuck. Now it's your

turn,'' he yelled as he squeezed the Smith & Wesson shotgun's trigger, the blast shaking him as the recoil and impact was contained between his own body and that of the sec chief.

The blast was enough to actually sever Harvey's head from his body, the bone and flesh of his throat and neck disintegrating under the charge. His nervous system spasmed in shock as it lost contact with his brain, and his finger squeezed again. The Colt Magnum Carry avenged his chilling by discharging into Ant's stomach before he had a chance to move away from the sec chief.

His scream of agony was high-pitched and despairing as he lost his own life in avenging the loss of his twin's.

Ryan emerged, taking in the carnage in one swift glance, also noting the retreating Jenna. He turned to follow, but was stayed by Krysty's hand on his arm.

"Leave her to me, lover,'' she said rapidly. "I can deal with her tricks. You get the nuke.''

Ryan agreed, but even as he did, the titian-haired beauty was already speeding off in pursuit of Jenna, her blaster poised as she ran, already making up ground.

One thing was for sure—there was no one else now between them and the nuke. He looked back to where Doc, Mildred and J.B. were approaching.

"Hurry, people,'' he called. "We've got a clear run, but who knows how much time.''

DEAN, JAK AND BLAKE had assumed their initial positions of cover, returning fire from the barricade and moving forward by degrees as the covering fire from behind drove the opposition down.

"How many they got?" Dean shouted to Blake.

"No more than a dozen blasters, most of 'em probably low on ammo now," Blake replied.

"Draw now," Jak called to Dean on hearing that.

The younger Cawdor knew exactly what the albino meant. He left cover and headed for an overturned barrow, deliberately slowing for a fraction of a second to show himself more clearly before executing a dive into cover. That fraction of a second drew three tempted marksmen into the open, showing themselves above the barricade.

Jak had been waiting for it. As the three men rose, so, too, did the albino with three leaf-bladed knives in his hand. In one fluid motion, the knives left his hand, flying with uncanny accuracy to their targets.

"Only nine now," he called as he took cover again.

On the other side of the opposition barricade, ville dwellers started to melt away into the units as much as possible, leaving only the sec men standing, firing back, hopelessly outnumbered and certain to be chilled.

The nine men exchanged glances. There was only one option.

Shouting to spur themselves on and try to work up a frenzy, the suicidal sec men mounted their barricade, firing at random.

The volley of blasterfire that tore into them ended the conflict in a matter of seconds. All caliber of shot tore into them, cutting them down before they were even over the barricades.

"Stop!" Blake yelled. The noise was so great he had to repeat himself several times before the noise ceased, and the suddenly silent air was filled with the spent smell of burned cordite.

"Guess it's over," he said quietly.

JENNA WAS GASPING heavily for breath. The slim, small mutie woman had never had much time for building her strength and stamina, and even the relatively light weight of the Uzi was slowing her. She threw it away as she ran, hearing it clatter to the floor behind her. She didn't need a blaster, she was confident of other abilities to save herself.

Turning into a side corridor, she took shelter in a sleeping unit, throwing the curtain back and leaning heavily against a wall, trying desperately to catch her breath.

Krysty saw Jenna throw away the blaster and made herself ready as she, too, turned into the side corridor, slowing to a halt as she tried to determine which unit the woman had hidden herself in. Krysty gripped her blaster with both hands, knowing she would need to have a steady grip before this encounter was over.

She walked slowly down the corridor, glancing from side to side.

"Here," she heard from behind her. Turning slowly, she saw Jenna standing by the entrance to one unit. She looked small and vulnerable until Krysty looked into those raven eyes. The whole world seemed to disappear.

Krysty raised her blaster and prepared to fire.

"You know you won't," Jenna said in those soft, sibilant tones.

Krysty felt the tendrils of darkness snake out and start to encircle her mind. The wave of nausea started in her gut, her ears blasted by the blow to her equilibrium. She fought to stay on her feet, to keep the darkness at bay.

Her hands trembled. She felt the urge to turn the weapon on herself. She gritted her teeth, grinding them to keep herself focused.

"You know you won't," Jenna repeated.

"It's ARMED, all right. And running."

Ryan stood over the nuke, feeling as helpless as a child. He looked at J.B., who was scratching his head. The Armorer pushed his spectacles back up the bridge of his nose.

"Dark night," he cursed softly, shaking his head, "Arms I know, but it's the comp on this that stops me. I just hope Doc and Millie can sort it out."

The two doctors stood over the incongruously painted nuke, examining the panel.

"There must be a series of codes that program it, and so there must be a series that deprogram, right?" Mildred asked.

Doc nodded briskly. "I believe I saw something like this in one of the files I was privy to study. Usually, it is a combination of letters and numbers that relate to those on the actual cone itself. Probably to trigger an association in an emergency—much like this one, but not perhaps under the same bizarre circumstances." He favored her with a ghoulish smile.

"Spare me the gallows humor, Doc. At least until this mother's stopped ticking," she said.

"Very well. Although to be pedantic, it cannot be

said to actually tick. Now, if we can just scrape some
of this paint from the cone," he added, tapping a
section of the nose cone with his swordstick.

J.B. stepped forward and began to scrape the top
layer of paint away with his Tekna. "Is this safe?"
he asked.

"Well, if we don't try, it will go off anyway," Doc
replied cheerfully.

"That makes me feel so much better," the Armorer
told him.

"Fireblast! This is so slow," Ryan muttered,
watching the countdown continue on the LED.

"Patience, friend Ryan, patience," Doc murmured
distractedly as the numbers came to light. He punched
in a corresponding series, but nothing happened.

"It's still going," J.B. said.

"Obviously," Doc replied without the slightest
sign of urgency. "There is a fail-safe backup I cannot
enter, something only the programmer would know."

"What?" Mildred exploded. "But you didn't mention that before, you stupid old buzzard. How the hell
are we supposed to know that?"

"Well, my dear Dr. Wyeth, I would deduce that
the programmer was someone in the redoubt we arrived in...and it would be something personal. A
name perhaps, six letters, and no more. They were all
six-letter codes..."

Mildred's mind raced. "Have you got any ideas?"
she said, making it a general question.

"Frankly, no," Doc said sadly, while Ryan and
J.B. just looked blank. For them, it could be anything.

But inspiration suddenly hit Mildred.

"It's our only chance, but it's a long shot," she stated, tapping in six letters.

The LED flashed, the figures frozen. Then, with a beep, it turned itself off.

"What the hell did you tell it?" J.B. asked her with a mixture of awe and admiration in his voice.

"I just put in the name Garcia." She smiled. Then, seeing their blank expressions, she laughed aloud. "It was just something on one of the posters from the redoubt... I'll explain it sometime. Let's just say you'll be grateful when you're dead."

"I very much doubt it," Doc said, bewildered.

THROUGH THE BLACKNESS and confusion, a wave of strength hit Krysty. Somehow, she had picked up on her friends and the wave of relief from them. It gave her strength, and within her mind she saw her mother back in Harmony, telling her about the power that could be wielded by those who worked together for a common good. It wasn't a power that could be measured like blasters or grens, but it had its own strength.

A strength that, for one moment, allowed her mind to clear from Jenna's influence.

Krysty's hands were twisted awkwardly and painfully toward her own body, pointing the blaster at herself. She straightened them, so that the blaster was pointed directly at Jenna.

The baron's wife realized that she had momentarily lost her grip on her adversary. In that second, fear entered those glittering black eyes.

It was all the relief that Krysty needed. She squeezed the trigger, and let fly a shot that entered

Jenna's forehead neatly between her eyes, puncturing
a small entry wound and a larger exit wound that took
a large chunk out of her skull, pulping brain tissue as
it did so.

The glittering raven eyes dulled and died.

Krysty, drained of all energy, fainted.

She was still unconscious when Jak and Dean
found her some minutes later.

Epilogue

It took several days for Blake—the new sec chief—to set straight the mess that Raw had become. The chilled bodies had to be disposed of, and those ville dwellers who had sided with Harvey had to be searched out. Those who didn't recant on their decision were to be exiled. Needless to say, all of them swore to be loyal to Alien. Blake wasn't so stupe as to believe them out of hand, and so established a list of those citizens who needed to be watched.

"Things will never be the same," he said sadly.

And they wouldn't be. Alien was a shadow of his former self. The knowledge of his wife's betrayal, and the depth of her depravity, had severely dented his belief in his ability to rule, and it would take him time to rebuild his barony. He attended the cremation of Jenna supported by Doc.

J.B. helped the Armorers set the armory straight, Mildred assisted the medical staff of the ville, and Ryan and Jak sat in with Blake as he attempted to build a new structure to the ville that took account of what had happened, but didn't stray too far from the precepts of Alien and his ancestors—the precepts in which Blake also believed.

Krysty took the entire period to recover from the psychic attack she had endured before chilling Jenna. Although she hadn't drawn on the Gaia power that aided her in times of great physical demand, she felt as though she had. She tired easily, ached all over and felt as though she could sleep all day.

Eventually, she was well enough for them to leave.

BLAKE ACCOMPANIED them to the exit that led out to the forest. Alien wouldn't go with them, wouldn't even acknowledge that they were leaving.

As they stood on the threshold of the ville, the new sec chief grasped Jak by the arm.

"I'm sorry to see you go," he said quietly. "I need all the good people I can get, and you're good people. If you ever come back this way…"

"Mebbe. Mebbe not wander some day," Jak replied, knowing that in some ways he would always be searching.

Blake watched them as they marched through the forest until they were out of sight, then returned to his own battle.

J.B. SIGHTED THROUGH his minisextant and took their direction. They were on the edge of the forest, back on the road out of old Seattle toward the valley of Samtvogel.

"Which way shall we head?" he asked Ryan.

"Can't go back to the redoubt and jump," the one-eyed warrior mused. "No way of getting back in there."

"Could follow the blacktop north," J.B. said.

"Mebbe find stupes with lasers," Jak added.

"That would be most interesting, always assuming they do not just want to chill us," Doc said wryly.

Krysty noticed that Ryan was staring at the horizon.

"What do you say, lover? Think they could be the key?"

"To the promised land?" he replied. "Mebbe. I feel like we've been cheated somehow, like we could have learned more in Raw if Jenna hadn't been a crazie. If the Illuminated Ones are still out there, still living apart from the rest of us, we could have mebbe learned something about them that would have taken us away from this."

"Maybe we still will," Mildred said softly. "But not out here. If there are any answers—and perhaps we're getting closer to finding that Erewhon—then we need to get to shelter before the sun goes down."

Ryan smiled. "Fireblast, I should be that smart, not just leave it to you. Let's head north toward the nearest redoubt."

J.B. sighted in his minisextant, plotting a course north that took them past old Seattle and up toward the old predark borders. Up toward the lands where the Illuminated Ones and the promised land were said to be.

James Axler

OUTLANDERS®

PRODIGAL CHALICE

The warriors, who dare to expose the deadly truth of
mankind's destiny, discover a new gateway in Central
America—one that could lead them deeper into the
conspiracy that has doomed Earth. Here they encounter a
most unusual baron struggling to control the vast oil
resources of the region. Uncertain if this charismatic leader
is friend or foe, Kane is lured into a search for an ancient
relic of mythic proportions that may promise a better
future…or plunge humanity back into the dark ages.

*In the Outlands,
the shocking truth is humanity's last hope.*

A journey to the dangerous frontier
known as the future...
Don't miss these titles!

JAMES AXLER

DEATH LANDS®

GDLBACK2